Avenger

Avenger

Book Three
The Tyke McGrath Series

by

William Woodall

Jeremiah Press · *Antoine, Arkansas*

Jeremiah Press
PO Box 3
Antoine, AR 71922

Cover image courtesy of NASA, and Dominic Forte of the University College, London.

First published by Jeremiah Press on 09/10/2013.

Printed in the United States of America.

This book is printed on acid-free paper.

ISBN 978-0-9833298-4-8

For Brennan, Jaden, Katlin, Briana, Jake, and Matthew,

Who asked for this book.

Curse-Breaker Books
by William Woodall:

The Last Werewolf Hunter Series

Cry for the Moon
Behind Blue Eyes
More Golden Than Day
Truesilver

The Stones of Song Series

Unclouded Day
Many Waters
Bran the Blessed

The Tyke McGrath Series

Nightfall
Tycho
Avenger
Freedom
Elysium

Unrelated Novels

The Prophet of Rain
Beneath a Star-Blue Sky
(short story collection)

The fool hath said in his heart, there is no God.

-Psalms 14:1

Thoughts of a Lost Boy
By Tycho Nicholas McGrath

"There's only one allegiance which no man or woman can ever deny for any reason, and that is to God."

"Facts are brutally honest things, and only a fool chooses to ignore what he doesn't understand."

"Our desire to know the one true answer to a question is a completely different thing than our desire to find that one particular answer rather than another is the true one."

"Unfortunately, people don't believe things just because you wish they would."

"All things have their unexpected beauties."

"Those who are most honorable and courageous themselves are almost always the ones most likely to praise others for the same things, and those who are most truly humble are usually those who are readiest to accept honor with simple thanks."

"Sometimes in the aftermath of a great deed, there comes a kind of quiet when you're not quite sure what to do with yourself."

"There are times when you know better than to ask for explanations. You just do what you're told and hope there's a good reason."

"I wonder how many kids go for years thinking they know everything there is to know about their dull mom and dad, and then suddenly discover some depth they never dreamed of. And vice versa, of course. It made me wonder if you ever really know your friends, or the people you work with, or anybody for that matter."

"Nothing has any value at all except what it holds through beauty, love, or usefulness. And I think that much at least is a very good thing indeed."

"Sometimes even a kid can see when his country is being led by idiots who either take no more thought for the future than a goose or whose heads are full of idealistic notions that any sensible person can see will lead to utter ruin if they ever came to pass."

"It's a very sad and obvious fact that rebels tend to have hard lives and die young."

Contents

Chapter One.. 9

Chapter Two...21

Chapter Three 32

Chapter Four.. 43

Chapter Five... 57

Chapter Six.. 70

Chapter Seven.. 76

Chapter Eight... 85

Chapter Nine.. 96

Chapter Ten.. 108

Chapter Eleven... 121

Chapter Twelve... 135

Chapter Thirteen... 146

Chapter Fourteen.. 156

Epilogue... 168

Freedom (Sample)... 172

Author's Note.. 193

Discussion Questions... 195

Bonus Material.. 197

Family Trees... 201

Chapter One
Saturday, February 21, 2156

They say life is full of surprises.

In hindsight, I think I could definitely agree with that. I never thought I'd become the first human being in history to set foot on the icy world of Titan, let alone that I'd make friends with an alien or join him in fulfilling an ancient prophecy from the beginning of time. Those aren't the kinds of things most people would ever anticipate doing.

I never expected to have to rethink my entire outlook on the supernatural, either, but maybe I'm getting a little bit ahead of myself with all that.

One thing I do know is, I was in no mood for any more adventures in space when this one suddenly got dropped in my lap. I'd had plenty of those already, and all I wanted back then was to settle down and live a quiet life on the beach for a while; no problems, no worries, no sweat.

When we moved to Hawaii back in November, it seemed at first like that was exactly the kind of life we'd get to have. It hardly ever rains on the southwest side of the island where we were, and it's never too hot or too cold. We were treated to nothing but warm sunshiny days and beautiful surroundings almost everywhere we looked. And if by chance we did get tired of perfection sometimes, we could always drive up to the summit of Mauna Kea to play in the snow for a little while if we liked, or circle around to the northeast coast and enjoy a rainstorm. Nowhere else on Earth does it get much better than this, and that's the truth.

But all that peace and tranquility didn't last near as long as we hoped it might. Hawaii may be the closest thing to paradise most people could ever imagine, but it turns out there are dangers, even here. Drew and Tabby were over on the northeast side of Kilauea with Josh a few months ago when a flash flood after a heavy downpour caught them off guard. Josh's body was the only one we ever found, and I can only hope they never knew what hit them. We buried him there and set up a memorial stone close to the place, but the loss hit us hard.

Nobody goes to enjoy the rainstorms very often anymore.

And then, Miss Amaya passed away in her sleep not long after that, adding to the tragedy. She'd lived a long and full life, of course, so I guess losing her wasn't *quite* like the other, but it still stung.

So we pulled a little closer together in Kailua Kona and rarely ventured out very much after that. When you're the last handful of human beings in the world and half your number are young children who have to be cared for, you learn not to take unnecessary risks. Seven boys and eight girls, none of us older than nineteen at the most, plus Aunt Joan to hold us all together. That's all that was left out of ten billion souls.

It was about to become decidedly more top-heavy with little kids, too. Jesse and Leah were getting married in June, and they wanted me and Danielle to do it the same day, and after that it likely wouldn't be long before we all had babies to think about. There was no reason to wait and a million reasons not to, after all. Every one of us had known that ever since Dr. Weiss laid down his rules about who could go to the Moon and who couldn't. He wanted equal numbers of boys and girls so we could pair off and repopulate the world most efficiently, while preserving as much sanity in the human race as possible by making sure to keep the male-female nuclear family intact. None of those calculations had changed one whit since then. If anything, the need was even more urgent now than it was then, since there were only half as many of us still left alive.

But in spite of knowing all that, I hadn't actually made any kind of formal proposal to Danielle, and I knew she was the type of girl who wouldn't be satisfied with anything less. She didn't like to be taken for granted, and I guess I couldn't much blame her for that. I'd have to bite the bullet and ask her eventually; there were no ifs, ands, or buts about it, and I knew I couldn't put it off for much longer, either.

I'm not sure why I kept dragging my feet so much about the whole thing; I really did love her, and I couldn't imagine being with anybody else. It's just that, well, it's a big step, you know. I don't know how to explain it any better than that.

But even though we didn't often leave Kona in those days, there were occasionally places we had to go whether we liked it or not. Once in a while we had to make expeditions across the mountains to Hilo to fetch things we needed, and rarely we had to go somewhere even further afield, mostly for my species repopulation project.

And then there was one other place, too. I know I always said I wouldn't do it, but I did occasionally drive up to the observatory on top of Mauna Kea, to look at the Moon and remember old times. Not very often, mind you; only when I was in a certain kind of mood.

It's sort of cold up there, and frost or snow is nothing unusual; very different from most people's idea of what a tropical island should be like. But it's usually in the fifties during the afternoon, which is good enough to get by with a jacket. I never minded the wintry weather so much; the Moon was a lot colder than that on a regular basis. In fact, Mauna Kea sort of reminds me of the Moon in certain ways; the barren ground where nothing grows, the silence, the loneliness. It's a good place to go when you're troubled at heart and want to be alone to think for a while.

Of course, whenever you've had your fill of brooding then you can always drive back down to the coast and strip down to shorts anytime you really want to, and that's nice. Ski resort to tropical beach in less than an hour. Isn't Hawaii wonderful?

Anyway, I went up there late one afternoon to kick some rocks around and think about the whole situation with Danielle and what I wanted to do about it and when and how. The Moon was already up by then, maybe half full, and when I went inside the station to warm up for a few minutes, I decided to take a look at it.

No particular reason, other than that rum mood I was in. But as I've often said about serendipity, it's almost always the accidental discoveries which turn out to be the most interesting ones.

I didn't see anything unusual at first. There were masses of clouds above the Sea of Tranquility, but the rest of the surface seemed mostly clear. Lakeside Station was right at the edge of the terminator, teetering on the very brink of dawn but still shrouded in darkness. I usually avoided looking at that particular region, mostly because my last memories of Lakeside were not such good ones.

That's when I saw the light.

It was right there where the station should be, flashing on and off in regular pulses. You could never have seen it with the naked eye; it was much too small for that. But the telescope at Mauna Kea is an excellent one, and on an object as close as the Moon you can make out details no more than three feet across.

I didn't know quite what to think about such a thing at first, so I focused the telescope on that area and scrutinized it a little closer. Sure enough, I wasn't mistaken. Three quick flashes of light, three longer ones, and then three short ones again. Then a pause for a few seconds, and the whole sequence started over again.

I didn't have the faintest idea what it might mean, if anything, but happily that was a question that could soon be answered. The observatory computer had access to every database on Earth that still worked, so I took the liberty of asking it if that particular sequence meant anything. Half a second later I had my answer.

Turns out it means SOS in old Morse code, and everybody knows what *that* means, even now.

Help.

For a second I was so stunned I couldn't think, and then I was so amazed I didn't know *what* to think. The only logical explanation was that somebody was alive up there at Lakeside, trying to signal for help. Never mind how that was possible, or who it was.

There was no way to signal back, of course, or at least none that I could think of. If whoever-it-was had been forced to rely on something as archaic as Morse code, then obviously they didn't have anything better to use. That made things difficult, because unless they had a good telescope and happened to be looking directly at Hawaii (both unlikely) they wouldn't see it even if I flashed a light at them. So what to do?

I finally decided there was no point in trying to communicate at the moment, however frustrating that was. But I didn't intend to just forget about it, either. It had to be one of the seven people we'd left behind; either Uncle Philip, Marie Bartow, Gina Breyer, Amos or Katrina McClendon, Bethany Weiss, or maybe even the arch-villain Dr. Weiss himself. There were no other possibilities. And if one or more of those folks were really still alive up there, then we'd have to make another trip to the Moon to rescue him or her or them as soon as possible. There was no question about *that*.

I couldn't help wondering which one or ones it might be, and how they could possibly have survived. It seemed unlikely to be Dr. Weiss; he was by far the oldest, and he hadn't seemed too keen on living the last time I saw him. Uncle Philip would have had the most skill at rigging up a signaling system like the one I'd seen, but I squelched that thought almost immediately. It wouldn't do to get my hopes up and then have them be crushed if it turned out I was wrong.

The trip itself didn't worry me too much, actually. The *Balboa* was spaceworthy enough to get us there and back with no major issues other than a little bit of discomfort; no worse than what we experienced on that first trip in the *Cabral*. But Jesse would have to fly her, and that meant I needed to tell him what I'd seen immediately.

I switched off the lights and left the observatory with no more ado, driving down the steep and winding mountain roads till I pulled into our driveway in Kona less than an hour later. I confess that I probably drove a little faster than I should have, but not too much.

Jesse was gone when I got there, but Aunt Joan was in the kitchen, cooking something that smelled like potato soup. Hunter, Tommy, Amie, Veronica, Derrick, Molly, and Lucia were all sitting at the table, working on whatever assignment she'd given them for school that day. Teaching them at home was pretty much the only option we had, and nobody was willing to let them grow up knowing nothing. The accumulated knowledge of mankind has been too hard-won to let it be lost in a single generation.

"Hey, Aunt Joan, do you know where Jesse is?" I asked when I got to the kitchen.

"He's out running, but I think he'll be back in a few minutes. It's almost time to eat," she said.

"Oh, all right. I'll wait for him, then," I said.

I didn't tell her about the light; at least not yet. Aunt Joan is a tough lady who can be hard as tempered steel when she has to be; she was a survey scout for the army back in her younger days, and she's told us some stories over the years that would raise the hair on the back of your neck. She laughs them off like they were nothing.

But I knew she was still grieving for Philip, and I knew exactly what she'd instantly think if I mentioned seeing an SOS signal at Lakeside. Hope is a wonderful thing, but it can also make you sick at heart sometimes, even to the point of being physically ill. I didn't want to put her through that for any longer of a time than necessary. I was having to keep a tight leash on my own feelings for that very reason, and I was nowhere near as close to Philip as Joan was. I felt bad even telling Jesse, but unfortunately there was no way around that.

I sat down to help Hunter with his algebra homework in the meantime, not really paying much attention because the problems were easy ones.

Jesse did come in before long, just like Joan had said he would. He still likes to run as much as ever, only now he's got a whole town to do it in and no traffic to worry about. He came in and washed up for supper, and I kept my mouth shut about everything till after we finished eating. Then I decided the time was ripe.

"Hey, Jesse, I need to talk to you about something," I mentioned casually, not letting on like it was anything important.

"Yeah, what's that?" he asked, and I cut my eyes toward the back door and nodded in that direction just the slightest bit. I didn't want Aunt Joan to get the idea there was anything suspicious afoot. Jesse looked at me strangely, but when I headed for the back door he followed along. I walked all the way down to the beach, where nobody could possibly overhear us.

Our house is one of the few beachfront places in Kona, actually. There are not nearly as many beaches on Hawaii as you might think; most of the coast is rocky. But there are a few, and we had one of the nicer ones. If you've got the luxury of picking any place in town you want, you might as well go for the best one.

"What is it?" Jesse finally asked.

"I saw something earlier, up at the observatory," I said.

"And?" he asked.

"Somebody was flashing an SOS signal at Lakeside," I said, not mincing words. His eyes got wide for a second.

"Do you think. . . " he asked, but I cut him off.

"I don't know who it is. But I don't know of anybody it *could* be, except Dr. Weiss or Bethany or one of the others we left behind. Maybe even Uncle Philip," I said.

"But I thought they were all dead," he said.

"Yeah, that's what I thought, too. But I got to thinking about that on the way down here earlier. That germ Dr. Weiss released wasn't actually the real thing, you know. It was a reverse-engineered copy, and those don't always work exactly the same as the original. It might not have been near as deadly as the real Orion Strain was. Obviously it wasn't, if somebody survived up there. Unless one of them was immune like Josh or Molly, but I kind of doubt *that,*" I explained.

I hadn't come to that conclusion without a lot of thought, and I'm pretty sure it never would have crossed my mind if it hadn't been for seeing the distress signal. But as it was, I thought it was a pretty solid bet. You *can't* ever be sure how a reverse-engineered copy will perform under actual conditions; not till you try it. Living things are unbelievably complex creations, and there are a hundred thousand things that can go wrong when you try to tinker with them. I knew that from personal experience, trying to re-create some of the lost species of Earth. Sometimes they turned out fine, but other times I got nothing but monstrosities that barely survived an hour or two. That's a discouraging thing when you're trying to do something good for the world. But there are always two sides to every coin, and if that same difficulty had caused Dr. Weiss's revitalized Orion Strain to turn out as a weak and feeble copy, or even as a *slightly* weaker copy, then I could only thank God for that and bless the complexity that so often frustrated me.

"I guess that might be true. But you know if there's somebody still up there, we'll have to go get them," Jesse said.

"Yeah, that's exactly what I wanted to talk to you about," I said.

"Well. . . I'm not too worried about getting there and back; not in the *Balboa*. It's almost brand new, after all. It's while we're there that worries me. You might be right about Dr. Weiss creating an imperfect copy of the bacteria, but if he did, then who's to say we'd be immune to that other version?" he pointed out.

"That's a possibility," I admitted. I thought we were fairly safe on that point, actually, but of course you never know for sure.

"We'll have to tell the others. We can't make a trip like that and keep it a secret," he said.

"No, but who should we take with us, do you think? You'll have to go because you're the only one who can pilot, but it wouldn't be safe to have you go by yourself," I said.

"I'd say you and me, plus maybe one or two other people, tops. We might need help, but we also don't want to risk any more than we have to. I know Mom will want to go, but we can't let her do that," he said, thinking out loud.

Well, *that* much was true. Aunt Joan was the linchpin of our whole family. She taught the kids and cared for the sick and the injured and held us all together by sheer determination, if nothing else. She was irreplaceable.

Well, maybe I should rephrase that. None of us were exactly *replaceable,* but you know what I mean.

I ticked off the other possibilities in my mind. Chris would have been a good choice, but he had a wife and a daughter to think about. Johnny was still too deep in his self-inflicted misery to be much use even if he did go. There were no other boys, or at least none old enough, except just barely possibly Hunter. He *might* do, if he could be trusted to keep a level head. Out of the girls, Leah wouldn't be any good for such a mission. She was a sweet and gentle person in many ways, but danger wasn't her thing. Emily had a baby to care for. That left no one else old enough except Danielle. *She* could definitely be relied on in an emergency, and I didn't doubt she'd agree to go. I was reluctant to put her in danger that way, but what other choice did I have?

"I think the only real choices we've got are Chris and Danielle, and maybe Hunter if you think he's old enough," I finally said. Basically our same old adventure group from the Moon days, minus Drew and adding Hunter.

"Yeah. . . but I doubt Chris can go, and I'm worried about Hunter. He's only fourteen," Jesse said, chewing on his lip.

"You think we'd be okay if it was just me, you, and Danielle?" I asked.

"That worries me, too, but like you say, Hunter is really the only other choice. I'll have to think about that, maybe talk to Leah and see what she thinks about letting him go. I'm pretty sure he'd want to, if he had the choice," he said.

"Well, you know, they *did* used to have cabin boys and things like that on sailing ships a long time ago. He's not exactly a baby anymore," I said.

"Yeah, true. Like I said, I'll have to ask Leah what she thinks," he said.

"Yeah, I better talk to Danielle myself," I said.

"Okay then. Let's not say anything to anybody else for a day or two, though. You talk to Danielle and I'll talk to Leah, and maybe Hunter if we decide he should go. Other than that we'll keep mum," he said.

"No problem," I agreed, and that was that.

Now that I had a purpose in mind, I set out down the beach for Danielle's place, fully intending to discuss everything with her. She lived two houses down from Aunt Joan, on the very same strip of beach we all lived on.

She was sitting outside on the porch when I got there. She and I had picked that house together when we first arrived in Kona, knowing we'd share it together someday soon. It was right on the seashore, a three-story white stucco place with a tiled roof, surrounded with palm trees and red geraniums in big concrete planters. There were big porches on every level on the seaward side so you could always enjoy the view of the ocean, and I looked forward to the day when we could actually live there together.

She came down the steps onto the beach to meet me, the sea breeze playing with her long brown hair in a way that seemed incredibly beautiful at the time. I'm sure she would have laughed if I'd told her such a thing, but I couldn't help thinking it.

She was barefoot, and I noticed she'd painted her nails with some sparkling blue polish, almost the exact same color as the ocean beside us. I ran the rest of the way across the sand and threw my arms around her, swinging her around in a hug that almost overbalanced us both, but I think even if we'd crashed on the sand together she still would have just laughed.

But we didn't, and after a sweet kiss I put her down.

"So to what do I owe the pleasure of your visit, my sweet boy?" she asked, in that semi-facetious way she sometimes had.

"Do I need a reason to come see the prettiest girl in Kona?" I asked, and she smiled.

"Flattery will get you everywhere, my love. But really, what's up?" she asked.

"Well, there *was* something I wanted to talk to you about," I admitted.

"Yup, thought so. You better tell me, then," she said.

"Okay, but come walk with me for a while. It'll be nicer that way," I said. I kicked off my own shoes and socks, and we walked hand in hand along the wet sand at the edge of the water, letting the waves come up and swirl around our ankles. It got the bottoms of my pants legs wet, but that was all right.

So I told her everything while we walked, about the light at the station and the plan to go back there in the *Balboa* to rescue whoever-it-was, and all the risks that might be involved.

"I guess I'll be coming along then," she finally said decisively, just like I knew she would.

"I wish you didn't have to," I said.

"No, it'll be all right. This won't be too dangerous; not in the *Balboa*. And besides that, it'll be a lot better than having to sit here and worry about you the whole time you're gone. I don't think you have any idea how awful that is," she said.

"Yeah, I think maybe I do, actually," I said, remembering when I thought she was lost at Shady Lake and might never turn up alive. Not knowing is a thousand times worse than anything else.

"Well, then, be glad, not upset. Do you think Hunter will come?" she asked.

"Don't know yet. Jesse said he'd talk to him and Leah tonight and figure something out. He wanted to take along enough people to have some safety in numbers, but at the same time not risk too many of us. Three or four is already a lot, out of only sixteen people," I said.

"That's probably good thinking," she said.

The next day, she and Jesse and I went to talk things over with Chris and Joan. That discussion went surprisingly well, actually. I guess when you have a certain set of facts, they tend to lead any logical person to the same conclusions. Nobody disagreed that we had a moral obligation to try to save whoever was left on the Moon, and it was pretty obvious that Jesse and Danielle and I were the only reasonable choices to handle a rescue mission like that. The only real friction was over whether Hunter should go, just like I expected. We finally decided the risk wasn't worth the benefit, in his case.

So it was that, two days later, we all assembled on the tarmac at the little airfield in Kona; three of us to head out on our rescue mission and the others to bid us good luck. Leah gave Jesse a long kiss before we left, and Danielle gave Derrick one and told him to behave himself till she got home. Aunt Joan hugged all three of us, and Veronica put garlands of red and purple flowers around our necks, just like you sometimes see in old movies about tourists when they first arrive in Hawaii.

But finally all the words were said and all the love was wished, and then it was time to leave. Jesse took his place in the pilot's chair while Danielle and I found seats in the main cabin and buckled in.

Then he took us up.

Chapter Two

It reminded me a lot of that first journey in the *Cabral*, actually. Unpleasantly so. We had more and better food this time, and warmer clothes, and generally speaking an easier time of it than we ever did before, but three days in space is never anybody's idea of a relaxing vacation, I promise you. Nobody threw up this time, but I'm pretty sure we all felt like it. I know I did.

It was re-entry that worried me more than the trip itself, though. Everything had gone perfectly fine the last time too, at least till we started to come in for a landing. But I remembered the crash all too well, and the memory made me ill at ease almost from the second we entered the Moon's atmosphere.

"Nervous?" Danielle asked. She was sitting beside me, and I guess she must have noticed the way I was gripping the armrests.

"Yeah, a little," I admitted.

I was braced for the trip through that canyon in the Snowy Mountains and all the bad memories *that* would bring back, especially if we caught a glimpse of the crash site and the remains of the *Cabral*. But it turned out Jesse didn't go that way at all. He avoided the high mountains altogether and came in from the west instead. I'm not sure why Mrs. Weiss didn't do that the first time, unless maybe there was a storm out there on the ocean that she had to avoid.   I thought I vaguely remembered her mentioning something like that during her tongue-in-cheek little welcome speech when we first arrived, but maybe memory was playing tricks on me.

Anyway, we landed this time without a hitch, just as smooth and pretty as you please.   As soon as the *Balboa* stopped moving I let out a long sigh of relief.

It was only about five days after sunrise at that point, just long enough that the snow had had a chance to melt off and the weather was almost at its nicest point for the month.   The hills were ablaze with flowers when we landed; it was the height of the morning bloom, and I gaped at it through the windows for a while.   I'd forgotten how pretty the Moon could be at certain times.

Jesse parked us right in front of the little building where the buggies and the airplanes were stored.   Then he shut down the engines, and we were officially there.

"Well, here we are," he said, coming out of the cockpit and rubbing his hands together.

"Yeah, here we are," I agreed uneasily.   In spite of my theory that our immunity to the Orion Strain should also be effective against Dr. Weiss's alternate version, it still made my skin crawl just a bit to think of opening the airlock.   We all stood there for a few seconds eyeing it, none of us wanting to go first.

Danielle was the first one who moved.

"Well, we didn't come all this way for nothing, did we?" she asked, and started turning the handle to open the inner door.   That shamed me into following her; if she was brave enough to pop the lock then surely I could be, too.   Besides that, she was right.   If we didn't mean to go out there and see what was what then we might as well never have come at all.

A few minutes later the outer door swung open, letting in a pungent whiff of that wet gunpowder smell I remembered so well. We went down the steps, shutting the door behind us, and then set out to hike the just-over-a-mile to Lakeside.

We didn't talk much, I guess because we were all tense about possible germs and also about what we might find once we got to the actual station. I could imagine lots of things; not all of them good. Worst of all was the notion that had popped into my mind right before we landed, that somehow that distress signal might have been some kind of malfunction in the station's computer system and we'd arrive in the lobby of the Institute building to find nothing but a group of skeletons waiting for us.

I didn't mention that particular idea to the others, but I think we all must have at least wondered about things like that.

We arrived at the chain link fence to find the gate standing open and the gravity enhancer still switched on. I noticed *that* immediately, but then of course I didn't know whether anybody had turned it off when they left the place or not. I doubted it, since the control room was inside the Institute building and therefore one of the first places to be contaminated with spores. Joan would never have risked lives by trying to go in there and shut things down. There was supposed to be an automatic hibernation mode that kicked in if nobody pushed a button or performed any kind of electronic activities at the station for a week, and it *should* have switched off the grav enhancer and some of the other high-power systems, to save energy. But then again, there was no telling whether it still operated properly or not. Like everything else at Lakeside it was old as dirt, and things don't always work the way they're meant to when they get decrepit like that. So maybe the simple fact that everything was still switched on didn't really prove much either way.

I was still trying not to get my hopes up too much, I guess.

The place was quiet and still except for the sound of the waves on the lake and the breeze in the Joshua trees. By unspoken agreement, we headed for the Institute building first. If there were any survivors, that was very likely where they'd be. If we found nobody there, the next place on the list would be the greenhouse, and then the cabins.

Jesse got there first and gingerly opened the door, letting us into the lobby.

There were no skeletons inside, at least. We quickly explored the rest of the building and found nothing unusual. That in itself was odd, though, since we all knew that was the last place Philip and the others had been.

"Where do you think they went?" Jesse whispered. The place felt spooky, like walking through a funeral home, making you not want to talk too loud.

"I don't know, but come on, there's nothing here to see. Let's go check the greenhouse," I said, deliberately *not* whispering. If you let yourself go that route, it's easy to develop a major case of the willies for no reason at all, and that wouldn't do *any* of us any good.

We left the building and headed across the compound to where the greenhouse stood, but then Danielle put a hand on my arm.

"Look," she said, and I turned my head in the direction she was pointing. Down by the lakeshore, right next to the basketball court we'd built last year, were six gravestones.

That was the first solid proof we'd yet seen that somebody must have survived up there at least for a while, so we immediately went to check them out. They were rough, made of white lunar stone. *Snowstone*, we used to call it. Each one had a name and a year, and silently we read them off.

Bethany Weiss, 2137 – 2155

Marie Bartow 2115 – 2155

Gina Breyer, 2113 – 2155

Robert Weiss, 2099 – 2155

Amos McClendon, 2119 – 2155

Katrina McClendon, 2125 – 2155

There was one name conspicuously absent from the list, and since *someone* had to dig those graves and mark those stones, we all knew who it must have been. Uncle Philip.

"But where *is* he?" Jesse wondered aloud, asking the question we all had on our minds. We swiftly searched the rest of the compound, and soon found unmistakable signs of recent occupation. There were vegetables growing in the greenhouse, obviously planted and tended. The cabin where Philip and Joan had once lived was plainly still being used. There hadn't even been time for weeds to start growing in the greenhouse. Philip had to be there, someplace. But as Jesse had said, where *was* he?

"Do you think he went fishing?" I finally suggested, uncertainly. I couldn't imagine where else he might have got off to.

"I doubt it. We took the *Moon Cat* when we left, remember? And if he wanted to fish from the bank he could do that right here without having to go anywhere," Jesse said.

"Yeah, true," I agreed.

The mystery was soon solved, though. We were still standing there frowning at the cabins when none other than Philip himself appeared in the eastern gate, wearing a bag of wrenches and tools. He didn't notice us at first, nor we him, but then Jesse spotted him. And then, forgetting all dignity and decorum, he ran to his father with a loud cry and threw his arms around him. When you unexpectedly run into someone you dearly love and have long believed to be dead, I guess you can be excused for such things. I would have liked to do the same thing myself, actually, but I forbore, for Jesse's sake.

But in time the emotion of those first few moments settled down, and we were able to ask some of the thousand questions we all had.

"I must have been unconscious for days, and then even after I woke up I was still sick for a long time. If we hadn't been in the cafeteria I don't think I would have made it. I know I couldn't have crawled anywhere. But there was food and water, and I gradually got strong enough to walk again. The others weren't so lucky," he said sadly.

"It's a miracle you survived," I said, and he nodded.

"Yeah, it really is. Maybe even literally," he agreed.

"So what happened next?" Jesse asked.

"I knew y'all were gone by then, so all I could do was try to keep surviving. I buried the others down there by the lake, and then for a while nothing much happened. The radio never did work, and I couldn't think of any way to use the computer to get in touch with anybody. All the email servers and phone networks on Earth crashed a long time ago, and I didn't know how else to find you. Then I finally thought of using the floodlights to signal somebody. I figured sooner or later one of you might get sentimental and decide to take a look at Lakeside through a telescope, so I rigged up the lights to keep flashing all the time whenever it was dark. I guess it finally caught somebody's attention," he said.

"Yeah, I guess it finally did," I said, feeling bad that I hadn't noticed sooner.

"Well, is there anything you need to take with you, Mr. Carpenter? We've got the *Balboa* sitting out there at the air strip ready and waiting. We might as well head home before it gets too hot," Danielle said.

"I wish we could, but unfortunately there's one more thing we have to do first," he said.

"What's that?" I asked, mystified.

"We've got to pay a visit to Tycho Crater," he said.

Now it so happens that Tycho Crater is one of the most noteworthy features on the Moon, in case you didn't know. When you look at the full moon you can even see it with the naked eye; it's down toward the south, and it has rays coming out from it in all directions. It's named after Tycho Brahe, just like I am, and I'd wanted to visit it while we were on the Moon last time. Not because it was anything special to see, most likely; I mostly just thought the name was cool. But I never got a chance to visit the place, partly because it was so far away; roughly 1500 miles, if I remembered right. That's a long way, even on the Moon. We couldn't fly the *Balboa* down there, either, because there was no place to land it.

"Why do we have to go all the way down *there?*" Jesse asked.

"I can't tell you that," Philip said, which left all three of us speechless for a second. I guess he could have made up a plausible-sounding story if he'd wanted to, but Philip isn't like that. He'll either tell the perfect truth or he won't talk at all, and when that happens then he'll usually come right out and tell you so. That can be jarring at times.

Not to mention *highly* unsatisfying, if you've got even a speck of curiosity in your bones. I had the devil's plenty of *that,* but I knew as well as the others did that we might as well not waste our time badgering him with any more questions. If he said he couldn't tell us anything, then that's the last word we'd hear on the subject, period.

There are certain times when the only choice you have is whether to trust somebody or not. Philip isn't capricious by any means, so if he thought there was a good enough reason to go all the way down to Tycho Crater before we left the Moon then I had to believe there must be, no matter how crazy it sounded.

The others must have reached similar conclusions, because nobody said a word more about whether we'd go or not. Philip had decided, and he was the leader, and that was that.

Aunt Joan used to tell us stories about her army days sometimes, and she's always been a firm believer in the proper chain of command and having respect for authority and all that jazz. She always said it's not that you have to believe the leader is always right, because he very well may not be sometimes. It's that you'd better *hope* he's right, because if he's not then you *might* end up dead, but if you argue and create dissension then you almost *certainly* will. She drummed that idea into all of us while we were growing up, and for the most part I think it's been a good lesson. It's a very sad and obvious fact that rebels tend to have hard lives and die young. There are times when principled disobedience is the right choice, of course; she simply told us to think long and hard about it first. She would have said there's only one allegiance which no man or woman can ever deny for any reason, and that is to God. In fact, she told me once that if she or Philip or anyone else in authority ever told me to do something ungodly, then she not only expected but ordered me to refuse immediately. . . but that had better be the only reason I ever had for bucking the rules.

But since this wasn't one of those occasions, all the training of a lifetime inclined me to do whatever Philip said.

"Is that other little plane still parked in the hangar out at the airfield?" I finally asked. If it was, then we could fly down to Tycho and land on the water somewhere nearby without too much trouble. That was exactly the kind of thing it was built for, after all.

"It's still there as far as I know," Philip said.

"We better go check it out, then," Jesse said.

So that's what we did. We stayed at Lakeside long enough to shut down the computer system and give Philip a chance to shave and put on some clean clothes, but other than that we were all glad to see the last of the place.

Then we encountered a problem. As soon as we reached the airfield, we discovered that the other plane wouldn't start. The reason was obvious once we lifted the hood; a rat had gnawed off the corner of the main circuit board for the inertial navigation computer and ruined it. Flying without navigation on the Moon is dangerous; you've got no compass, no radio, nothing to keep track of where you are or even what direction you're headed. So if the navigation system won't operate for some reason, there's a built-in safety switch on those planes that won't even let the engine start. Jesse probably could have found a way to work around it with a little luck, but then again, those safety switches are in place for a reason. It really *is* dangerous to fly blind, and you're begging for disaster if you try it.

"Well, that's out," Danielle said glumly.

"There might be a usable boat over there at the fisheries station on the west coast. If there is then we could use that to skim along the shore like we did on the way back from Mount Hadley that time. We'd have to walk it, though. There's no airstrip over there," Jesse said.

"How far is it?" I asked.

"Two hundred miles, maybe two-fifty. But at least there's a road all the way," Jesse said.

"That's a long way to walk, just for a maybe. I'm sure I don't need to remind you what this place is like with no shelter, do I? How blistering hot it gets, how stormy and dangerous it can be?" I asked.

"No, I promise you I remember all that real well," Jesse said.

"It's not as bad as you think. We can take the buggy and be over there and back in only a couple days, before it gets really hot," Philip said.

"But we wrecked the buggy. Chris broke the axle," Danielle said.

"Yeah, I know he did. But I haven't been sitting on my hands for a whole year. I went out there a few months ago with a portable welder and fixed it," Philip said.

"A welded axle still won't be as good as the original," Jesse said doubtfully.

"No, but it'll do. We won't be racing across the desert; we'll be driving down the road like civilized people," Philip said.

"Well, in that case, we could probably haul the boat back here and use the canal system to head south instead of sticking to the coast. It'd be a lot safer, probably," Jesse said.

"What do you mean, probably?" Danielle asked.

"We wouldn't have to worry about storms at least. But anywhere down south of the Caloosahatchie valley is a dangerous place to visit. There's a lot of radiation because of the mountains, and I know they turned loose some pretty vicious monsters down there, too," Jesse said.

"Monsters?" I asked.

"I don't know what else you'd call them. Genetically engineered creatures designed to be aggressive, bloodthirsty, and bad tempered. Things for the big game hunters to get a thrill from," he said.

"I don't remember hearing about them before," I said.

"They only live down there on the other side of the swamp. They were designed not to be able to swim, so they couldn't cross over and bother anybody up here in this neck of the woods. I read about them in the Map Room one time, but it never mattered much since we never went down there anywhere we might see one," Jesse said.

"So it's a choice between storms or monsters? Sounds wonderful," I said.

"Well, no. Like I said, they can't swim and they hate water. Long as we stay on the canal we shouldn't have a problem. That's one reason why they built it in the first place, you know. A lot of people like to have those fake adventures where there's never really any danger, like one of those safaris where the animals are trained to act mean but then just stand still till the customer shoots them. The folks who wanted a taste of *real* danger could always go off to hunt monsters on foot, and the ones who only wanted some cheap thrills could stay safely on the canal like good little tourists. Something to please everybody, that way," Jesse said.

"That sounds stupid," I said, and it did, too. But no stupider than a dozen other half-baked ideas the terraformers had built in to this unendingly strange place. Sometimes it reminded me of a gigantic amusement park.

"Maybe so, but it's the safest and quickest way of getting to Tycho Crater that I can think of, since we don't have a plane," Jesse said.

Nobody could think of anything better, so Jesse's plan was accepted by mutual agreement.

The highway that ran west out of Lakeside only barely deserved the name. It was supposed to be all-weather gravel, but fifty years of lunar storms will do a number on almost anything. There were several washouts and potholes we had to be careful of, but most of the bridges were still intact, at least.

We soon dropped down out of the Lakeside Hills into the wide desert of Yucca Flats, so named because almost nothing grew there except yucca plants. We talked about this and that along the way, but it was mostly just dull. It was nice weather for riding, though, and I actually enjoyed that part of our little adventure. Finally we went up and over a pass in the dark brown Chocolate Mountains, and soon found ourselves right there on the coast of the Stormy Ocean.

It didn't seem too stormy at the moment, but we were all wary nevertheless. Weather on the Moon can change fast.

The fishery was trashed. That's the kindest word I can use to describe it. I'm sure it had been taking the full brunt of storms for years, and there was no high bluff to protect anything from the waves as there was at Barnaby on the north coast.

But still, those little Moon-boats were tough; they had to be. We soon found one that floated, at least, though that was about the best you could say for the thing. It was called the *Elsinore*, and it hadn't escaped its own share of battering over the years. The motor and battery were shot, and it was missing a few other pieces it ought to have had, but other than that it seemed to be in better shape than any of the others.

"I think we can work with this. We've got plenty of spare parts back at Lakeside," Philip said, examining the boat critically.

We rigged up a rickety trailer to haul the boat back to the hangar at Lakeside, and before long Jesse and Philip were able to refit the old girl into a working ship again. While they were working on the motor and such, Danielle and I were sent to the cafeteria to fetch food and supplies for the journey. There was still a goodish amount of canned and preserved food in there which might as well be used. We needed what was on the *Balboa* for the trip home.

"So, whatcha hungry for, babe? Stale sardines? Ancient ham, maybe?" she asked, looking at cans.

"Gee, what a choice," I said.

"Yeah, I know. Reminds me of Sunday dinners when Gina used to pass out a can from the store room so we could have something besides fish and cornbread for a change," she said.

"No doubt. Only problem is, now I'm *used* to eating good. Fifty year old sauerkraut and weenies just doesn't do much for me anymore," I said.

"Me neither, but since this is all we've got, we'll have to make do again for a while. I guess we should be thankful it's here," she said.

"Yeah, I know, and I am. We better grab a good variety of stuff, though. It'll probably take a month or so to reach the crater, and anything gets old after a while," I said.

We loaded up a decent supply, along with some honey and dried milk and other things like that, not to mention flatware and various other necessities. Then we hauled it all back to the hangar where Philip and Jesse were still working on the *Elsinore*. We stowed everything in the hold, and then there was really nothing left to do except wait for them to finish with the motor.

It was getting on towards the hottest part of the day when they finally got her fixed up, but none of us were inclined to wait till evening to get started. The first part of the trip would be to cross the wide Okechobee, and since the open water wouldn't be near as hot as the land, we all thought we could tough it out.

So we hauled the *Elsinore* down to the beach and launched her with great fanfare, and then before long the four of us were all on board, headed south across the lake.

Chapter Three

It was a lot like I remembered from a thousand fishing trips; big slow-moving swells of blue-green water topped with glassy whitecaps from the wind. It looked rougher than it really was, but Jesse is a good sailor. The ship gave no trouble, and we zipped across the lake in only a few hours' time.

Heat and humidity came back with a vengeance as soon as we entered the channel where the Caloosahatchie River cut south through the swamplands on the southern shore, but at least the moving boat created enough breeze to keep us from getting baked alive. Instead of following the river itself down to the Sea of Tranquility like we did when we fled to the Summer Isles, this time Jesse turned aside after a few hours into a channel that cut back to the southwest.

That's when the real adventure began.

I learned a lot about the Moon over the next several days, not all of it nice. The Land of Snow is a manicured, prettified place intended from the very beginning to attract tourists and retirees with fun, beauty, and grandeur, and a lot of that intensive effort still showed. But once we crossed the swamps, all obvious traces of the terraformers' handiwork vanished. We soon found ourselves in an ugly land of bald mountains pockmarked with livid green crater swamps. We passed through a lot of those, in fact, since the canal took advantage of natural low spots whenever possible. The whole area looked unhealthy, and I guess it probably was, for that matter. Those mountains got hammered with a lot of hard radiation; ten times what there was at Lakeside, if the guidebook was to be believed. I bet the frogs in those swamps had six legs apiece and glowed in the dark.

"I sure am glad we never had to live *here,*" Danielle said, looking at it all.

"Yeah, me too," I agreed. I think all of us would have come away with a very different impression of the Moon than we did, if we'd crashed just a few hundred miles farther south. In fact, I don't know that we'd ever have survived.

We hadn't seen or heard any monsters yet, and I was glad to keep it that way. I'd never even seen a picture of one, but Jesse was glad to provide us with a lurid and horrifying description, full of such wonderfully colorful details as the fact that they had a mouth full of teeth shaped like needles, sharp enough to slice through flesh and bone like a hot knife through butter. He has a real talent for that kind of thing.

The trees along the canal were mostly cottonwoods, considerably larger and thicker than I was used to seeing around Lakeside, and sometimes I couldn't help staring at the darkness under the canopy, shifting my weight uneasily on the deck and halfway believing I saw needle-sharp teeth glinting in some momentary finger of light. I could imagine whole packs of monsters snuffling and growling out there just out of sight, waiting for an opportunity to pounce as soon as we got too close to the bank. It was a tad bit scary to think about, even in the middle of a golden afternoon. Yeah, I know I was being a little bit paranoid, but that was my reward for listening to Jesse's gruesome stories too much.

To hear him tell it, monsters weren't the only big game animals the terraformers had installed on the southern part of the peninsula, either. There were bears and panthers and other things out there, too, or at least there had been. It was hard to say which ones or how many Dr. Weiss's modified bacterium might have killed off, but if Uncle Philip survived then it wasn't too much of a stretch to think that some of the other living things on the Moon might have survived, too. That's the problem when you're dealing with an unknown quantity; you simply don't know, and I don't like guesswork when lives might be at stake.

The canal hadn't fared much better than the highway when it came to storms and such, and that slowed us down considerably. It was full of logs and sandbars, and several times Jesse had to get uncomfortably close to the bank, giving me vivid images of monsters leaping out from amongst the trees. There were also islands and other hazards which had to be navigated.

But it was the heat that was worst of all. We couldn't sail the *Elsinore* fast enough to get much relief from the breeze anymore, and the air itself was dead still. Lakeside had always been that way for several days each month, true, but at least that had been a dry, desert-like kind of heat. Bad enough in its own right, but nothing compared to this. *This* was the humid, suffocating heat of a tropical swamp on the hottest day you ever imagined. Think of southern Louisiana during a hundred-year heat wave and you might get some faint idea of what the crater swamps of the Altai Mountains on the Moon are like on a normal day. We had to take turns steering the boat around obstacles, and the rest of the time we spent cowering below decks with the air conditioner running full blast. It was miserably hot even then, and I almost wished we'd risked the Stormy Ocean instead. I was ready to face a thousand hurricanes one right after another, as long as I didn't have to be hot.

It gradually got a little bit better as the sun sank ever-so-slowly into the west, although we all knew it was only a temporary reprieve before the freezing cold night arrived.

We pressed on for as long as possible in the twilight, till it got too dark to see our way. We had to stop then; there was too much danger of hitting a log or a rock and sinking the boat. Jesse tied us up to a gnarly cottonwood tree at the tip of an island, and then let the *Elsinore* drift slowly downstream until the rope caught it. If the monsters didn't like water, then that was the safest place we could be for a while. We were far south by then, over three quarters of the way to our destination, if we calculated right.

Soon a heavy fog rolled in from the Cloudy Sea to the west, thick as split pea soup, and before long it was mixed with cold rain. It was strange to see fog and rain together like that, but at least it wasn't anything dangerous.

"Nasty weather," I commented, looking out the doorway. We were all settled in the cabin below decks to stay dry, wrapped in blankets so we could put off having to turn on the heater for as long as possible. The battery was supposed to contain enough energy to keep the ship's cabin warm or cool for at least two weeks without the motor running, just in case a research crew got stranded somewhere and no one could come to their rescue for a while. But those components were fifty years old, and none of us wanted to lean on them any harder than we had to.

"Yeah, I hope it's not like this all night," Danielle said.

"Might be better if it is, actually. It'll keep us a little warmer, at least. Fog insulates pretty well," I said.

Danielle looked like she was about to say something else, but just then we heard a bone-chilling shriek from somewhere outside. We all jumped to our feet without thinking; you tend to do that when something freezes your very blood like that.

"What *was* that?" I asked.

"Uh. . . if I had to guess, I'd say it's one of the monsters," Jesse said, slowly sitting back down and wrapping his blanket around his shoulders again.

I don't think I've ever heard a more horrible sound in my life than the scream of those genetically engineered monstrosities on the Moon. I don't doubt they were intentionally designed to sound that way, and all I can say is, as many beautiful things as the geneticists created for the Moon and as much love and care as they poured into the Summer Isles or the Red Rock Desert, their work had a dark and horrifying side, too. One which I'd never seen (or heard) till that moment.

The fog made it worse, because it muffled and distorted sounds and made it impossible to tell how far away they were or even what direction they'd come from. We seemed to be enclosed in a dark gray capsule that shut out the whole world except for the boat itself. That monster might have been screaming at us from the tip of the island for all we knew, not fifteen feet away. That was a truly terrifying thought.

Eventually the rain switched over to snow, just like it always had at Lakeside, and soon enough we found ourselves locked in ice and buried under deep drifts. That suited me just as well; I definitely felt safer that way.

There's not much to tell about how we spent that long lunar night. Once in a while we heard the scream of a monster, faint and far through the snow, but mostly it was nothing but tedious waiting. We talked, we ate, we slept a lot, sometimes we played cards or told stories or whatever else we could think of to while away the time. I guess it helped that we were all used to that kind of thing from the last time we'd been on the Moon, even though the cabin of the *Elsinore* was a lot tighter quarters than we'd ever had to share before.

But at long last the sun rose and the snow and ice melted away. At first I had visions of the raging torrent the Lucky River had become during the morning melt, but thankfully the canal was nothing like that. Yes, it overflowed its banks and flooded for a while, turning the water thick and dense with chalky-white mud. It reminded me of a joke I heard once about a river that was too thick to drink and too thin to plow. It felt almost like we were sailing on a lake of condensed milk.

But it wasn't dangerous, and what little current there was didn't affect things much. We were able to go on almost as soon as the ice broke up.

In hindsight, it might have been better if we hadn't.

For a while we made good progress, zipping along the swollen canal without a care in the world. We were pretty confident we'd make it the rest of the way to Tycho Crater within a few hours, and maybe even all the way back to Lakeside before sundown, with a little luck.

Unfortunately, it didn't work out quite that way.

I don't know what it was we hit, but all of a sudden there was a loud *thunk* from underneath us, and the boat left the water at an alarming angle. It's hard to turn over a catamaran, but you can certainly do it if you hit a submerged object in just the right way. We barely had time to realize we must have hit something under the surface, before the hull flipped over and dumped us out into the canal.

I plunged under the surface without hitting bottom, and came back up gasping for air. I saw the others all swimming for shore, so I quit worrying about them and concentrated on saving my own skin. Since it wasn't really all that far to the bank (or the treetops where the bank would be later on, I guess I should say), I made it with no particular problems. I pulled myself up into a cottonwood tree near the others, covered from head to toe in thin chalky mud, and looked out across the river again to see if I could find any of our things.

The boat was floating upside down in the water, slowly drifting back downstream. I soon realized there was no saving it; we didn't have the strength or the leverage to flip it back over before it sank. Not out in the middle of the water like that. My fear was soon confirmed when the *Elsinore* slipped beneath the milky flood, disappearing with all our food, tools, and everything else. We were stranded, barefoot and soaking wet, in the middle of those monster-haunted hills.

The thought filled me with dread, and for pretty danged good reasons, too. We were well and truly in trouble this time. It was no use to head back to Lakeside on foot. Even if the monsters didn't eat us along the way, we'd never make it back across the Caloosahatchie swamps with no boat. We'd never recover the *Elsinore*, either; not after all the silt settled out and buried her in mud ten feet deep.

I had the panicky kind of feeling that a rat must have when he finds himself caught in a trap with no hope of escape, and that's a bad feeling to have.

I told myself sternly to get a grip and think logically. You can't give up just because you hit a rough patch; it only means you have to toughen up a little, that's all.

The first thing I did was to feel in my pockets to see if I had anything useful in there. It turned out I still had my knife, and that was *something*, at least. I also had the stub of a pencil and a soggy, crumpled up note with some indecipherable writing on it, but I didn't see how those things would be much use at all. It looked like

Danielle had had the presence of mind to grab a piece of flotsam while she swam; a backpack that might contain almost anything.

"There's a facility at Tycho Crater. They might have another boat!" Philip said, yelling so we could all hear him. I didn't overlook the fact that he only said there *might* be another boat, but I latched onto that slim hope like a hungry man snatches at a piece of bread. Even a small hope is ten thousand times better than none at all.

"Everybody swim to solid ground. We can't afford to wait for the water to go down," he went on. That was good sense, so we all swam through the flooded trees till we reached an actual solid bank, and then stood there shivering in the chill breeze.

"So what do we do now?" Jesse asked.

"We'll have to try to reach Tycho on foot; it's no use to head back to Lakeside from here. But we'll have to keep following the canal so we don't get lost," Philip said, and we all nodded. Mountains and hills on Earth have been shaped by water for so long that they have at least a semi-predictable shape and form, and you can almost always find your way out of them simply by following water downstream. The Moon isn't like that at all. The hills there are full of random pockets and valleys that go nowhere, little streams which will lead you into nothing but crater swamps or (even worse) quicksand beds, and you could wander for days without finding your way out. And time is the one luxury you usually don't have on the Moon; you're always under the constant threat of freezing, roasting, drowning, or getting fried by an afternoon electrical storm. It's never a matter of *if* one of those things will happen, either; it's only a matter of how long it will take, and which one of them will get you first. So if you know of a path to get you where you want to go, you better stick to it if you can.

"Let's see what's in here first, before we go," Danielle said, unzipping the backpack she'd saved. It turned out to contain a canned ham and several bottles of Gatorade. I remembered packing it, now that we had the bag open.

"That won't last long, among four of us," Jesse pointed out. It was a glum thought.

"No, but it's a lot better than nothing. We'll have to ration it the best we can," Philip said.

There was nothing else to be said, so we struggled on southward as best we could, grimly determined to either reach Tycho or die trying. If we didn't find some kind of food before the ham ran out, then there was little doubt what the outcome would be.

The water level dropped over the next few days until the canal returned to its normal level, and after that things were a little bit easier. But the blistering heat also returned with a vengeance, and we dared not exert ourselves too much. The shade of the cottonwood trees helped a little bit, but not nearly enough. When it's that hot, you can get sun-sick even in the shade.

We survived on ham and Gatorade for as long as we could make it last, stretching it out to the uttermost drop and crumb. Then we did without.

In a perverse kind of way, knowing what we were up against stiffened my courage. If a thing has to be endured, well then it has to be, simple as that. No use crying over it. I know people who fall to pieces when things get tough, and I can't help wondering what good they think that will do. Some or all of us might very well die before we could make it home; well, that was simply reality. We'd do all we could, and if we failed then at least we could die knowing we didn't give up.

Still, the fastest speed we could manage was only a snail's pace compared to the boat. We were just north of the Stöfler-Faraday Crater when the *Elsinore* sank, and that's a large crater swamp about sixty miles across. A big, putrid, stinking mess. But also useful, because the old rim-walls of the crater were elevated above the surrounding land and gave us a really dry and firm place to walk for a while.

Five days after the wreck we were *still* on those rim walls, if you want some idea of how big that crater is. The ham was long gone by then, and my stomach was rumbling with nothing to satisfy it. My head ached from the heat, and my eyes burned from the sweat that trickled down into them and blurred my vision. It felt like I was wrapped in a warm, wet towel, which I guess I almost was; my shirt and pants were soaked with sweat which couldn't evaporate in the humid air. The only things blessedly absent were the flies and mosquitoes, since those things don't live on the Moon.

The others must have felt just as miserable as I did, because it wasn't long before Philip decided it was time to call a halt for the day. We needed to sleep for a few hours if possible, hard as that would be in the stifling heat.

We were almost forty degrees south of the lunar equator by then, roughly the same latitude as New Zealand, so that meant it wasn't *quite* as hot as it would have been farther north. I'm not sure we could have survived at all, if it had been. It was still bad enough as it was.

I drank the last of my Gatorade, then picked my way down to the edge of the crater for a quick swim to cool off and wash some of the grime and sweat from my body, even though the water was far from the cleanest I've ever seen. I wished longingly for the hook and line that we'd lost when the boat flipped. As much as I always swore I'd never eat another fish, I would have been glad to sink my teeth into one right then.

"Do you think it's safe to drink the water?" Danielle asked when I got out, looking at the fetid pool behind me. It was a good question, since the Gatorade was all gone.

"Well. . . the terraformers never introduced a lot of those nasty germs and parasites you might find in a swamp on Earth. So yeah, probably," I said. I wasn't at all sure of that, honestly, but it sounded like a good guess.

"Probably?" she asked.

"You never know for sure till you try it, I guess. But I don't see that we've got much choice. We have to have water," I said.

"I know. But I'd feel a lot better about things if we had some of those purification tablets or some other way to make sure it's safe," she said.

That gave me an idea.

"You know, I think we might just have a way to make that work," I said.

"How's that?" she asked.

"I'll have to show you. Come on, let's go cut down one of those big pieces of bamboo over there," I said. She shrugged and came with me to the canebrake, willing to see what I had in mind. I got out my pocketknife and started sawing on one of the segments while she watched. Turns out cutting down bamboo as thick as your calf with a pocketknife is pretty hard work, but soon enough I had a ragged segment about as long as my forearm.

"What's that for?" Danielle asked.

"Watch and see," I said. I then proceeded to pack the bamboo segment with alternating layers of sand from the beach and ground-up charcoal from our campfire till it was full.

"Now we've got a filter. Pour some water in the top and catch it when it runs out the bottom. It ought to be a lot cleaner," I said.

"Where'd you learn that?" she asked.

"Aunt Joan used to have one of those pitchers that filter tap water, several years ago. Me and Jesse took it apart one day to see how it worked and then got in trouble because we couldn't put it back together again," I said smugly. I remembered the incident very well; we hadn't been more than nine or ten years old, and Aunt Joan had made both of us wash dishes for a week to make up for breaking her pitcher. . . the most hated of all chores. But if that old memory could save our bacon now, then I'd gladly wash dishes every day for the rest of my life.

Sure enough, after the swamp water had flowed through the sand and charcoal it looked clear as a mountain stream. I gingerly took a sip, not quite trusting it. I thought it still had a muddy, fishy kind of taste, but I might have been imagining things.

The canal itself ended at Stöfler-Faraday, but the waterway continued in the form of a broad river which flowed out over the southeastern lip of the crater. If all went well, then about sixty miles downstream we'd meet the drainage river coming down from Tycho, and we could follow that up to our destination. And then, with a little luck, we might actually find a boat, or maybe even some food. I was much more focused on that goal at the time than anything else, and to tell the truth I'd almost forgotten to wonder anymore why Philip had originally wanted us to visit the place. Who cared about that, when survival was at stake?

After the incident with the bamboo filter we found a sandy place under some cottonwood trees to sleep for a few hours, taking turns on watch. Then after that it was back to the same old slog, putting one foot in front of the other till I felt almost hypnotized by the movement.

There was nothing left to eat, and gnawing hunger is not a nice feeling, I promise you. Whenever it got unbearable I drank some filtered river water to fend it off for a while. You can actually go for quite a long time on very short rations, if you have to. After the first few days you won't even be hungry anymore. But it's a dangerous thing to do, because you'll start losing weight fast and it won't take long before you start getting weak, too. An occasional wild grape or edible mushroom foraged from the woods wasn't going to cut the mustard for long.

We reached the place where the river met the other one, and quickly headed upstream on the new course. We made pretty good time on that, too, in spite of the fact that it was steeper terrain. The sun was sinking pretty low in the west by then, and we needed to find that facility at Tycho so we'd have a warm place to spend the night. We hadn't seen any caves recently, and we'd never survive in the open with no shelter.

We heard the sound of water pouring over stone long before we saw it. But soon the river swung around a sharp bend, and we found ourselves walking westward, directly into the setting sun. Not long after that, we reached the source of the noise.

It was a line of rocks that stretched across the river, and the water came pouring over and through them with a loud roar. It wasn't quite a waterfall, but it was something more than just rapids, too. Beyond it, the high rim-walls of Tycho Crater reared up suddenly out of the hills, and the river came down through them in a deep gorge.

We'd finally made it.

Chapter Four

I'm not sure what I expected to see when we climbed and scrambled our way up to the top of the rim-walls. If anything, I had a vague notion that it might turn out to be another nasty crater swamp pretty much like a hundred others we'd seen. That's what tends to happen after a while, as a crater gets filled up with silt washing down from the mountains. But there are exceptions to that rule; the ones with high rim-walls that don't let in a lot of runoff tend to turn into lakes, not swamps. Tycho was one of that kind. It was only swampy in a few spots around the very edges, and most of it was open water, blue as a sapphire under the sky. It was a little smaller than Stöfler-Faraday; maybe forty-five miles across, and besides the clear water and the unusually high rim-walls, the only thing even slightly remarkable about it was the fact that it had a rocky island in the exact center, maybe three or four miles across. I guess it was the remains of whatever piece of rock smashed into the Moon and formed the crater in the first place. We could just barely see it, in spite of how high up we were.

"That's where we need to go," Philip said, pointing at the island.

"Yeah, but how do we get there from here?" I asked, eyeing the lake down below us. There were still twenty miles of open water to cross, with no boat. Some people might be able to swim that far, but I doubted any of us could do it.

"There are some trees and things down there next to the shore. We might could build a raft," Jesse said. He sounded doubtful, but I had to admit I couldn't think of anything better to try.

So we made our way down to the shore and collected some limbs from the cottonwood trees, tying them together with some tough vines. When we got done it looked like a pitiful excuse for a raft; the kind that might fall apart if you looked at it cross-eyed.

"Do you think that's safe?" I asked, looking at it.

"No, probably not. But it'll be even less safe to spend the night out here with no shelter. We've got to make it to that island one way or another. If the raft falls apart, we can probably grab hold of some of the loose wood to stay afloat. The water should be warm as a bathtub this time of day, so if we stick together then maybe we could finish swimming the rest of the way, if we had to. I hope," Jesse said.

He was right, of course, so we launched our little craft and paddled out into the lake, headed directly for the island. Our only reference point was the sun, and the crater walls behind us. The raft floated dangerously low in the water, or so it seemed to me. We were sitting in several inches of water at all times, and more than that whenever a wave lapped over us. But we did our best to ignore those things, and kept paddling toward the sun till we glimpsed the summit of the island rising above the water in the distance. We'd been out on the lake for several hours by then, and I was ready to get my feet on solid ground again.

It was several more hours before we managed that, though, and when we reached the island itself we found that it was surrounded by swampy shallows all around, much too thick for us to get the raft through.

"How do we get through *that?*" Danielle asked, staring at the gooey water distastefully. I couldn't blame her; it looked disgusting, and from the occasional whiff we got when the breeze wafted our way, it probably smelled even worse than it looked.

"We'll have to either swim or walk, depending on how deep it is. It's not far," Jesse said.

"There's nothing out there that'll eat us, is there?" she asked, only half joking.

"Of course not. Might get a little nasty, that's all," I said.

A little nasty was putting it kindly. We tied up the raft to a cottonwood tree and half-swam, half-walked through algae-choked water dark and full of swamp gas bubbles, and the mud on the bottom was so foul it made us all gag. We reached the island stinking like we'd just come from a swim in a sewer.

"That sure was pleasant," Danielle commented dryly.

"Oh, babe, even sewer gas smells beautiful on you," I said, and she laughed.

"You're such a liar, Tyke, but thanks anyway," she said.

They say Tycho Brahe got in a sword-fighting duel once and ended up getting his nose cut off. I know I used to feel sorry for the poor man, but right then I was almost ready to take out my pocketknife and cut my own nose off, just like my namesake. I'm not sure but what he didn't end up with the better deal, after all.

Philip headed inland, and it wasn't very long before we reached the summit of the little island. And there at last was the facility we'd been struggling toward for weeks.

It wasn't especially impressive. Just a more-or-less cubical building about twelve feet square, built of snowstone blocks that almost certainly had come from somewhere near Lakeside. It had a steel door and a perfectly ordinary hasp and padlock on it. It was obviously something the terraformers had put there, for whatever unfathomable reason they might have had.

It was surrounded by a chain link fence topped with razor wire, and there was another heavy padlock on the gate. I half expected to see a warning sign about how trespassers would be shot on sight.

We didn't have anything to break the lock open other than maybe a rock, but I really didn't much feel like climbing over razor wire, either.

"Any ideas?" I asked, looking at the padlock.

"I'd be willing to bet this fence was built to keep out animals, not people. They might have left a key around here somewhere, if we look for it," Philip said.

That was a worthwhile idea, so we fanned out to look for one. I circled the perimeter, trying not to overlook anything, and soon found a metal box attached to one of the fence poles behind the building. Inside was a key on a ring, and I laughed. People are so predictable.

"Found it!" I yelled, and then jogged back around to the front gate to try it in the lock. It turned smoothly, and the lock snapped open and fell to the ground.

"Good deal," I said in satisfaction.

We swung open the gate and walked boldly up to the building itself, and when I got close enough I noticed that the padlock on the door seemed to be the twin of the one on the gate. They might even be keyed alike, so I shrugged and gave it a try. That seemed to be the case, because the lock popped open just like the other one had.

I reached tentatively for the handle on the big steel door, half curious and half wary. Philip had no compunctions about it, though, because he immediately grabbed the door handle and yanked it open while I hesitated. I felt a wash of cool air spill out, and there was light inside from a skylight, too. Other than that I couldn't see much except a bare stone wall. Then Philip looked at me and made a gesture that I should go inside.

"What, me?" I asked, and he nodded.

There wasn't much to be seen through the door except a bare room and the top of a metal stairwell that led straight down into the ground, so I shrugged and went inside.

"There's nothing in here except some stairs," I said, turning my head to tell the others. They quietly filed in behind me, and we all stood there staring at the stairwell. Then I put my foot on the top step.

It wasn't actually all that far to the bottom, as it turned out. Maybe thirty feet or so, before we came to the last step. At that point there was a narrow tunnel with snowstone walls, very dimly lit by what little light filtered down from above. No doubt there used to be electric lights in the place, but those were long-since defunct.

I don't much like dark, narrow places deep underground. You always have to wonder what might be lurking down there in all that inky blackness. It wasn't quite as black as ink in the tunnel, but it was a lot darker than I would have liked, and the walls were uncomfortably close together. The floor sloped gradually downward, until we suddenly reached a place where the walls opened out on both sides into a wide chamber. I could barely see it, but I felt the change in the air around me. I didn't think it was a good idea to walk blindly out into empty space without knowing what was there, so I turned and followed the left wall instead.

There was a distinct curve to it, and before long I found myself led gradually in a circle until I came back to the starting point. There was no other exit from the room, which puzzled me. Why dig a tunnel and go to so much trouble for no reason?

I went back out to the foot of the stairs where the others were waiting.

"Did you find anything?" Danielle asked.

"No, just a room with no other way out. But I couldn't *see* anything," I said.

"There must be lights in this place, somewhere. We might get them working again, with a little luck. It sure would be nice, if we mean to spend all night in here," Jesse said.

"I guess so," I agreed.

The building had solar panels on the roof, and once we followed the wiring we located an electrical box behind the stairs.

"This looks simple enough," Philip said. He turned a knob and flipped two switches, and then all of a sudden the lights came on. Dusty and old, to be sure, but perfectly workable. The room at the end of the tunnel was lit up bright as day, nothing sinister or mysterious about it anymore, so I went down there to take a look at it in the light.

The only thing in the room was a little pedestal in the exact center, and on top of it one of those things like they have at jewelry stores to hold necklaces. Not too surprising, I don't guess, since that's exactly what was sitting there.

It was nothing particularly unusual; just a clear crystal about the size of a big marble, in a cage of silvery wire attached to a chain. Weirder and weirder.

I don't know why, but something made me handle it respectfully. I didn't just grab it and go. I carefully lifted it off the holder, and then for lack of anywhere better to put it, I hung it around my own neck. Then I turned to Philip.

"Is this what you wanted us to come here for?" I asked, holding the crystal up.

"Yeah. I never thought I'd see that again," Philip murmured, which, needless to say, only added to the strangeness of it all. I glanced at Jesse and Danielle, but they both seemed as clueless as I was.

There was still a little time before it got dark, so we quickly made a round trip along the shore of the island to see if there was a boat we could use.

Unfortunately, there wasn't. The only man-made thing on the whole island was that little building with the underground chamber, and that was bad.

"We'll never make it for two more weeks with no food," I whispered to Jesse when we were alone on the north shore of the island.

"Yeah, I know. This time we've got nothing to fish with, either," he agreed, sounding worried.

"Is there anything else we could eat?" I asked. I didn't really expect him to know; I was more or less thinking out loud.

"I'm not sure what all grows down here. It's a lot different climate than Lakeside," he said.

"Yeah, I noticed that. I did see some cat-tails growing back there, though. I always heard you could take the roots from those and make bread out of them," I suggested.

"Do you know how to do that?" he asked.

"Well. . . no," I admitted.

"Then it won't do us any good. We've got to find something we already know how to use," he said.

I tried, but I had a really hard time coming up with anything. There were a few wild grapes in the canyons and we quickly collected those, but that wouldn't last even a day. There had to be something better than that.

"What about some of that algae? I know it's disgusting but it'd be a lot better than nothing," I finally suggested. It looked like *Spyrogyra,* the so-called maidenhair algae because it grows in long delicate filaments that look something like a girl's long hair floating in the water. If her hair was bright green, of course. It tastes unspeakably nasty, but it's not poisonous at least. Jesse sighed.

"You really know how to bring a dude down, don't you?" he said, shaking his head and looking at the algae with distaste.

Nevertheless we collected as much of it as we could, taking our shirts off and using them as sacks to hold the stuff. You can almost always find *something* to eat practically anywhere, if you know what to look for. It might be utterly disgusting, but at least it'll keep you alive for a while.

We hauled our catch up to the building, where Danielle and Philip were waiting.

"What's that?" Danielle asked, staring at our dripping shirts.

"We found some maidenhair, down there on the shore. There's plenty more, but we better go collect as much as we can before it starts to get rainy and cold out here," I said.

Nobody argued, and within a few hours we had a fairly good-sized pile of it inside the building, spread out on the floor to dry. It'd keep longer that way, and if we had to we could grind it up into a kind of flour and make flatbread out of it. It might even taste a little better that way. Doubtful, but we could always hope.

But soon enough that heavy pea-soup southern fog rolled in off the Cloudy Sea and forced us indoors for the night, and not long after that the rain began, slow at first and then steadily intensifying. It beat on the roof of the building like a drum, and I found myself once again lost in memories of many a night at Lakeside.

One thing I've noticed about bad weather is that it can be an enjoyable thing under certain circumstances. Whenever you can shut it outdoors and savor your immunity to it, then rain or snow and all those other things are awesome. But when you can't do that and you have to suffer with whatever the sky decides to throw at you, then it's not nice at all. That night at Tycho Crater was a mixed bag. The building kept us dry, but it did little or nothing to keep the cold from seeping in.

There wasn't just snow that night, either. There was a full-blown blizzard, with the wind howling and blowing the snow in swirling clouds across the rock-solid ice of the lake. The ground up on top of the hill was scoured completely bare except for where it collected in the gullies here and there. I went to the door a few times to peep outside and watch it all by Earthshine, and shudder at the thought of what might have happened if we hadn't reached the building in time.

That night, I had the strangest dream of my entire life. It was vividly, unbelievably real, just like I was standing there wide awake and in person. But it was also deeply weird, because all I saw was a castle made of glistening ice, with lofty spires gleaming white in orange-tinted twilight under a cloudy sky and surrounded by dark jungle. I'd never seen anything remotely like it.

And that was all. A single vivid image burned brightly into my mind, along with a sense of urgent necessity that we had to find that place and go there. I've never in all my life experienced anything so intense. It had none of that hazy, easily-forgettable quality that dreams often have, either. I doubted I'd ever forget it for the rest of my life.

I might have written it off as a fluke, if it had only happened just that once. God knows I had plenty of other things on my mind at the time. But then I had the exact same dream the next night, and then again on the third. That was stretching the limits of coincidence pretty far, and I found myself forced to take the matter seriously.

Katrina McClendon always used to tell us the world is full of strange and inexplicable phenomena which we shouldn't expect to understand immediately. She told us that sometimes even the greatest scientists in the world are forced to simply describe what they see, without a clue as to what it means. When Isaac Newton formulated his theory of gravity, he didn't even attempt to explain how it worked. In fact, the only thing he said was that he framed no hypothesis on the subject, which is just a fancy way of saying he didn't have the faintest idea.

Well. Here I was, like Newton, confronted with a phenomenon which I couldn't remotely explain. Vivid dreams about ice castles and black jungles had no place in the universe I thought I understood. But facts are brutally honest things, and only an idiot chooses to ignore what he doesn't comprehend. I fully intended to get to the bottom of the issue, but for the time being I could only imitate Newton and say that I framed no hypothesis.

I didn't mention the dreams to the others immediately, but that didn't mean I didn't think about them a lot. There wasn't much else to do except sit there and think for the next two weeks, huddling together for warmth and nibbling on pieces of dried pond scum. But try as I might, I couldn't come up with any kind of explanation that made even the slightest kind of sense. After a while it started to drive me crazy.

I don't suppose I ever would have solved the problem on my own, but as it turned out I didn't have to.

Several days after we arrived, I finally got around to asking Philip about the purpose of our little expedition.

"So what's *this* about?" I asked, holding up the crystal which was still around my neck. We were in the middle of trying to grind up some maidenhair into dark green flour for pancakes, which we'd found was the least disgusting way to eat the stuff. We had nothing to grind it with but rocks; a tedious job, and Philip seemed glad for the distraction.

"It's a long story, but suffice it to say it's called a Guardian Stone. There are only three of them, and they're very precious and holy things. I've already got the other two at home, so that one you're wearing is the last one left. We couldn't leave the Moon without taking it," he said.

"So they're some kind of family heirloom type thing? Is that it?" I asked. That made some kind of semi-sense, I guess; I don't know that I personally would have made a trip all the way down there to fetch something like that, but I could at least see the motivation for it.

"I guess you could say that, in a way. We've had the other two for a long time, but we could never locate that third stone. I've been trying to find it for years," he agreed.

I noted in passing that Philip must have had an awfully serious and long-term sort of interest in those Guardian Stones, the way he kept talking about years of looking for them, and that made me curious about why he was so curious, if you know what I mean.

"How'd you find out it was at Tycho Crater, then?" I asked.

"I found a notation about it in the Map Room. I don't think the person who wrote the article really knew what it was. He only said that building was ordered built by the chief Project scientist at Barnaby in 2085, but he didn't specify who that was or what the reason might be. I'm sure if we wanted to do a little research we could figure out who the head scientist was in that year. But it doesn't really matter. They had a picture of the necklace beside the article, and I knew what it was as soon as I saw the photo of it," he said.

"I guess so," I said, noncommittally. Collectibles are nice things, but definitely not worth risking your life over.

Then he dropped the bomb.

"These things are special, though. If you wear one of them long enough, you'll start having dreams. Not all the time, but once in a while," he said.

My mind leapt immediately to that castle of ice and the urgent desire to find it, but I bit my tongue at the last second before I blurted out something I couldn't take back. At least I wasn't quite as surprised to hear such a thing as Jesse and Danielle were, though.

"What kind of dreams?" I asked neutrally, and I could have sworn Philip hesitated a second before he spoke.

"Things about the future, to show you what you're supposed to do," he finally said, and I know my eyes widened. I honestly didn't know what to think at that point, but Danielle had no such hesitation.

"You're crazy," she said flatly, and even though Jesse would never have *said* such a thing, I knew him well enough to see that he was thinking the exact same thought. People do lose their minds sometimes, especially after they've just suffered through a year of solitary confinement like Philip had.

"Now you see why I didn't tell you all this before? I knew even my own kids wouldn't believe me," Philip said.

I was ashamed when he said that; as I've mentioned before, I've never, ever known Philip to lie, not even as a joke. But he was right. If he'd told me something like that to begin with, I wouldn't have believed him any more than Jesse and Danielle did. Oh, I might have *tried* to, in an abstract kind of way, as long as there was nothing much at stake. But I knew as well as Philip did that I wouldn't have believed him enough to risk my life on a dangerous trip to Tycho Crater. I would've thought he'd lost his mind from being trapped alone on the Moon for too long, just like the others were thinking. I know I turned red in the face, and hung my head so he wouldn't see.

It might seem like it didn't matter near as much anymore at that point, since we'd already made the trip and recovered the Stone, but it *did*. My faith in him as a trustworthy leader was shaken to the core, and if it turned out he was wrong then I wasn't sure I'd ever be able to rely on him again. Yes, I'd been having dreams exactly of the type he described, but I still had no proof they were anything real, much less that they had anything to do with the necklace.

I think in reality I was struggling with something altogether different, though. The whole tenor of my mind and everything I'd ever learned at the Academy had trained me to distrust anything that smacked of mysticism or magic or whatever you want to call it. And however much I might say I framed no hypothesis about the dreams, connecting them to an old crystal like that came dangerously near to stepping all over every sacred cow I'd ever been led to believe.

I found myself thinking uneasily about something else Katrina McClendon always taught us. . . that a scientist must never make the mistake of slipping into an unconscious faith in naturalism; that is, the idea that the universe is all that exists. We may have to operate on that assumption while working, but we mustn't become so accustomed to it that we take it for granted as a proven fact. It is in fact an unproven and unprovable assertion which is not at all self-evident; it's merely a useful tool for research sometimes. She always sternly insisted that we keep science and philosophy strictly separate in that way. The distinction is critical to remember, and I wondered if I might be slipping over the edge into letting philosophy affect my logic.

The very thought horrified me.

Robert Weiss may have taught me more technical skills about genetics, but it was really Katrina McClendon who taught me how to think. I can almost hear her now, lecturing us about the honor of the intellect and following logic wherever it leads you, no matter where that may be nor how high the cost. Oh, she was a fiend for intellectual integrity. She told us many times that our desire to know the one true answer to a question is a completely different thing than our desire to find that one particular answer rather than another is the true one. She spent a lot of time praising the first outlook and heaping scorn on the second, to the point that we all developed almost as passionate a love for the truth as she had. I say *almost* because I'm not sure anybody could ever have been as passionate about the truth as Katrina McClendon.

Except possibly Philip Carpenter.

So I deliberately cleared my mind of any and all preconceived notions about the nature of reality, and decided to perform a few experiments of my own, just to see where the evidence would lead me.

I'd been wearing the necklace all three nights when I dreamed of the castle, so the obvious thing to do at that point was to see if there were any difference between wearing the necklace and not wearing it.

For the next several nights I tested Philip's theory, and sure enough, on the nights when I didn't wear the necklace I never dreamed. When I did wear it, I sometimes saw the castle of ice again. But not always, and I have to admit that weakened the correlation I was trying to make. I would have liked more time to collect data, but based on the few nights we spent at Tycho Crater, I felt I was justified in forming a tentative conclusion that yes, the necklace did in fact have something to do with the dreams, however unlikely that seemed. And that astounded me.

But for the moment at least, I kept my conclusions to myself.

"You know, if we leave early enough in the morning, I think we could walk across the ice and not have to worry with that raft anymore," Danielle suggested one day. No one seemed to want to talk about the necklace anymore, and if anybody noticed my experiments in wearing it some nights and not others, then none of them saw fit to mention the fact. I think the whole subject had become somewhat alarming, actually; we all had a tacit agreement to focus on practical things, like how to get home. The question of whether Philip was crazy or not could wait.

"It'll be awfully cold that early. We don't have warm enough clothes to be out there for long, and besides that we'll get bogged down in the snow as soon as we leave the crater," Jesse said.

"Yeah, but it'll save us some time. We won't have to wait for the lake to melt, and we can dig a cave in the snow as soon as we get to shore to wait till it warms up before we try to go any farther. I'm ready to get off this rock," she said.

I think we all shared *that* sentiment, at least, and so it was that we left the building at the very crack of dawn so we could walk across the ice before it melted. Jesse was right about how frigid it would be, but at least there was no wind to make it worse.

The surface of the lake itself was mostly swept bare, but there were immense drifts of powdery snow piled up against the rim-walls. And when I say immense, I mean absolutely gigantic; a hundred feet tall or maybe even more. The only reason we ever escaped at all was because we found a place where the rocks jutted out into the crater a bit more than usual, and the snow had piled up on both sides while leaving that area bare. So we picked our way back up to the top, and in the dim half-light of sunrise looked out across the jumbled land to the north, still covered in snow.

We dug a chamber in the snow near the top of the rim-wall, to keep warm while we waited for everything to melt and the morning floods to subside. I chewed on a maidenhair pancake for breakfast, barely tasting it anymore.

"I think the best thing to do would be to follow the coast back up the fishery station, and then cross back to Lakeside on the highway. It'll be a lot better than trying to pick our way back through the mountains again. It'll be a lot faster, and a lot cooler during the heat of the day, and hopefully not as many monsters," Jesse said.

"Won't we still have to cross the swamps?" Danielle asked.

"Yeah, but I hope there might be some barrier islands right there where the swamp meets the ocean. That way we'd have an easier time," Jesse said.

"And if there aren't?" I asked.

"Well, in that case the only thing I know to do is to try to build a raft and skim along the edge of the ocean. If a storm blows in we'll be dead meat, but it's a risk we might have to take," he said.

"It sounds like a good plan to me," Philip said.

So that's what we did. As soon as it was safe, we started following the Tycho River downstream again, headed for the ocean.

Chapter Five

Several hours later, just when we were beginning to think about taking a break to sleep for a few hours, we heard the monster.

One of those bloodcurdling shrieks came from the woods, *way* too close for comfort, and then another one even closer. We looked at each other fearfully. We'd been awfully lucky so far about avoiding the beasts, but it seemed that our luck had finally run out.

There was a small island in the middle of the river not far downstream at that point, a rocky outcrop barely big enough to support a few scraggly willow trees. It was our only hope of refuge.

"Can they swim at all?" I whispered.

"I don't think so. It said in the survey notes they hate water," Jesse said.

"I hope you're right," I muttered.

"Come on, let's get over there while we still can," Philip said.

But this river wasn't the same slow, placid stream that the canal had been. The current was swift, and the rocks were literally sharp as knives. They always are, on the Moon. There hasn't been time for them to get rounded and softened by flowing water yet. The river was full of them; not so much where we stood, but just a little way downstream was a set of rapids which was chock full of them.

It was an open question as to whether we'd have time to swim to the island before the current swept us downstream and sliced us to ribbons against those rapids. I thought for a second about those algebra word-problems I'd been helping Hunter with at Aunt Joan's supper table right before we left, about how far downstream a boat would float by the time it crossed a river with a current of thus-and-such. I'd always been pretty good at stuff like that.

I almost laughed, and wished it could be that simple. Math is great, but it won't help you at all if you don't know what numbers to plug in. I didn't know how fast I could swim, or how fast the river was moving, or even exactly how far it was across. The best I could do was eyeball it and try to make the best guess I could. And hope.

The river was clear and cool when we waded in, swirling pleasantly around my sore feet. I waded a little deeper until the water was around my waist, and the current was fairly strong but not impossible to deal with. Then I pushed off with my feet and started swimming as hard as I could for the middle. The current grabbed me immediately, just like I knew it would. But I didn't try to fight it, just let it carry me downstream while I grimly kept swimming straight ahead.

The island wasn't really all that far offshore, maybe a hundred feet or so. We started out a good distance above it so we'd have time to cross the current, and I refused to think about what might happen if one of us missed it.

My hand scraped bottom suddenly, and I wasted no time putting my feet down to see if I could touch. I was still about ten feet from the island, but I found myself able to stand up in about waist-deep water. I almost lost my footing several times when I stepped on sharp rocks, but soon I slogged my way up onto dry land and found that the island was about twenty feet long and maybe ten feet wide. Like I said, it was stable enough to support a few sickly willow trees and cottonwood bushes, but there wasn't enough dirt for any grass to grow.

I only hoped the monster hated water as much as Jesse said they did.

As soon as everybody was accounted for, I turned to look back at the bank. I still couldn't see anything under the shadows of the trees, but I could hear the monster crunching sticks and such as he moved around. He was that close.

Then a blood-chilling howl split the quiet morning apart, and I nearly jumped right out of my skin, eyes wide and heart beating wildly in my chest. Even knowing he was there, the sound of that howl was horrifying at such close range. I barely had time to think before another howl came, and then the sound of several large and heavy creatures moving closer through the woods on the riverbank, right where we'd just been a few scant minutes ago.

I kept telling myself over and over that the monsters couldn't swim, as if repetition would make it true. In the meantime, I could hear them crashing and banging around not a hundred yards away.

They must have smelled us, or heard us, or whatever it was they did, because after a while I saw several dark shapes gather on the riverbank and even wade out several steps into the river, and that's when I got my first good look at the things.

Jesse's description didn't do them justice. They vaguely reminded me of a beaver, if you can imagine a beaver the size of a bear, with no tail and a mouth full of sewing needles. That's what their teeth reminded me of, long and thin like that, poking out of their mouths like a crocodile's teeth might have done. They had needle-like claws, too, curved and wickedly sharp.

They didn't dare go out too far into the water, though, and they stood on the bank for a few seconds howling in anger and frustration, knowing we were there but unable to reach us. The noise was ear-splitting, that near by.

After a while they disappeared back into the woods, and I started to hope they might actually have given up and gone to look for easier prey. Then I heard a splintering and crashing sound, and to my horror watched a huge cottonwood tree fall into the river with an incredible splash that sent waves crashing against the rocks of the island. They were trying to build a bridge!

"You never said anything about them being that smart," I said, turning to Jesse with more than a little fear in my voice.

"The notes didn't say they were," he said, his eyes still glued to the fallen tree. It only reached about two thirds of the way across the river, but that was too close for comfort. Several of the monsters reappeared on the shore, but most of them hung back. One of them, though, set his weight carefully on the makeshift bridge and began making his way across it toward the island.

We stood there frozen in horror, watching him approach. He slowly inched along the tree, seeming to distrust the water beneath him. Every now and then he lifted his snout and snuffled like a dog on a scent, so maybe he paid more attention to our smell than anything else. I don't know. His teeth gleamed white in the sunlight, even from that far away. Eventually he came to the branches on the tree and that slowed him down, but some of these he broke loose and threw in the river, and others he simply brushed aside. Finally, though, the trunk had narrowed to the point that it would barely support his weight, and the dark water was swirling about his feet. He was still at least thirty feet from the island, and he lifted his face to the sky and howled his frustration.

Maybe the monster was smart enough to know that the water would get shallower near the island, because he began to creep even farther along the thin trunk. I had no idea how far out the shallows might reach, or how deep a monster could wade.

"Maybe we should swim to the other bank," I said.

"Let's wait a little bit first. I still don't think he can make it," Philip said.

The monster growled again when he heard us talking, but he kept on inching his way along the submerged trunk just like before.

Then I heard a sudden crack of wood and a huge splash as the beast fell into the river. He must still have been in deep water, because he gave a terrible cry as he went under. None of the others still standing on shore made any move to help him, but after a second he pulled his head above water by holding on to one of the tree branches. He must have had a grip like steel, because I thought at first he might actually make it back out onto the trunk. But no, with more snapping of branches and flailing of arms, he fell back into the water again with a shriek that froze my bones. This time he never came back up.

The others had seen all this and drew back from the water as if it were the very Lake of Fire itself. They stood staring at us for a long time, and I could almost feel the force of their hunger and hatred. But presently they turned away as a group and melted silently back into the woods. I let out my breath when they disappeared, not even realizing until then that I'd been holding it.

"We probably better hang tight for a little while, make sure those things are really gone. It's about time to catch a few hours of sleep, anyway. We might as well do that here, and then whenever we get up we'll move on," Philip said.

I hadn't noticed I was tired till he mentioned it, but as soon as he did, I couldn't control a huge yawn. Maybe it was the power of suggestion, or maybe reaction was finally setting in after the monster attack. Either way, I decided sleep was an excellent idea.

I found a place where sand had collected in a mound, and after checking to make sure it was dry I used my hands and feet to form a kind of body-shaped hollow that I could lie down in. I put down some willow branches to lay my head on, partly for the extra comfort and partly to keep the sand out of my hair while I slept. Not much of a bed, true, but a lot better than the rocks. I squirmed a little, to shape the sand a bit closer to my body. I was hungry and cold and my feet hurt from walking barefoot all day, but there was nothing to be done about any of those things, except sleep.

I woke up several hours later even colder than before, but considerably better rested. I rubbed my hands together and clapped them against my sides to produce a little warmth, and before long I decided it was time to get up.

Everybody else was still asleep in whatever semi-comfortable spot they could find, and I was loathe to wake them. So I quietly walked around the island for a while to help work the stiffness out of my muscles, and down on the eastern shore I stumbled across a nasty surprise. The body of the monster had floated to the top while we slept, and the current had carried it down near the bottom tip of the island. Now it was caught in the branches of a willow tree, face down.

I stared at the waterlogged fur of the thing's back, and shuddered at the memory of how close we'd come to getting eaten yesterday.

But I'd never seen a monster so close up before, and I crept closer in morbid curiosity.

The fur was thick and fine-textured, again like something an otter or a beaver might have had, but that was about all I could see of the thing. The rest of it was hidden underwater. I grabbed a long piece of driftwood that was caught in one of the trees, and with beating heart I came closer still, until I could reach out and poke the thing with my stick.

I jumped back almost instantly, even though nothing had happened. I gained a little courage from that, and poked the body again without flinching this time. Nothing happened that time, either, so then I reached out to touch it with my bare hand.

The fur was cold and wet, just like I'd thought it would be, and my hand came away with a funny musky smell that reminded me of sweaty clothes. But it was surprisingly soft and creamy-textured, like a rabbit or a chinchilla. One of those animals they use to make expensive fur coats, anyway.

Curiosity satisfied, I soon lost interest in the body of the monster, and turned to look at the river to think about how best to get back across and continue our journey.

I soon realized we'd never make it back to the eastern bank. Even if we started out from the very upper tip of the island, we still wouldn't have enough time to swim that far before the current sucked us down into those rapids.

I crossed the island to look at the west bank instead, and the channel was considerably narrower over there. I was pretty sure we could make it across, on that side. The only problem with that idea was that it would put us on the wrong side of the river from where we needed to be. It wouldn't matter immediately, but sooner or later we'd have to find a place to get across again, and then we'd have to swim the whole width of the river at once, instead of only half of it. Not only that, but the farther downstream we went, the wider it was likelier to be.

I tapped my foot and sighed, thinking again about how stupid the whole thing was. Had we survived the onslaught of an entire pack of monsters, only to starve to death in the wilderness simply because we couldn't swim far enough to cross a river?

The thought of food made my stomach hurt again, and I tried to drink some water to ease the pain. But my body was having none of that; not today. Almost as soon as I swallowed the water I felt sick, and soon after that I bent over and threw up almost all of it. That made me feel ten times worse than I had before, but it did have the side effect of erasing my hunger for a little while. I cupped my hand in the river and washed my mouth out to get rid of the nasty taste, and then lay back down on my sandy bed for a little while until I felt almost normal again. What I wouldn't give for a steak!

The thought of meat brought my hunger back in full force, and with it came another idea. We *did* have meat, as a matter of fact, if we were willing to eat it. The monster was almost as big as a bull. All we had to do was cut off some chunks and roast them.

There was no telling what the beast might taste like, but at that point I hardly cared. It couldn't possibly be any worse than algae cakes, and we'd been surviving on those yummy little delicacies for two whole weeks. In any case it was the only game in town, and I was willing to try anything once. Therefore I got up and went back to where the body was lodged in the willow tree, and surveyed it critically.

I grabbed hold of his fur and dragged the dead monster half up on shore, then rolled him over on his back so I could start gutting and cleaning him. I knew how to butcher an animal, of course; Philip loves to hunt, and he taught me all that stuff ever since I was knee high to a grasshopper. But that was mostly with deer, and I'd never had to deal with anything even half so big as this before. It also didn't help that I had nothing to work with except my pocketknife.

Well, I managed, but it was a nasty, messy, bloody job before I was done. I was glad I could stand in the water to do it. As soon as I was able to hack out some ragged chunks of meat, I left the rest of it to finish later. Then I rinsed my arms and body in the river and set about gathering enough driftwood to build a fire. Monster steak was one thing, but eating it raw was more than I could stomach.

After a few tries I was able to get the wood to catch, and soon I had a roaring blaze. I spitted the meat on some long sticks, and then shoved it over the fire to cook.

Before long an almost unbearably delicious smell began to fill the air, and it was all I could do to keep from yanking the meat off the spit and eating it half cooked. I think the smell must have woken the others, because one by one they got up and gathered round the fire to wait for their own piece.

"Where'd the meat come from?" Jesse asked, still yawning.

"I found that monster from yesterday caught in a willow tree down at the foot of the island, so I decided to cut him up and see what he tastes like," I said.

"It sure does smell good," Danielle said.

"Yeah, I'm trying not to think too much about that," I said.

We waited as long as humanly possible, and then pulled the spits out of the fire. The meat turned out to be a little bit burned in several places and barely cooked in others, but I was beyond caring about that. I gingerly took a small bite to see what it might taste like, and then I threw caution to the winds and ate, literally, like I was starving.

I couldn't hold as much as I'd thought I could, but that was all right. The pleasure of being full was almost too good to be true.

"Is there any more?" Jesse asked.

"You can have the rest of mine, if you're still hungry," I said.

"No, it's not that. But I thought we might slice up the rest of him and take it with us. It'll be a lot better than anything else we could find," he said.

"Yeah, there's quite a bit of him left. I only dressed him out and cut off a few chunks. The rest of him is still over there on the bank," I said.

We all four returned to the body of the monster and methodically cut out several dozen pounds of flesh, slicing them into thin strips so they'd cook faster. It went a lot quicker with three more people to help, even though the others had nothing to cut with except some sharp rocks from the river bank.

"You know, maybe we should stay here for a few days. The meat will be a lot easier to carry and it'll last a lot longer if we let it dry first, and it seems like we're pretty safe here in the meantime," I suggested.

"I think that's a good idea," Philip agreed.

So that's what we did, and I guess things could have been worse. Drying and smoking meat is not the most enjoyable chore in the world, but if it kept us fed for a while then I was all for it. It took us almost a whole day just to finish cutting up the carcass, and three more to dry it all. But when everything was finished, we had enough monster jerky to last us for weeks if we conserved it properly. That was a major relief.

While we were at it, I decided to keep the fur, too. It was big enough to make a fine blanket to keep out the chill of the night, and besides that, I felt like I deserved a trophy for killing my very own monster. After all, those game hunters used to pay big money for the chance to nail an awesome beast like that, and I was sure *they* wouldn't have left the fur behind. We lacked the tools to stretch the hide and dry it properly, but we made do as best we could by sharpening sticks and driving them into the ground through the edges. Then I scraped the hide clean and rubbed it with fat before leaving it alone to cure for a while.

Finally, I decided to keep the teeth as a souvenir. I could imagine what everybody back in Kona would think when I showed up with a monster-tooth necklace on. Bragging rights are always nice, and even if you were actually scared half out of your skin at the time, it still sounds good later on to tell everybody how you bravely stared down the horrifying monster with nothing but a rock in your hand and a steely gleam in your eye. I smiled at the thought.

"What are you smiling at?" Danielle asked, and I flinched guiltily.

"Oh, nothing really. Just thinking about saving those teeth and maybe making a necklace out of them," I said.

"I see. Need any help?" she asked.

"Sure," I said.

It turned out to be harder than I thought. The teeth wouldn't come out just by pulling, and they were sharp as razors. We finally had to smash them out with a rock, which wasn't the most ideal tool by any means. We ended up breaking most of them or losing them in the river, but when all was said and done I found myself the proud possessor of five perfect specimens, each one about as long as a finger. They were shaped almost like sharks' teeth, only much thinner and longer, dark slate blue at the base and gradually fading to bright white at the tips. I put them in a little pile next to the hide so I wouldn't forget where they were when it came time to leave.

There wasn't much else to do other than wait for the meat to dry and the fur to cure. Once in a while we added a little more wood to the fire, but that was all. I didn't mind so much, other than the boredom and the steadily increasing heat.

On the third day it was gray and overcast, with a threat of thunderstorms, and that was enough to make us leave a little earlier than we'd planned. The island was low, and if it rained very much then we might find ourselves in serious danger of getting swept away. There was flotsam and driftwood way up high in the branches of the willow trees, so we knew the water got at least that far up sometimes.

Floods on the Moon are no joke, and we had no intention of taking any chances on one. The meat was more or less dry by then, and the hide was at least green-cured so it wouldn't stink. There was no reason to stay on the island any longer.

Therefore me and Jesse and Philip took off our shirts and used them as bags for the monster-jerky, just like we had when we collected the maidenhair at Tycho Crater. Then I rolled the hide into a tight ball like a sleeping bag, and we were ready to go.

We waded out from the western shore of the island as far as we could without needing to swim, so as to have as much leeway as possible. The current wasn't nearly as swift on that side as it was on the east bank, but there was no point in being careless.

I made certain my shirt sleeves were tied securely around my chest so I wouldn't lose my food supply, and I soon found that the monster hide floated like a cork in the water. I tucked the hide under one arm and swam the last thirty feet or so without mishap, crawling out onto the shore with a deep sigh of relief.

Then, with no more ado, we set off purposefully downstream.

It's roughly two hundred miles from Tycho Crater to the coast of the Cloudy Sea, and we made fairly short work of it. Three days after we left the island, we found ourselves standing on the sandy shores of the ocean, at long last.

The Cloudy Sea is one of those ancient names they never changed, but it's a pretty appropriate one, at that. The water is cold because of the far-southern latitude, and that leads to mist and fog almost all the time, sometimes offshore, sometimes right up on the beach. I suppose the same conditions would have occurred in the far north, if we'd ever had a reason to go and see. It was an interesting phenomenon at first, especially since Lakeside was never like that. The Land of Snow is right smack in the middle of the lunar tropics, and even though the storms were worse, it was rarely if ever foggy.

But the fog sometimes dissipates even down there in Tycho-land, as Jesse took to calling that whole area. Not that there was much to see when it did; the cold, steel-gray ocean on one side and the jumbled hills and crater swamps on the other. A thin strand of gravelly beach ran right between them, flat and straight for as far as the eye could see, and that was just about the extent of it.

We used the beach to good advantage, running northward as fast as we could manage and still keep up the pace. You can run for a long time on the Moon without getting tired, believe it or not. The low gravity makes you feel light as a feather, and in some ways it's more like bounding along the sand like a rabbit than running. Every time your foot hits the ground you spring off almost ten feet in the air and thirty feet along the ground, and how awesome is that? I'd forgotten how cool it really was.

But it *is* still running, and you *will* get winded after a while no matter how careful you are to conserve energy. So you can't run forever, and you can only cover about a hundred miles a day even if nothing causes you any problems. There's an almost unbroken strand of beach all the way from the mouth of the Tycho River up to Cape Carmel on the southern fringe of the Caloosahatchie swamps. We took to calling it the Thousand Mile Beach, because that's almost exactly how far apart those two points are. It varies from rocky to sandy and everything in between, but none of that matters on the Moon. You just run and run and run, like an ostrich across the desert, nothing but beach up ahead and beach left behind, and even though you might have run a hundred miles before you have to rest, you feel almost like you haven't moved an inch from where you stopped last time.

The ocean gradually changed from murky gray to clear green as we trotted north toward the lunar equator, and the fog disappeared, too. We never heard or saw any monsters down there on the coast, for whatever reason. I guess they didn't like to venture so near the water, but that's only a guess.

We made the whole trip in nine days, just in time for sunset again. It was already dark and misting rain by the time we came out on the rocky point of Cape Carmel and saw the Caloosahatchie valley spread out below us, the old plain of the Sinus Medii, now filled with eighty miles of swampland. And on the far side, even though we couldn't see them yet, was the southern tip of the Chocolate Mountains and the thousand-times-blessed Land of Snow. I'd never in my life been so happy to know that it was so close. No more monsters to worry about, no more quicksand and pea-soup fog, no more ugliness at all. Only beautiful and amazing things whichever way you cared to look, in a land on which the terraformers had lavished every bit of love and idealism they possessed. There was a time when I used to think some of the names and places up there were cutesy, but I promise you I'll never think so again, not after that trip down south. I felt almost like Moses must have felt when he first saw the Promised Land.

But there wasn't time to cross over right then, so we holed up in a cave on Cape Carmel, resigned to spending another lunar night in the wilds. We still had plenty of jerky to last us that long, and I guess we did all right. As usual, there wasn't really much to say about it. Cold and snow and wind and rain, just like usual.

But when morning came, we set out quickly along the beach again. There *were* some barrier islands between the swamp and the sea, just like Jesse had hoped for, but there was no more unbroken strand like we had further south. There were plenty of spots where the sand disappeared into cypress and mangrove swamps and we had to struggle along at barely a quarter the speed we could make on the beach. It took us three days to make it across, most of that time spent splashing and swimming through ice-cold mud. It was still early enough in the day that we didn't have to worry too much about storms, but we paid for safety by freezing half to death.

Nevertheless, there came a moment when we actually did set foot on the northern shore at long last, and when that happened I immediately bent down and kissed the ground. You can think it's funny if you want to, but you might have felt the same way if you'd just been through the kind of ordeal we'd all been through for the past three months.

We got there just in time to catch the morning wildflower bloom in the Chocolate Mountains; our reward for coming home again, I suppose. We kept following the coast all the way up to the fishery station, and from there we took the old highway through the mountains and across Yucca Flats to Lakeside. By the time we got there it was just beginning to get uncomfortably hot again.

The first thing we did when we got to the station was to jump in the shower and have a really good scrubbing for the first time in a while. All of us still had clean clothes in our old cabins, and we gratefully changed into some of them. As soon as that was done it was time to leave, which is exactly what we did.

Immediately.

Chapter Six

I had no regrets at all about leaving the Moon for the second time. The first time, yeah, I was kind of sentimental about it then. But that was when we'd just left Philip behind and were headed out to a very uncertain future on Earth, if we even survived to make it there. Now we had Philip with us and we were headed for a fairly happy and comfortable life in Hawaii on the *Balboa*. Two very different situations.

So I was pretty laid back and relaxed, and even happy now that the whole thing was over. We all four sat and talked for hours while the ship took us home more or less on autopilot; there wouldn't be much for Jesse to do until it was time to land.

It turned out to be an uneventful trip home, and that's exactly the kind I like.

At least, it was uneventful until we landed at the airstrip in Kona, and left the *Balboa* to a hero's welcome. Everybody was excited, but I really think it was seeing Philip and Joan that made it all worth it. They ran together and held each other tight for a long time, and we all had a celebration that night in the best Hawaiian style; cookout on the beach and music and dancing till midnight.

"I'm really glad we went," Danielle told me while we were dancing barefooted in the sand that night.

"Yeah, me too. This is the first time I've seen Aunt Joan really happy ever since we left the Moon," I agreed.

After a few days things settled down to a sleepy routine again, which reminded me in some ways of how we used to live at Lakeside. I finished curing the monster fur and used it as a bedspread, and ended up giving the teeth to Derrick to hang on his wall.

I didn't exactly forget about the Guardian Stone or that vision of the icy castle it had given me, but I didn't think about it too often, either. I wore it all the time, to see if any more dreams would come, and after a while I barely noticed it was there anymore. Danielle told me it looked very cool and bohemian, especially whenever I walked around barefoot on the beach with no shirt on. So naturally I made sure to walk around that way whenever possible. Not during the day, of course; that was a good recipe for a vicious sunburn. But later in the evenings and at night when we cooked out, and even sometimes in the early mornings, that was very much my taste in fashion for a while.

Not quite a month after we got home, I had another dream.

It was like the other one in a way. There was the same black jungle, the same orangey twilight. But it was different, too, because this time it was no castle I saw, but a steep and craggy mountain rising hundreds if not thousands of feet above the jungle, white and glittering as ice. The summit was flat, with a three-sided pyramid built there. And again there was that deep desire to find this place and go there, so strong it was almost like a physical thirst. And this time, there came with it an equally strong wish to take the three Guardian Stones to that place.

I woke up early, more confused than ever by the whole bizarre phenomenon, with that same restless urge from my dream still very much alive in my heart.

I got up quietly and dressed, then headed out to the beach to take a walk and try to sort out my conflicted thoughts.

Philip was out on the rocks when I got there, fishing. He'd been up for hours already by then, early riser as he always was. Kona isn't Lakeside; there's not near as much that has to be fixed or maintained, and we had more food than we could ever eat in ten lifetimes. So as a result, Philip didn't have very much to do anymore except fish and things of that sort. No doubt he'd find something else to occupy him sooner or later, but in the meantime he could relax for a while. I don't think anybody grudged him some down time after everything he'd been through lately.

But my heart was heavy and I felt very alone at the time, so I made up my mind to have a talk with him and see if he might give me any new wisdom. God knows I was fresh out of my own. I climbed over the rocks till I stood beside him, and for a minute I didn't say anything.

"Catch anything?" I finally asked.

"Not yet. Still early, though," he said.

"I had a dream last night. A true one, I think. Not for the first time, either," I said, fumbling to get the words out. There was no point in dancing circles around the issue, though; it was time I fessed up and admitted he was right, just like I should have done to begin with.

"Yeah, I knew you would, sooner or later," he agreed. No rancor at all, and certainly no trace of that smug I-told-you-so triumphalism I so thoroughly hated in certain other people I've known.

"I'm sorry I didn't believe you," I said. It was hard to say that, too, but I felt like it needed to be said.

"Well, I don't know that I would have believed me, either. Don't worry about it, bubba," he said, and clapped me on the shoulder with his burly paw and ruffled my hair.

"I think I found out something, though," I said.

"Yeah, what's that?" he asked.

"We're supposed to take those three stones somewhere," I said.

"Where's that?" he asked, sounding interested.

"I don't know. A castle made of ice, or maybe a pyramid; that's all I saw," I said.

"Are you sure it was ice, and not just white stone?" he asked.

"No, I'm certain about that part. It was definitely ice," I said.

"Well, there couldn't be too many places where you'd find something like *that,*" he said.

"That's the problem. I don't know of *anywhere* you'd find something like that, except maybe high in the mountains somewhere or else on one of the ice caps. But this place was nowhere remotely like that. In fact, if I didn't know any better I would have said it was in the middle of a jungle," I said, laughing a little self-consciously. In hindsight, that was the most puzzling thing about the dream. Such a place as that was impossible. Buildings made of ice don't survive for long in a tropical rain forest.

"Maybe it's not on Earth," Philip said calmly, and that floored me.

"Are you serious?" I asked.

"Absolutely. If you've seen a place which you know couldn't exist in this world, then it's not so strange to think it might be elsewhere, is it?" he asked.

"But there's nowhere on the Moon like that, either, and we don't have the capability to go *much* past that," I said.

"I'm not talking about other stars or anything like that, Tyke. I know that's impossible. But there are lots of places right here in this solar system besides the Earth and the Moon. Go down to the library and study awhile. Find out where it might be possible to have an ice castle in the middle of a jungle, and then maybe we'll see what we see," he said.

"I guess so," I admitted, thinking hard. I could eliminate most bodies in the solar system pretty quickly. Anyplace with no atmosphere was out of the question, since I'd seen clouds in the sky. That wiped out ninety-nine percent of what was out there. The gas giant planets wouldn't work because there was no surface to build anything on. Venus was too hot. Mars? Well, possibly. I'd have to look into that some more. The only other options were a few of the moons of the outer planets. Europa and Io around Jupiter had atmospheres, and so did Saturn's moon Titan and Neptune's moon Triton. But I was hazy on the details of any of those places.

So I did exactly what Philip suggested, ignoring the fact of how insane it still seemed that I should be basing serious research on a dream. I was following logic wherever it led me, and that would have to do. So I walked down to the public library, found a book on space science, kicked back in a chair, and started reading.

It didn't take me very long to figure out there was only one place that fit all the conditions to see something like the castle in my dream, and that was Titan.

I put the book down, aghast at the very idea. No one had ever been that far, or even *close* to that far. There hadn't even been any manned trips to Mars, yet. Saturn was so impossibly far that it might as well have been in another galaxy.

Well, maybe it wasn't *quite* that bad, but almost. The only space vehicle we had was the *Balboa,* and I was certain it was never intended for a voyage like that. It hadn't even been meant to go to the Moon, let alone Titan. I'd have to talk to Jesse and see what he thought about it, but I was none too hopeful.

I took the space book with me when I left the library, looking down at my feet the whole way home and lost in thought.

The last hundred years or so has been a bad time for scientific research and space exploration, with a few notable exceptions, of course. It's been a bloody, violent century full of wars and social problems, and that tends to disrupt most major projects unless they've got something to do with the military. I'm not a political kind of person myself and I neither know nor care about such things for the most part, but sometimes even a kid can see when his country is being led by idiots who either take no more thought for the future than a goose or whose heads are full of idealistic notions that any sensible person can see will lead to utter ruin if they ever came to pass.

That's how things had been for a long time before the Orion Strain came along and solved the problem; a world full of fools and fanatics of all stripes and colors, with the rest of us caught up in the fray whether we liked it or not. In that kind of atmosphere, there's precious little room for pursuing curiosity and new things, because of the simple fact that people like that are so certain they already know everything that matters. The very definition of a fanatic is a person who thinks he knows it all and can't possibly be wrong, and it's quite possible to be a fanatic about *anything,* unfortunately.

That's why there hadn't been much if any space exploration in a very long time, not even probes. The Lunar Terraform Project had been one of the notable scientific exceptions, of course, but that was done by a private company who hoped to make money and then ended up going bust. Not much really new exploration there, either.

Apparently, that was about to change.

Chapter Seven

As soon as I got home I went looking for Jesse, and found him (naturally enough) studying a pilot's manual.

"Jesse, how far do you think the *Balboa* could go, if it absolutely had to?" I asked. No chit chat, no small talk; I got directly to the point.

"That depends," he said, shrugging. He didn't seem terribly interested in the question at the time.

"Depends on what? I really need to know," I said.

"Well, theoretically speaking, there's really no limit to how far the *Balboa* could go, *per se*. It'll keep going till it either runs out of fuel or something breaks which can't be fixed. Or until the crew runs out of food and starves to death, I guess. Why do you ask?" he asked.

"Do you think it'd make it to Titan and back?" I asked, ignoring his question. For a second he looked like he thought he'd misheard me, but he recovered quickly.

"You mean the moon of Saturn?" he asked skeptically.

"Yeah, that's the one," I said.

Jesse must have thought I'd flipped my lid, but I have to give him credit. He took the question seriously and gave me a straight answer.

"Not without unacceptably high risk," he said.

"What do you mean? And how high is unacceptably high?" I asked.

"I mean the *Balboa* could probably get there, true enough, subject to those same problems I just now mentioned about running out of fuel or something breaking. Titan is a really long way, Tyke. If you want my honest opinion, I don't think we'd survive a trip like that. I doubt we'd have the fuel, and even if we did, there are a dozen other issues that come to mind without stopping to think about it. I'd give us a ten percent chance of making it there and back, tops, and that's probably being generous," he said.

"How long would it take, if we did make it?" I asked.

"Depends on how much fuel you're willing to use and how much cargo you've got, not to mention how much acceleration you can handle. Among other things," Jesse said.

"Okay, assume that fuel isn't a problem, bare minimum cargo and crew necessary to make the trip, and however much acceleration you think we could handle," I said.

"Well. . . in that case. . . maybe a month, just to get there," Jesse said, working out the math in his head.

I furrowed my brows and thought hard.

"I think we can handle that," I finally said.

"Hey, slow down a minute. We're only talking about hypothetical situations here, not real ones," Jesse said.

"Not so hypothetical anymore," I said, and proceeded to tell him all about the dream and everything else.

You're serious about this?" Jesse asked when he heard it all, almost like he couldn't believe it.

"I've never been more serious in my life, buddy," I said solemnly.

"But. . . " Jesse said.

"Yeah, I know, you think it's crazy, right?" I said.

"The thought did cross my mind," he admitted.

"You think I like it? As far as I'm concerned, I'd never leave Kona again if it was up to me," I said.

"Well, you know, Tyke, it really *is* up to you, when all the water is boiled out of the pot. Nobody's forcing you," he said.

"Jesse. . . " I began, and then trailed off. I couldn't think of what to say so he'd understand how important this was. Not surprising, since I didn't understand it myself. No one who hadn't had one of those dreams himself could possibly appreciate what it felt like. All I knew was that it absolutely had to be done, but unfortunately people don't believe things simply because you wish they would.

On the other hand, Jesse has always been the type who found danger to be slightly intoxicating in certain respects. Not as much so as Chris, to be sure, but he definitely had a streak of that same trait. He likes adventure, and always has. People with no taste for that kind of thing don't become pilots, and they don't read stories about famous explorers or daydream about leading expeditions to Mars. Jesse might *say* he didn't like this whole plan of going to Titan, and I guess on a rational level he probably didn't. But then again, on another level it was right up his alley; the kind of thing that would have made his eyes shine with excitement a couple years ago, before the Moon adventure. Maybe he'd had his fill of such things for a while, but I knew him well enough to know that deep down, there was certainly a part of him which still thirsted after far horizons.

Even if he wouldn't admit it.

"Hypothetically speaking, would we have to land on the surface? I doubt there are any runways, and the *Balboa* can't land anywhere else," he asked grudgingly, and I knew right then the battle was won. He might not have agreed quite yet, but if he was already nibbling the bait then it was only a matter of time.

"Yeah, we'll definitely have to land," I said, thinking about that ice castle. Jesse frowned, chewing his bottom lip while he thought about that.

"There are some small landing pods we could try. They're not really built to go with the XR's but we might clamp one to the hull, I guess. That would get us down to the surface while we left the *Balboa* in a parking orbit, and we could set down pretty much anywhere as long as it was solid ground. Maybe even move around a little. They're not really made for repeated use, though. We'd be seriously limited as to how much we could travel, and I doubt we could trust them to make more than one trip back up to the *Balboa*. They're also small, so we'd be limited as to how much food and such we could carry down with us. We'd only have a week or so on the surface, at the most. Is that enough?" Jesse said.

"I don't know. I guess it depends on how long it takes us to find that castle," I admitted.

"Well, I sure would hate to travel all that way and then turn up empty-handed," he said.

"So you'll do it?" I asked hopefully.

"It's against my better judgment, but I'm sure I'll probably end up saying yes. I always do, don't I?" he asked, with a sigh.

"Yeah. . . that you do," I said, and that was all we said about it.

In spite of Jesse's semi-willingness to go, we couldn't just take off for Titan the next day. There were things to be considered and preparations to be made for a long and dangerous mission like that. We had to fetch some extra thorium from Mrs. Weiss's old laboratory in Tampa, not to mention a landing pod from MacDill while we were there. Jesse was right about those; the craft looked pitifully small and rickety. There were food and water stores to be thought of, and the all-important question of who all should go. Jesse and I had no choice about going, and when all was said and done, the only other member of the expedition turned out to be Philip. This was almost as much his project as it was mine, so he was the logical choice.

"Why can't I go?" Danielle asked me that night, frowning. We were sitting on the beach together, alone for the time being, and I could sympathize with how she felt. None of us *wanted* to go, but if the thing had to be done then it was in some ways even harder to stay behind.

"If you go, it'll be one more person to have to carry food and air for. You know that. We're already on tight limits as it is. Every bit of extra cargo we have to add only cuts down on our chances of coming back alive, which are already not so great," I reminded her.

"Yeah, I know," she said softly, and squeezed my hand.

"I hope you know, though, how much of a comfort it'll be for me, knowing you're back home safe, and not up there in danger with us," I said, and she sighed.

"Yeah, I know that too," she agreed.

"But I tell you what, beautiful. Whenever I get home, will you marry me and live happily ever after?" I asked, and she laughed then.

"Tyke, you knew the answer to that before you even asked," she said.

"Yeah, but I kinda thought you might like to be asked, you know," I said.

"You know me too well," she said. She put her head on my shoulder and I put my arms around her, and for a long time neither one of us said anything else, looking out at the stars over the ocean. They say all things have their unexpected beauties, and one of the few unexpected beauties of the Orion Strain is that the Earth is dark from pole to pole, in a way it hasn't been in centuries; no city lights, nothing like that to break the darkness, and as a result the sight of the stars is almost incredible nowadays, big and bright like diamonds on black velvet. I think I could sit and watch them for hours, especially when Danielle was with me.

I idly let my eyes drift to where Saturn shone amongst the stars, and couldn't help wondering if we'd ever really make it there, let alone make it back. How much I would have preferred just to stay home with Danielle, I don't think I could even put into words.

"I'll pray for you while you're gone, every single night. Every morning, too," she murmured after a while.

Danielle has never been the type to say things like that very much. She's actually a deeply religious sort of person, but she's also the type that if she meant to pray for you, she'd normally just do it and never mention the fact. Telling me something like that only showed how worried she really was about this whole expedition.

Living at the Academy for so long had made me sort of the same way, though. Jesse had always been handsome and popular enough that he could get away with talking about anything he pleased and wearing his Christianity on his sleeve for all the world to see, and people loved him for that just like they loved him for everything else he ever said or did. It made him, in that time and place, just enough of a rebel to be charming, just like his hayseed mannerisms or his silly jokes. Things were harder for me. I was never popular enough to have that option, so I learned to keep quiet about what I thought and believed. After a while, it made me shy of talking about such things at all, even in private with the one person I loved most in the whole world.

Then I told myself not to be ridiculous.

"I'm sure God will watch over both of us," I said staunchly.

"I'm sure He will, too. But I sure will miss you while you're gone, mister," she said.

"I'll miss you too, beautiful," I agreed.

"Well, bring me back a souvenir or something, then. Even if it's only a rock," she said, trying to lighten the mood.

"I doubt we can, babe. It's so cold out there that the rocks are made of water ice, and they'd melt if we tried to bring one back," I said, but she only laughed.

"Well, in that case, you can bring me a little bottle of water back and we can pretend it's Titanian lava. I guess it would be, wouldn't it?" she asked.

"Yeah, I guess it would, at that," I agreed.

"They sell water lots of places for souvenirs, anyway. I went to Saint Augustine once and we bought a little bottle of water from the Fountain of Youth over there. Nastiest stuff I ever tasted," she said.

"Yeah, I've been there, too, now that you mention it. It really *was* disgusting, wasn't it?" I said.

From there the conversation meandered in a hundred different directions, but that was all right. We were close, and we were loving each other with every word we said, even if those words were only about touristy places back home in Florida.

But still, I walked home with a heavy heart after I kissed her goodnight, no matter how sweet the evening had been. I knew we'd be leaving all too soon, and then it was a very real possibility that I might never see her again. It was more likely than not, as a matter of fact.

I let myself wonder for a little while what she'd do if I never came home. Probably grow old alone, if I had to guess. There wouldn't be any other boys for her to marry, unless she ended up with Hunter or Tommy, and both of them were so young that it seemed highly unlikely. I didn't foresee Chris ever breaking up with Emily, and Derrick was her blood kin. There was Johnny Weiss, I guess, but those two were so unalike that it seemed impossible she'd ever be interested in him, or vice versa for that matter. That exhausted the entire list of possibilities. So it was most likely either me or nobody, as far as she was concerned.

Some people might have enjoyed the idea of being so indispensable, I suppose, especially if they had a dash of the vain and selfish type in them. But all it did was make me sad, actually, knowing that she stood to lose nearly as much as I did on this mission. Maybe more, in some ways. Her whole life was at stake just as much as mine was, only in a different manner. I was certain those things hadn't escaped her attention, either, even if she hadn't said anything about them. No doubt trying to spare my feelings, dear heart that she was.

But there was nothing I could do about any of those things except to offer up my own humble prayer, which I did before I went to bed that night. The gentle susurration of the waves outside my bedroom window soon lulled me to sleep, and for a little while I forgot about all the potential sorrows in the world.

The next morning it was time to head out, and just like last time, everybody came out to the airfield to see us off. But the mood was a lot more somber this time, and nobody even pretended to smile. We all knew how risky this mission would be, and how bad the chances were that we'd ever return.

But soon enough all the hugs and kisses were over, and then there was nothing left to do except board the *Balboa* and pray we made it back.

I remembered thinking what a long and dreary trip it was to reach the Moon, and that had only lasted three days. What would a whole month be like?

Well, I'm here to tell you, it's no picnic. It gets very, very boring after a while, when you can never go outside and you've only got a narrow path down the middle of a spacecraft cabin to pace back and forth, and even that not the whole way. The back end of the passenger cabin was stowed with all our food and other supplies.

For a long time there was nothing much to see, either. You might think we'd have to pass by Jupiter or Mars or at least a few of the asteroids, but we never did. The planets were far around on the other side of the sun, and as for the asteroid belt, well, even that's no more than a wispy ghost, like finding one piece of gravel in an area the size of a football field. Space is mostly exactly what it sounds like; empty space, nothingness, for millions and billions of miles in every direction. In a way it's awe-inspiring, and in another way it's kind of terrifying, to be honest. It has a tendency to remind you how incredibly small and insignificant you really are, and how cold and pitiless the universe can be sometimes.

But it's also very unwise to let yourself dwell on those kinds of thoughts for too long. I've read real-life stories of people who went crazy out there, got in their space suits, and went out the airlock intending to head back home on foot, so to speak. Insanity, of course, but that's exactly what comes from brooding too much on how scary a place you're in. It'll make you bonkers after a while, and then you're liable to do just about anything.

It's much better to keep your mind and body busy with other things. Exercise, reading, socializing, watching movies; anything except dwelling on the great unknown. After a day or two, we deliberately kept the windows covered so we wouldn't see what was outside the ship, and Jesse seldom if ever went to the cockpit except to check things over every morning.

But after a long, long time, Jesse mentioned that he could see Saturn, and we did go up to the cockpit to check that out.

It was nothing particularly exciting at that point; just an unusually bright star among many others. But it gradually got bigger and brighter over the next few days, until it dominated the whole sky on that side of the ship. The rings are every bit as spectacular as you might think, especially up close like that, but you can't see them unless you're at the right angle. They're razor-thin, and if you look at them straight-on then you can't see them at all.

But Saturn itself was only an afterthought on this trip, and soon enough we came in sight of the real object of our attention: Titan.

Titan may technically be a moon, but don't let the name fool you. It's bigger than the planet Mercury and almost a third the size of Earth. It's by far the biggest moon in the solar system, if you include the atmosphere. If you don't, then Jupiter's moon Ganymede is very slightly larger, but since that moon is airless then Titan definitely wins out in the visual size department. Hence the name.

I don't know that it would win too many beauty contests, though. It looks like an almost featureless orange ball, with a bluish haze surrounding it. That's mostly because it's always got a hundred percent cloud cover, but still, I would have liked to see the surface a little sooner, after traveling so far to reach the place.

But we could afford to wait a few more hours, while Jesse slowed us down and carefully put us into a parking orbit. The navigational computer could maintain that for as long as we needed it to.

We had to make a spacewalk to reach the landing pod, and that was ticklish business. We went outside, tethered together and to the *Balboa* just in case, and then crawled slowly and carefully along the underside of the fuselage until we reached the spot where the pod was attached. Then we quickly switched our tether from the *Balboa* to the pod. That was a dangerous moment; it always is, when you're out in space and not attached to anything. But we got it done as fast as possible, and then all three of us had to manually throw the clamps attaching the pod to the ship. That was another dangerous maneuver, since the pod immediately began to fall away from the ship. It wouldn't have taken half a second to get crushed between two big pieces of metal or even cut to pieces against the clamps if things hadn't gone right.

But thankfully nothing like that happened, and we entered the pod with a sigh of relief.

It was awfully crowded in there. It was a more-or-less circular room about twelve feet across, but most of the space was taken up with food, water, exploratory and scientific equipment, and things of that nature. There was barely room for the three of us to squeeze in, even standing elbow to elbow.

Chapter Eight

We wouldn't need space suits down on the surface, of course. Titan has a thick, heavy atmosphere and the air pressure is plenty high enough that we could do without space suits. What we *did* have to have were thermal suits, but those are quite a bit easier to move around and work in. I believe I said earlier that the past hundred years have been kind of a hostile time for scientific research, and that's true as far as it goes, but thermo-resistant fabric is one of the nice little exceptions. You can make a suit out of it which is loose and comfortable like street clothes, and then you don't have to worry about extreme temperatures. There are limits, of course; you couldn't exactly go swimming in a volcano or anything. But as long as you stay within the prescribed temperature range, you'll be all right.

Titan hovers around 94 degrees above absolute zero, give or take 20 degrees or so. That's down at the very extreme limits of what a thermal suit is supposed to be able to handle, but they do work better against cold than heat, so we had a reasonable hope of getting by all right with just that and a respirator.

We quickly changed into them, and I was glad to get that cumbersome space suit off. Then Jesse sat down at the controls and took us down into the atmosphere. It turns out Titan has a blue sky as long as you're above the clouds, jarringly Earthlike for such an alien place. The clouds themselves were thick and orange, with whitish tendrils here and there. We still couldn't see a thing when it came to the actual surface, but we all knew that would change once we got down below the cloud deck.

"Here we go," Jesse murmured, and the pod quickly slipped from the blue, sunlit world above into dense orangey haze that grew steadily darker as we descended.

"Do you have any idea where we need to go?" Jesse asked.

"All I know is that it looks like a castle made of ice. I'll know it when I see it, but I don't know where it is on the surface," I said.

"I'll bring us in near the equator, then. If there's anything alive down there, it'll probably be in the tropics, don't you think?" Jesse asked.

"Sounds like a reasonable theory to me," I said.

Long ago, back when people still spent money on such things, they sent a few probes to Titan. Enough to find out the temperature range and some of the geography and things like that, and one result of those missions was the surface map I held in my hands. It was only partial, and there weren't a lot of details, but most of the prominent features were named and that much at least was useful.

We dropped below the clouds over the mountains of Xanadu (according to the map), and those are glistening white hills of solid ice. The entire range is roughly the size of Australia; quite a lot of the features on Titan are oversized like that. It was awfully hard to see much; the light level was more or less like deep twilight on Earth, and everything was cast in an orangey tint because of the clouds. It was weird and unearthly-looking, which I guess shouldn't have surprised me.

We were near the western edge of Xanadu when we spotted something.

"Look there," Jesse said, pointing at the screen quite unnecessarily.

It was a castle, made of glittering blocks of ice-rock. It rose up in tall spires and thick walls, and although I don't think it's the kind of building any human would design, it was the first obviously *built* thing we'd yet seen. It was situated on a prominence overlooking the black desert of Shangri-la to the west, as if keeping watch.

"I can't believe it was that easy," Jesse muttered.

"It may not be. I don't see any jungle around there," Philip pointed out.

"Well. . . we won't know if we don't check it out. Let's stop and see if anybody's home," I said.

Jesse landed us maybe a mile away from the castle, coming to rest on a flat hilltop that we christened Sugarloaf Mountain, after the highest point of land near Tampa. Not that that amounts to much, you know, but home is home.

Strictly speaking, my mother and Aunt Joan were from Texas, and so was my father for that matter. Uncle Philip was from Arkansas, so I guess me and Jesse are transplants, of a sort, even though we were both born in Tampa and lived all our lives there until the Orion Strain changed everything. Since then we'd lived in Hawaii and even on the Moon, and I couldn't help wondering just a little where we'd ever come to rest. It's all fine and well to be a rolling stone for a while, but there comes a point when you start to want some peace and stability for a change.

"So, who gets to have his name in the history books?" Jesse asked while we waited for the airlock to bleed out. I knew what he meant; he was thinking about which one of us would be the first one to set foot on Titan. It's a sad but true fact that everybody remembers Neil Armstrong, after all, and Buzz Aldrin is forever a footnote.

"Go ahead, Jesse. Make your mark," I said tolerantly. He deserved his moment of glory, after risking his life to come all this way. It was the kind of thing he'd been dreaming of ever since he was three years old, and I of all people would never take that from him.

"You're sure?" he asked.

"Yeah, I'm sure. Go ahead," I said.

The airlock door swung open and we left the pod cautiously, not quite sure what to expect. We stood for a minute at the top of the steps, and the first thing I noticed was the *cold*. I could feel it even through the thermal suit; a deathly chill like a freezing winter's morning. The suits have to allow a certain amount of body heat to escape or else you'd roast, but it's not much. If I still felt that much cold even through my suit, then I hardly wanted to imagine what it must have been like out there with no protection. I knew it was frigid on an intellectual level, of course. I knew what the temperature was and what that meant as far as conditions on the ground might go. It's cold enough that water is solid rock and a human being without protection would flash-freeze in less than a second. But knowing all that in my head was a completely different thing than feeling those cold fingers tickling my ribs.

I shivered, and not entirely from the cold, either.

Then Jesse went down the steps and left the first human footprint on that icy world, and even though there was no one to witness it except me and Philip, we both clapped and hooted and made a big deal over it, and Philip took some pictures. I couldn't see Jesse's face through his helmet, but I'm sure he was practically bursting with pride.

But we had actual business to do besides looking for photo ops, so after a few minutes Philip and I joined Jesse at the foot of the steps.

We soon discovered that the ground was slick and greasy; imagine an ice cube soaked in kerosene and you'll get a pretty good idea of what the surface of Titan is like. The very first thing I did when I set foot on the place was to slip and fall right on my rear end. It didn't hurt too much because of the low gravity, but it would never do to go slipping and sliding along like that.

"We'll have to wear some cleats and stay roped together," Philip said.

Jesse went back inside the pod to fetch some steel spikes that attached to the bottoms of our boots, to bite into the ice-rock and give us some extra traction. Then we all tied ourselves together and headed out for the castle.

Xanadu was named after a mythical country in a poem by Samuel Taylor Coleridge, a long, long time ago. He certainly didn't have Titan in mind when he wrote it, or if he did then he was either crazy or drunk. The place is actually much more like the deepest circle of Dante's *Inferno,* where the souls of traitors are condemned to eternal torment in the frozen ice.

Besides being slick as snot, the ground was rough and broken almost everywhere, and that made the footing extremely treacherous. One slip at the wrong time and you were apt to go hurtling right off the edge of a steep cliff into a canyon or a dry river channel, and then you very well might not make it out again. Titan is not the Moon, either; fall from too high up on *that* place and you're dead meat, even if you don't rip your suit open and freeze to death. I thanked God many times for those metal spikes on our boots, and we always, *always* stayed roped together. More than once, that was all that saved one or another of us from falling. The low gravity helped, especially since we were used to that from our time on the Moon, but nevertheless, it's a dangerous place. Added to that, I don't doubt the stench would have been incredible if we'd been able to breathe the air.

"This sure is a nasty place," I muttered as we trudged along.

It took us about two hours to reach the castle, mostly because we had to be so careful. Once we got there, it was easy to see that the place had been abandoned for who-knows-how-long. The stones were weathered and old-looking, and a few of them were cracked and fallen. In front of the walls was a well-beaten road that came up from the desert below and then disappeared into the hills after passing the castle. I couldn't help wondering where it came from and where it went, but of course there was no way of knowing.

"We might as well look inside, while we're here," Jesse said, and I shrugged.

We walked through the gate into a kind of courtyard, but most of the buildings had collapsed long ago. Probably the only reason the walls were still standing was because they were so thick and strong. Although that fact alone got me to wondering what kind of danger there might be in this place which led these people to think they needed such thick walls in the first place.

"Well, *this* was a sight to see," Jesse said dryly, surveying the ruins.

"Oh, come on, Jesse, you're not excited about the first alien buildings any human being has ever seen?" I asked.

"Sure, but I'd be a lot *more* excited about them if they weren't falling to pieces," he said.

It started to rain while we stood there, and we sought shelter under what was left of the gateway, looking out across the black desert while we waited for it to end.

It was an odd kind of rain; liquid methane, of course, and not water. No doubt that was what made the hills so slick and greasy. If you can imagine orange clouds that rain a substance very much like gasoline in drops big as marbles that fall slow as snowflakes, you might get some idea of what it looked like. And amongst all that, blue-white lightning and wind that drove the rain in sheets against the castle walls.

Then I spotted something.

"Is that another castle?" I asked, pointing across the desert.

"It sure does look like one," Jesse said, scrutinizing it. It was maybe five miles away, as best I could judge, and it seemed that the road ran straight towards it.

"Maybe we could go check that place out when it quits raining. I don't think anybody's lived in this one for a long time," I commented.

"It's worth a try," Philip said.

The rain turned out to be only a brief shower, and when it was over we headed down the road toward the desert. I'm not sure we could've gotten back to the pod right then anyway; the ground was so sludgy and slick from the rain that it was probably impassable even with our metal cleats on.

The desert brought its own set of issues, but on the whole I think it was less dangerous than the hills. There were black dunes that stood hundreds of feet high and stretched for hundreds of miles in both directions, line after line of them, with only narrow ravines in between. The ground in those ravines reminded me of thick, wet clay, the kind that sucks your shoes off sometimes if you step in it the wrong way. There were rounded ice-rock boulders down there in places, washed down out of the hills by the rivers I suppose.

The road followed one of the wider ravines between the dunes, built up in places with ice-rock cobblestones to keep travelers from sinking thigh deep in the tar-like mud. It was almost as dreary a place as the hills.

That was before we found the oasis.

Well, I guess that's what you'd call it, anyway. It was a pool of liquid methane not far from the foot of the hills, fed by an underground aquifer no doubt. It was maybe a hundred yards across, clear and smooth as glass. It looked just like water, and the ice-rock boulders around the edge were actually kind of pretty. But what really interested me were the trees.

That's right, you heard me. Trees, the first actual living things we'd seen on Titan. Weird, twisted, alien things. They reminded me of elephant ears, more or less, if you can imagine elephant ears which are jet black and twice as large as usual and which have trunks. We stumbled across a thicket of them growing right beside the pool, with the leaves hanging over the side. I didn't recognize them for what they were at first, till we got close enough.

"Do you see that?" I asked, keying my radio.

"Yeah, I see them. Looks like plants," Jesse said.

"Let's go see," I said.

"We better be careful, don't you think? They might be poisonous or anything," he said.

That was a good point, so we crept up to the elephant ears with extreme caution. It turned out to be semi-justified; the trunks were covered with wickedly sharp thorns that reminded me of a cactus. I touched one of the fronds, and when nothing happened I carefully tore a piece loose. That was another anomaly; it didn't rip the way you'd expect a leaf to rip. It stretched and tore, almost like taffy.

"This is really weird stuff," I said, turning it over in my hand. It had what looked like a vascular system of veins running through it, and the leaf was covered with tiny hairs. I was fascinated.

But even while I watched, the "plant" melted like chocolate in my hand, I guess from the little bit of heat that came through the thermal suit, and it didn't stop there, either. Once it turned to caramel-colored goop in my palm, it actually boiled away, leaving my hand empty and clean as a whistle. I turned my palm over to look at it, wondering.

I suppose that even on Earth, any substance you can imagine will either boil or catch fire sooner or later if you apply enough heat. Nothing strange about that. As far as these cold life forms on Titan were concerned, my hand was literally hotter than a blowtorch. It was sort of strange to think about things that way, but it was true. If there had been any oxygen in the atmosphere then we might have ignited a massive explosion just by walking around and handling things like we did, but since there wasn't, we only boiled things alive.

Nevertheless, I was determined to study them at least a little bit while I had the chance. Nothing like this could ever grow on Earth, or anywhere else that I knew of, for that matter. One of those elephant ears would catch fire and burn up almost instantly if it ever got transported back to Earth somehow.

So I carefully cut off a leaf and sealed it up in a bag so it wouldn't come anywhere near my hot little hands, intending to examine it more closely once we got back to the ship.

"You'll never be able to take that inside the pod, you know. It'll melt," Jesse pointed out.

"Yeah, I know. I can move some equipment outside for a little while if I have to," I said.

"You think it'll stand up to the cold?" Philip asked.

"I hope so," I said. He had a good point; Earth-made instruments are not built for use under those kinds of extreme conditions. They might crack or freeze up or any number of things. But I hoped I could get them to work at least for a little while.

There were fish in the pool, too. I only call them that advisedly, because they were nothing like the fish you're thinking of. They were gray and leathery, and they reminded me more of eels than anything else. They were fast, though; much too fast for us to think about catching one. We watched them feeding on a type of black algae-like substance that grew in the pool, but that was as close as we could get. There seemed to be awfully few species, but of course the oasis was a limited area. I was eager to move on and find out more.

The castle out in the desert turned out to be not really a castle. It was more of a large but simple building, with windows to the outside and very obviously not built for defense against anything. It was made of ice-rock, to be sure, but it reminded me more of a warehouse than a castle. In any case it was a bust, too. Nothing but ruins, just like the other one.

"Maybe we should think about looking somewhere else. There are supposed to be some big lakes and things up at the north pole, if the map is right. That might be a better place to look than here," I suggested.

"I guess we should. Will the pod get us that far, Jesse?" Philip asked.

"Well. . . yeah, I guess so. We better not use it more than we absolutely have to, though," he said.

We made our way back across the desert and the slippery hills to the pod, and as soon as we stepped inside the airlock, the methane and other gases started boiling off our suits as the temperature rose. It made a foul mess of the atmosphere, and we had to wait for the ship to cycle the air purifier long enough to remove them so we could breathe and not contaminate the rest of the ship when we opened the inner airlock door.

"We better think carefully about exactly where we want to go before we lift off. We can't make *too* many trips in this old tub. We need to make this one count, if we can," Jesse said.

"Well, I tell you what. Why don't you two think about that for a little while, and in the meantime I can go outside and study those plants from the oasis," I said, my fingers itching to get started.

"That's fine, Tyke, but don't get too wrapped up in all that. Take a few hours, sure, but be ready to leave whenever we make up our minds," Philip said.

"Sure thing," I agreed, and then grabbed a microscope and some other tools and headed back outside.

It was hard to accomplish much, under those circumstances. The darkness hampered me, and so did the lack of a table. The cold made most types of chemical analysis useless. What I might have discovered under proper conditions I can only begin to imagine, because the little bit I *did* discover astounded me.

On Earth, the basic energy molecule is sugar, namely glucose. Plants store energy and build up their tissues out of sugars and complex polymers of sugars. Even wood is only a bunch of sugar molecules tacked together. Plants use sunlight to break up water molecules and combine them with carbon dioxide to form those sugars, and then they (and animals) reverse that process to release energy.

Very simple, very efficient, and utterly unworkable on Titan. Partly because water is a solid rock, and partly because there's not enough carbon dioxide.

This plant (if you wanted to call it that), did nothing of the kind. Its body tissues were built up from tars and polymerized hydrocarbons, and when I studied the thing's metabolism I found that it used sunlight, hydrogen, and liquid methane to build up acetylene as an energy storage molecule instead of sugar. That's the same stuff they use as fuel for welding torches. Respiration took the opposite path, breaking down acetylene for energy and releasing methane and hydrogen. It was somewhat analogous to the way glucose is used on Earth, and it was fascinating.

I probably could have spent a lifetime studying Titanian body chemistry, but that wasn't really what we were there for, no matter how alien and incredibly interesting it might be.

After several hours, Philip called me inside and I reluctantly had to abandon my research.

"We're headed up to the north pole where all the lakes are. If there are still any people here, it's more likely they lived there than anywhere else. Easier to find food and all that," Jesse said, which was pretty much the decision I'd expected them to make.

"Yeah, vegetables made out of tar and fish soaked in gasoline. Yum," I said, and Jesse laughed.

"Sure, maybe they'll invite us over for supper and we can trade recipes," he said.

"They'd probably think our food is just as nasty," I said.

"I'm sure they would. But seriously, though, let's see what we can find near the water," Philip said.

"You mean the methane," Jesse said.

"You know what I mean. Find us a lake," Philip said.

Turns out Titan is pretty much a desert by Earthly standards. There are no oceans, and there are only a few oases in the equatorial regions. There are some pretty big lakes, though, a few of them bigger than Lake Superior or the Caspian Sea. Most of those are near the north and south poles, and they grow and shrink with the seasons. Only a few are wide and deep enough to be permanent.

Jesse took us to the largest of them all, the Kraken Sea, named after the famous sea serpent, and then we nosed our way along the coast to see what we could see. It was early summer in the northern hemisphere, which we hoped meant living things would be at their most active and easiest to find.

Chapter Nine

The Kraken coast is mostly rocky, with high cliffs of ice-rock in most places, shining pale white even in the twilight. Here and there are bays with white sand beaches of ice crystals, and on top of the cliffs there are whole forests of the black elephant ears. We found flying things, too, which apparently lived in crevices in the cliffs and now and again swooped down on black, leathery wings to snatch fish from the sea.

"They remind me of eagles, a little bit," Jesse said, watching them.

"Yeah, a little. The fish-catching part, at least. I don't think I ever saw a black eagle with no feathers, though," I said.

"It sure is *ugly* here. It seems like everything on the whole dadgummed planet is either black, white, or gray," he said.

"Aw, now, don't forget the clouds," I said.

"Yeah, you're right. How could I forget that? They cast such a lovely orange tint all over the black, white, and gray," he said wryly.

I stopped teasing him, because he was right. Everything really *was* either black, white, or gray, all of it tinted with dull orange from the dim light filtering down through the clouds. It was a depressing color scheme after a while.

By and by we came across another castle, though it was unlike the one we'd seen before. It was more delicate and thin-walled, with soaring spires and bright white walls stained orange from the dim light. I think it was the first really beautiful thing I ever remember seeing on Titan.

"That one looks a lot more like the one I remember. Let's go check it out," I said, and Jesse cautiously set us down as far back from the cliff's edge as he could without getting entangled in the dense jungle of elephant ears. Then we quickly emerged from the pod and started hiking toward the building.

That cliff itself was probably three hundred feet high, and as I said before, Titan is *not* like the Moon. Falling off a cliff like that would have crushed us like bugs on a windshield. Therefore we stayed well back from the edge, not trusting the slippery ice.

But it was a pretty view, sort of. The Kraken Sea stretched out as far as the eye could see, almost smooth as glass if it hadn't been for a gentle swell. It looked almost like ripples in the surface of a mirror. The black birds flew back and forth, diving for fish, but there was nothing to be heard except the gentle sigh of the breeze in the elephant ears.

It wasn't till we nearly reached the castle itself that we saw our first A'rum. That's the name they call themselves, which we learned later on. The apostrophe stands for a clicking noise which we don't have in English and which makes their language practically unpronounceable as far as I'm concerned, but then I guess that ought not to have surprised anybody. The closest I could ever get was *Akrum*. The name means something like *the Beautiful People*, which might have seemed conceited if that's all you knew. But really it's just a form of their word for Titan itself, which they call A'rath, the Beautiful Land.

Well, maybe it's a beautiful place for the A'rum, but I still don't think any human being would ever think so.

I'd been trying very hard not to form any expectations of what the castle builders might look like or how they might act, knowing how unlikely it was that I'd guess anywhere even remotely close to the truth. But I suppose you can't shut down your brain entirely, and it works subconsciously to build up ideas you're not even aware of. So however hard I tried to expect nothing, the A'rum still managed to surprise me.

The first one we saw was about ten feet tall, I suppose, covered in that same leathery gray-black hide that covered every other creature we'd seen so far. No surprise there. It had four limbs like a human, but that was the only point of similarity. It reminded me more of hairless bat than anything else, with large protuberances on its head which could only be ears, and loose skin connecting the arms and legs. Maybe it was more like a hairless flying squirrel, come to think of it. It had large golden eyes with cat-like pupils, and a small mouth with sharp black teeth hanging outside its lips like a crocodile, or like the monsters of the Altai crater swamps for that matter. No nose or tail, but it did walk upright on two feet.

When we first saw it, the thing was carrying an armload of black leaves which I assumed had come from the elephant ears, but when it saw us it dropped them and let out a high-pitched screech so loud it hurt my ears even through my helmet. Then it immediately took flight, but not the way you might think. It didn't flap wings or anything like that; it swam through the air like a human being might swim through water, and almost before you could blink it was gone.

"I wonder if that was the owner of our castle," Jesse said.

"I guess we'll find out soon enough. He looked scared, but maybe if we wait here for a while he'll get curious and come back," I said.

So that's what we did, and sure enough, before long the welcoming committee arrived. Five of the creatures emerged from the castle doors, approaching us cautiously and stopping when they were still several yards away. One of them seemed to be the leader, since he was the one who spoke. He had a high-pitched voice which was almost too far up the scale for us to hear, squeaky and thin like a mouse. We didn't understand a word he said, of course, or vice versa. But he must have been fairly intelligent, because as soon as he grasped the fact that we didn't know each others' language, he sat down and started working to learn it.

I suppose there are certain gestures that are so obvious to any observer that their meaning is universal; that would be an interesting question for a language specialist, no doubt. But however that might be, when he tapped his chest and said a word, we guessed he must be giving us his name. I couldn't even begin to try to pronounce it the way he did, not with those confounded clicks; the closest I could get was N'grumth. Or something like that. I'm sure I mangled it, but I think it was close enough for him to understand. He didn't do much better with our names, either, though. Thus we became Tick, Yissy, and Pillip for the rest of our stay on Titan.

I'm sure he was trying his best, but honestly. . . Tick? And I used to think *Tyke* was bad. The things we have to put up with for the sake of interplanetary diplomacy.

N'grumth invited us back to the castle, by means of a beckoning gesture. We followed, talking quietly among ourselves.

"Do you think it's safe to go with these people?" I asked in a low voice.

"I don't know, but if we don't then we'll never learn anything. They haven't attacked us yet, at least," Philip said.

"Yeah, it's that *yet* part that worries me," I said.

"Aw, don't be such a worry wart, Tick," Jesse said. I should have known he'd immediately pick up on *that* juicy little tidbit. I could hear it now; he'd be needling me from here on out about how I was the biggest tick he'd ever seen, and asking me if I really liked the taste of blood or whether I considered mosquitoes to be professional colleagues, and such similar hogwash.

"You're so funny, Yissy," I said, but somehow that didn't sound nearly as comical. I wondered enviously why *he* couldn't be the one who got slapped with the toad-sucker nickname for once. But there was nothing I could do about it, so I put the whole thing out of my mind and tried to focus on something more practical. We were just entering the castle, and I had more important things to think about than what the A'rum called me.

We entered a dim courtyard of sorts, similar to the one we'd seen in Xanadu when we first landed. It was paved with ice-rock cobbles and surrounded with buildings made of the same substance. I noticed there were lots of windows, but no glass in any of them. Instead there were black curtains made of some kind of woven fabric, which could be drawn for privacy or to keep out the rain or snow. The same thing was true for most of the doors.

N'grumth paid no attention to these things and led us directly across the courtyard, then pushed his way through a set of black curtains into one of the buildings. After a second's hesitation, we followed. It was awfully dim inside, but when our eyes adjusted we found ourselves in a room with a large ice-rock table surrounded by black cushions where several A'rum were sitting, eating from bowls. I don't know what the food was; it looked like black salad. They all stared at us for a long minute, making me intensely uncomfortable, but then went right back to their meal as if nothing had happened. One of them offered me a bowl of food, and since I didn't know how to refuse I accepted it.

There were torn-up leaves that might have come from the elephant ears, mixed with chunks of a meatlike substance that might have come from anywhere. God only knows what it must have tasted like; I'm not sure I even want to imagine it. Tar sprinkled with gasoline is my best guess. But it didn't really matter, since there was no possible way I could eat it anyway. It would vaporize the instant it touched my lips, and freeze me in the process. And even if I did somehow choke down a bite, it would either make me violently ill or maybe even kill me; I'm not sure which. So I didn't try to eat the stuff. I merely picked at it with the Titanian equivalent of a fork; that is, a sharpened piece of bone with which you could spear your food. It was every bit as black as the salad, and I noticed it was already starting to soften and melt in my hand, just like the leaf had done at the oasis. I quickly put it down on the table, not wanting to destroy anybody's property.

* * * * * * *

That was the first of many visits with N'grumth over the next several days, and we gradually reached the point that we could communicate in a basic kind of way. The computer on the pod wasn't powerful enough to help much, but we linked to the *Balboa* and let the computer up there work on translating the A'rum language as if it were a nice tough problem in stellar navigation. That provided some valuable insights, and so did our own efforts.

We found out quite a lot of things about them as time went by. Human words and concepts don't really fit very well when you're talking about aliens, so we often had to rely on analogies. Otherwise we never would have understood anything at all.

It soon turned out that the castle belonged to N'grumth's family, although that was one of the very first misunderstandings we had. The A'rum don't mean the same thing by family that a human would. There's no such thing as male or female on that world, and therefore no reproduction of the kind that allows for close but varied genetic relationships like humans have. I don't know what to call them, actually; there are no human words to describe it. They're not male or female, they're not hermaphrodites, and they're certainly not neuter. But what other words are there?

Each adult A'rum reproduces by releasing millions of single-celled zygotes into the rivers, and the babies wash downstream where they grow and develop in the sea for nearly five whole Titanian years until the very few who survive long enough eventually come ashore and get scooped up by the older ones to finish growing up at the castle. I gathered that the younglings remember the taste of their home river, sort of like salmon do, and always return there when they're ready to emerge from the water. In the meantime, all but a precious few of them get eaten by fish and other predators, and sometimes even by each other. The whole thing didn't seem to trouble N'grumth one single bit, and he seemed puzzled as to why I thought it was so horrifying.

In any case, all the genetic material for a baby comes from a single parent, with no need for any mixing. I guess you'd call it a type of budding, but it's a type I've never heard of on Earth before. What it means in practical terms is that a child is physically identical to his parent, and his grandparent, and to all his siblings and cousins, and to his own children, and so on forever and ever. They do cherish the babies who survive long enough to come up out of the water, though. They're still barely old enough to walk or talk at that point, and the entire group raises them together.

All this produces a very tightly bonded clan of genetically identical individuals, and *that's* what an A'rum means when he says family. N'grumth's clan had nearly a hundred members of all different ages, and I was never able to tell one from another the whole time we were there. *They* could tell, of course, and in spite of being genetically identical you shouldn't think that meant they all behaved the same way. They were very much individuals, with their own personalities and quirks, just like humans who are identical twins may behave and see the world in completely different ways.

Love was another word we had difficulty with. They understood what it meant in the platonic sense, but romantic attachment is an utterly foreign concept to them, and one which N'grumth at least (once I could get him to comprehend it at all), seemed heartily glad to do without. His reaction reminded me of the way little kids think love stories are icky, actually.

Most of their time was spent farming, fishing, and hunting, as you might expect. But they also did other things. They were fond of storytelling and some of them who had a taste for it enjoyed carving ice sculptures or weaving fabric from the fibers that came from the elephant ear trees. I never understood their music; it was so high-pitched it sounded like a swarm of buzzing mosquitoes to me. They seemed happy and I think they liked each other, at least within their own clans.

They were really cruelly limited on what they had to work with. The only stone available was the ice-rock, and there are no woody-type plants on Titan, only succulents. They had no metals at all except for a few little nuggets of meteoric iron, rare as hens' teeth and prized among them like jewels. N'grumth had one of those, which he wore around his neck on a braided string. They had no glass. They knew nothing about fire. They couldn't read or write. Such tools as they had were made of bone from the animals they hunted. But in spite of being poor as church mice in some respects, they were wonderfully inventive with what they did have.

It was something vaguely like finding a late Stone Age society, I suppose, except of course it wasn't even really that, since you can't make tools out of ice-rock. It's too brittle. Maybe I should call it a Bone Age culture instead, except that I knew with no metals to work, they'd never progress any further.

It was a fascinating culture, actually, and I wish we'd had time to study it longer than we did. As it was, we barely had time to scratch the surface.

They had a government, of sorts. Every clan had a leader who decided everything, although how he was chosen I never did understand. And then in addition to that, there was a "king" who ruled the whole area and to which many dozens of clans owed allegiance. It turns out there are three kingdoms on Titan, and always have been. The Land of Dilmun, where we were, includes everything north of the equatorial deserts. The Land of Tsegihi includes everything south of the deserts. And then the Land of Belet includes the deserts themselves and the mountainous "islands" that poke up through the black sands here and there. The hill country of Xanadu where we first landed belongs to no one, it seems, sacred ground where all three kingdoms meet but none of them holds sway.

All three kingdoms have their own languages and customs, although of course they have certain things in common, too, just like all humans have certain things in common no matter where they may live. Truthfully we never got to spend any time with the people in Tsegihi or Belet, so I don't know a thing about their language or the way they live, except for occasional things the people of N'grumth's clan told me. Mostly derogatory things, actually, since the three tribes for the most part don't like each other at all.

It gradually emerged that the A'rum were a fiercely warlike and territorial people, and they fought each other regularly in bloody battles that could sometimes last for days. They fought mostly with bone clubs, slings, and something similar to a cat-o-nine-tails; a braided whip with sharp pieces of bone attached to the tip. They were pretty inventive with their weaponry, too, in spite of having only bone and string to make them.

But the odd thing (well, one of the many odd things) about them was that, in spite of how ferocious and bloodthirsty they could be, they rarely seemed to fight about the things a human would fight over. To give you one example, it seemingly never crossed anybody's mind to enlarge their territory at the expense of another kingdom or to try to conquer each other. The borders were simply the borders, as much of a given as the sunshine or the rain. When I tried to explain to N'grumth about how kingdoms on Earth frequently went to war to take over each others' lands, I think he found the whole concept utterly incomprehensible.

On the other hand, they very frequently fought over things which seemed frankly ridiculous to me; the most minor and obscure infractions of honor and courtesy were taken quite seriously as excellent reasons to go to war. N'grumth was interested in Earthly customs and when he heard that we also had a tradition of fighting for honor at times (although nowhere near as bloody as theirs), I think it raised his opinion of us by light-years. In fact, when he heard about how people used to duel with knives and pistols in single combat over points of honor, he was absolutely delighted with the idea, to the point that I was afraid I might have inadvertently introduced a brand new blood sport to a place that already had more than its fair share of such things.

I guess the biggest difference between the A'rum and humans when it came to warfare was that the A'rum were so calm about the whole thing. They didn't fight out of anger or hurt feelings, they fought purely for the cool and unruffled principle of the thing, even though they also enjoyed it tremendously and looked for any excuse to pick a fight. That was hard for me to comprehend, on both counts.

Xanadu was the only land that bordered all three kingdoms, and there, it seemed, was where they fought their frequent wars with one another, at some prearranged date and location that suited the adversaries. Anywhere within Xanadu was fair game for a battle, and there was enough variation in topography to suit whatever was needed. No fighting ever took place elsewhere.

Well, I should say anywhere in Xanadu was fair game for a fight, except for one place. Near the center of that land was an ice-rock mountain, the tallest on Titan, which N'grumth referred to in reverent tones as Muwamanth, or roughly translated, the Pillar of Heaven.

And there upon the very summit of Muwamanth, there stood a three-sided pyramid roughly two hundred feet tall, with a flat top maybe a hundred feet across. It was built of glittering ice-rock, just like every other structure on Titan. The building itself was too far away to visit, but I did see a sculpture of it. To judge from that, the blocks it was built from must have been huge, but N'grumth solemnly assured me they were fitted together so tightly that no one could have slipped even so much as the tip of a thorn in between them. There were stairs ascending the middle of all three faces, and in that way it reminded me more of a Mayan pyramid than an Egyptian one, except that Mayan pyramids have four sides and not three. In fact I'd never seen anything quite like it anywhere on Earth, and I suppose I would have been shocked if I had.

How long it had been there even the A'rum didn't know; N'grumth told us it had been there "since the day the world was made". And that was it. No other temple or holy place was there in all the three kingdoms, and there the Kings came on each equinox to praise God and offer thanks. Twice a year for them, or roughly every three and a half years in Earth-time, and on those days at least, all violence was strictly forbidden.

Anyone could go there at other times if he wished, to pray or meditate or even to make works of art depicting the place, and many of the A'rum did so for a little while, especially the young ones. It was a favorite subject of the ice sculptors and the musicians, and in the black jungle at the foot of Muwamanth there was a colony of individuals from all over the world who were there to care for the temple and minister to travelers and I guess live a quiet and reflective life for a year or two; one of the few places on Titan where such a thing was possible. You could call them temporary monks, I suppose, although again I'm grasping for words that don't really fit.

Indeed, it soon emerged that the A'rum are a deeply religious and reverent people, whatever else they might be. Now and then one of them will leave his clan to live as a solitary hermit out in the wilds, where he supposedly dreams of the future and makes prophecies. There hadn't been a holy hermit like that for a long time when we came to visit, but whenever such a one did arise the other A'rum respected him deeply and he was welcome anywhere in the world he chose to go; a favor granted to no other individual on the planet. Ordinary citizens were killed instantly if they blundered into places they didn't belong.

N'grumth told me all these things as we talked, and I gradually learned quite a bit about him personally, too. He was only fourteen years old; barely more than a child among the A'rum, but he'd already served a year in the temple at Muwamanth and he was generally seen as a rising star in his clan, I believe. As I've said before, I don't even pretend to understand Titanian politics, but N'grumth had an almost unheard of amount of respect and authority within his clan for one still in his early youth. Brilliance and bravery will get you a long way amongst the A'rum, it seems, and so will holiness.

I liked talking to him, once we reached the point that it wasn't impossibly difficult to understand each other. He was amazingly swift to learn English, although that high-pitched twitter and occasional clicks thrown in where they didn't belong made it hard to decipher what he meant sometimes. But I could usually understand well enough to get by.

He told me some of his combat stories and how his iron nugget necklace was a gift from the King of Dilmun for exceptional bravery at the Battle of Bloody Creek, where he saved the wounded King's life by single-handedly killing three mighty soldiers of Tsegihi with only his sling. For that reason among other things he was what the A'rum called an *Akiri,* one who had displayed extraordinary courage and steadfast honor in the face of danger. It was their only title of nobility, I guess you could say, and it could only be earned by doing something really exceptional. Even then, it could only be granted by someone who had already earned it himself.

But one of the most interesting things he told me concerned his quieter days at Muwamanth. It seemed that on top of the pyramid, at the apex of each corner, there stood a small pedestal with a depression on top about the size of a peach pit. All three were empty.

"What are those for?" I asked him.

"They have been empty since the beginning of time. But it is said that someday a stranger would come from a far place, bearing three crystals to fit in those spots, and then we all should have dreams, and God would be hidden no more, and the Kings would be at peace all the time, and not just twice a year. But in all our history, that has never happened," he said sadly.

It seemed like an awfully odd thing for one of the war-loving A'rum to prophesy. It was hard to imagine any of them looking forward to a day with no more fighting. It seemed to cut completely against the grain of everything they believed in and cared about. But then, as I've said before, it's very hard to understand a truly alien mind.

But later that afternoon I pulled Jesse aside.

"You don't think those holes at the temple were made for the Guardian Stones, do you?" I whispered.

"I was just wondering the same thing. I don't see how that could be, since apparently the temple has been here since the beginning of time. And besides that, we're on *Titan,* for goodness' sake. How could they have ever even known about them, before now?" he asked.

"I don't know," I admitted. But all the same, I couldn't help thinking of my own dreams back at Tycho Crater and even in Kona. It didn't make sense that I could have seen a castle of ice, or a pyramid atop a mountain which was surely Muwamanth. None of it made any sense. But I remembered very well that strong desire to carry the three Guardian Stones to Titan, and now N'grumth was telling me the A'rum had been expecting something like that for who-knows-how-long. I didn't understand how any of it could be, but in the meantime there was nothing stopping me from taking it at face value for a while. Explanations could come later.

"I think we should show them to N'grumth and ask him what he thinks," Philip said.

"Do you really think that's wise?" I asked.

"It's a risk, definitely. But we'll never find out anything if we don't ask," Philip said.

Chapter Ten

We resolved to meet with N'grumth at the first opportunity, to show him the three Guardian Stones and ask him if he thought they were the crystals foretold in the prophecy.

But before we had a chance to do that, N'grumth himself showed up at the pod, full of excitement. The King of Dilmun had sent word that he'd like to see us, it seemed, so that involved a trip to his palace on an island in the Ligeia Sea, many hundreds of miles away. It was a great honor to be invited, apparently. I understood the A'rum well enough by then to grasp the flip side of that, too; it would be viewed as a deadly insult if we *didn't* go, and believe me, the one thing you never, *ever* want to do is to insult an A'rum, let alone the King.

There was still time to ask about the Stones, though. Philip brought them out, holding all three in his right hand by their chains. The instant N'grumth saw them, he became utterly still and silent, staring at them. That's an A'rum's way of showing awe, something like what a human would mean by falling to his knees and bowing his head.

"We wanted to ask you about these. We believe they might be the crystals for Muwamanth," I said, watching N'grumth closely. And again he surprised me.

"You must put those away and never show them to anyone again before you take them to Muwamanth. And most especially you must *not* tell the King," N'grumth said. For an A'rum, that verged on treason.

"Why not?" I asked.

"Because he would take the stones and kill you immediately. The King is one of those who wish the prophecy not to be true. If he thought you were about to fulfill it, your lives would be worth no more than yesterday's garbage," he said.

That was a fairly alarming thought. It wouldn't take much to kill us on Titan; a simple rip in our thermal suits would do the job nicely. Or if the King thought that was too dangerous because of the heat from our bodies, then all he'd have to do would be to throw us in prison and wait till we starved or suffocated. It wouldn't take long.

"We won't even go see the King at all, in that case. We'll head directly for Muwamanth," Philip said, and N'grumth nodded; an odd habit he'd picked up from watching us.

"Be swift as a diving eagle," he said, one of the A'rum's favorite proverbs in circumstances when speed was required. It referred to the way the black birds on the coast dived down to snatch fish from the sea, and it carries connotations of good luck and finding whatever you seek. Like a delicious and flavorful eel made of tar and gasoline, no doubt.

But the A'rum also have another proverb, about how whispers fly faster than stones from a sling. The atmosphere on Titan is very thick, and what that means in practical terms is that you can hear things from a long way off. If you've ever knocked two rocks together under water, you know how loud it makes them sound, right? That's because water is denser than air. Well, the air on Titan does the same thing, and the A'rum have very sharp ears to begin with. They have to, living in such a dimly lit environment. Sonar is one of the main ways lots of creatures there find their way around, including the A'rum themselves at times, when they're flying in the dark.

What it amounts to is that you never know who might overhear what you say, even if there's nobody close by. Secrets are hard to keep, and there were enough A'rum in N'grumth's clan who knew a smattering of English by then that speaking in a foreign language wasn't much help.

Someone must have overheard our conversation with N'grumth, or part of it at least, and whatever else they may be, the A'rum are not fools. Everyone in N'grumth's clan had heard about the King's invitation, and they all knew about the Prophecy of Muwamanth, too. Some of them had probably suspected from the very beginning that we might be the ones meant to fulfill it, and there were plenty of folks besides the King of Dilmun who didn't like that idea.

But whoever was eavesdropping and whatever they heard, they sure didn't waste any time taking action. Before we even had a chance to board the pod, we found ourselves surrounded with grim-looking A'rum, armed with bone-tipped weaponry of all sorts and kinds.

We didn't try to run or fight, not when a single prick from one of those weapons would mean instant death if it punctured our thermal suits. Not so N'grumth. He instantly launched himself off the cliff nearby and scuttled out across the sea faster than the proverbial diving eagle, with several other A'rum in hot pursuit. He was still a youngling and therefore one of the fastest fliers, but whatever might have been the case with *him,* we didn't have that option.

Our captors twittered darkly amongst themselves while they herded us back to the castle, and as soon as we got there they took us down a set of stairs carved into the living ice to a bare room about twelve feet square. Then they left us there in the dark by rolling a heavy slab of ice across the top of the stairs like a trap door.

Well, it wasn't *quite* dark, actually. A very little bit of sunlight filtered through the ice from outside, barely enough to see each other.

"Looks like we're in for it now," Jesse said, and even though privately I couldn't disagree with that assessment, I felt like I needed to say something more positive. Jesse is usually more optimistic than that, but on those rare occasions when he *does* slip into a funk, it tends to be a bad one.

"Maybe they'll let us out in a little while," I said, even though I didn't really believe it.

"No they won't, Tyke. You heard what N'grumth said. They'll kill us, one way or another. In fact, all they have to do is leave us locked up down here for a while to take care of *that,*" Jesse said.

"Then we've got to break out before that happens," I said.

"Yeah, good luck with that. We're locked up in a dungeon of ice, billions of miles from home, and even if we did get out there's no telling what they've done with the pod," Jesse said.

"I don't think it's time to despair quite yet, son. Calm down and think carefully. I've still got my hand laser, and we might have some other things, too, if we take stock. We're far from helpless," Philip said.

It gave me some momentary hope when I heard that he still had the hand laser, until I remembered it was almost useless against anything transparent. Like ice, for example. We could pick off the A'rum one by one if they ever came back for us, of course, but it didn't take a genius to know that that was a losing proposition in the long run. Sooner or later the battery on the laser would die, or we'd run out of air, or they'd nail us with a piece of ice-rock from a sling. There was no hope that way.

"I don't see how the laser can help us get out. We can fight them, yeah, but there are so many more of them than there are of us, they'll find a way to outmaneuver us sooner or later," I finally said.

"Could we melt our way through the wall with our body heat? If we all three pushed our backs up against the same place, it ought to melt the ice pretty fast," Philip suggested.

"Yeah, but probably not fast enough to get us out of here before we run out of air. We don't know how thick the walls are, or where we might come out at. That area over there with all the light coming in would probably have us poke out right through the cliff wall over the ocean," Jesse said.

"What about that slab they slid over the door? It's probably thin enough to melt through. We might even be able to lift it, for that matter. We're a lot stronger than they are," I said.

"I'm sure they've got guards out there to deal with anything like that. What we really need is something either completely stealthy so they don't know we're escaping, or else a major diversion so they don't have time to deal with us," Philip said.

That gave me a dose of sudden inspiration.

"Uh, Jesse, how much heat are these suits rated for?" I asked casually.

"The label says anywhere from a hundred degrees up to about a thousand," he said immediately. He gave the figure in degrees Kelvin, of course, just like anyone would have done when speaking in a scientific or engineering capacity. All sensible people abolished the tired old Celsius scale a long time ago. Kelvin is much better for science, since you never have to deal with negative numbers. Zero degrees Kelvin is *really* zero degrees; absolute zero, the coldest possible temperature, the point at which all molecular motion stops. That didn't mean, of course, that we couldn't still use Celsius or Fahrenheit or anything else we liked for colloquial and specialized purposes like weather forecasts and cooking and so forth. We frequently did use Fahrenheit for those purposes, actually, since the degrees are smaller and it's quite useful in those capacities.

But in this case, the history of thermometers wasn't really relevant. What I cared most to know was whether those suits would protect us from the heat of an explosion.

That's right, an explosion.

As I mentioned before, the atmosphere of Titan is full of highly flammable hydrocarbons like methane and ethane, the same things that make up natural gas. But since there's no oxygen in the air, they don't normally catch fire or explode even when there's a spark, say from a lightning bolt. But the three of us were carrying bottles of oxygen on our backs, and we were locked up in a sealed room. That meant if we opened our air hoses and released some oxygen into the room, we'd create an explosive mixture of gases which would ignite at the tiniest spark, causing a massive explosion which would (hopefully) blow the slab off the stairs and maybe even crack the walls. For the A'rum, who'd never seen fire before, it would be a horrifying experience.

It wouldn't blow up the whole world, of course; it was limited by the amount of oxygen we could release. But it might provide us with a way out of the dungeon, not to mention the major diversion we needed to escape. My only concern was whether we'd survive such an explosion ourselves.

I quickly explained my plan to the others to see what they thought.

"I'm not sure about that, Tyke. The suits are meant to stand up to heat, not explosions. It might even rip one of them open," Jesse said.

"Yeah, it might. I didn't say it wouldn't be dangerous. But have you got any better ideas?" I asked.

"As a matter of fact I might. Well, it's a variation, anyway. We could use our backpacks to hold the oxygen instead of just letting it go free in the room. Then we'd have a sort of localized bomb. It wouldn't take as much gas, and we could stay farther away from it, too," Jesse said.

"That's a good idea. Let's give it a try while we've still got air," Philip said.

So that's what we did. We unshackled each other's backpacks from our thermal suits, leaving the bottles attached to the suits themselves via their hoses and carrying the bottles in our arms. It wasn't quite safe to do things that way, but it worked.

Then we inflated the packs with oxygen from our breathing tanks, zipping them up as tight as possible so they wouldn't leak so fast. When all was said and done, we had three bloated bags of (hopefully) highly explosive gases, which we piled together at the top of the stairs.

"Here goes nothing," Philip whispered. We were standing together at the bottom of the stairs beside the door, out of the way of whatever blast might come down. Philip stuck the tip of the hand laser around the very edge of the door jamb, pointing it as near the direction of the bags as he could, and then triggered it. The thing might not have been much use as a weapon against that many enemies, but it made an excellent long-distance ignition device.

For a second there was nothing, and then a horrendous explosion rattled the ice all around us, blowing orange flame mixed with acrid black soot into the dungeon. It was louder than you'd believe anything could possibly be, and I'm sure it must have deafened every A'rum in the castle, with their sensitive and tender ears.

"Come on!" Philip cried, and together we ran up the steps even before the smoke cleared. The slab of ice at the top had been blown to pieces, and we emerged from our former cell to behold a courtyard full of A'rum knocked senseless from the blast, and others who hadn't been quite as close were practically gibbering with fear.

They'd moved the pod into the courtyard, the better to guard it, I suppose. But that only simplified things as far as we were concerned. We immediately ran to the airlock and scrambled inside as fast as we could, and Jesse took off from the courtyard in such a hurry that I'm sure he must have left a crater in the cobblestone floor ten feet wide. Not to mention he probably vaporized a few unlucky A'rum who happened to be too close when he took off.

"Where are we going?" Jesse yelled as soon as we got out of the castle.

"Head for Muwamanth!" I yelled right back.

The explosion at the castle might have stunned and traumatized most of N'grumth's clan members, but however that may be, they did have criers to spread the word, and the pod was none too fast. All they have to do is howl to each other like wolves in that thick atmosphere, and in that way news can travel like a flash of lightning from one side of the world to the other in almost no time. There might not be any telephones on Titan, but they sure do have the next best thing.

We made it quite a long way before anything happened, though; in fact we were almost at the southern border of Dilmun where the black-sand deserts begin. Then we saw a cloud of A'rum flying toward us in that odd swimming flight they use.

"That doesn't look good," Philip said, watching them.

"Maybe they've got nothing to do with us," I said hopefully.

But they did. The A'rum attacked the pod with their bone clubs, obscuring Jesse's view and destroying several of the sensors located on the outer hull. Several of them were killed or even melted by the heat from the engines, but that didn't seem to deter the others at all. They clung to the pod, doing whatever damage they could do, and their weight plus the beating was dragging us down. Finally one of them must have smashed the camera, because the screen suddenly went black and dead.

Jesse slammed his fist on the table in frustration and switched to a backup, bringing back a blurry image. We were out over the desert by then, and alarmingly low to the ground. The Dilmunese had abandoned the attack after we crossed the border into Belet, but that wouldn't help us.

"We're going down," Jesse said grimly, and even though I knew what that meant, I refused to think about it.

We'd never had a chance to take off our thermal gear in the first place, but we quickly put our respirators back on, fully prepared for a breach of the hull when we crashed, and Jesse did his best to land us gently.

He didn't succeed very well. We crashed on the upper slopes of Mount Tortola, which is one of the many volcanic cones in the northern part of the Shangri-la desert. Even though the impact didn't cause as much damage as it would have on Earth, it still crumpled the hull and tore it open. All three of us were thrown violently against the controls, while cans of Spam and bottles of water from the stores rained down on us painfully from behind.

Everything inside the pod was instantly coated in hoar-frost as the water vapor in the air flash-froze as soon as the hull cracked open. But we must have been near the summit, because we punched right through the rim and found ourselves sailing through the air again, but only briefly. We soon landed with a huge splash in the lake at the bottom of the caldera, and for a second I really thought that was the end of us.

But it wasn't, or at least not quite. The pod sank quickly, and before I knew it we came to rest on the bottom. We could still breathe because of our respirators, of course, and we were still protected from the liquid methane because of our thermal suits, but how we'd ever get out of there was another question altogether. The rip in the hull was too narrow to fit through, and it was an open question whether we'd ever get the airlock to work.

I stood up painfully, or at least as well as you can manage to stand while you're submerged in liquid. Getting pummeled with Spam is an excruciating experience; believe me, I know. One of the cans had lobbed me right on the back of my neck, and I could feel the tender beginnings of a baseball-sized bruise back there. I probably had others I hadn't noticed yet, and I didn't doubt Jesse and Philip did, too.

"Is everybody all right?" Philip asked.

"I've been better," Jesse said, and I had to agree. That's when I noticed the rip in his suit. It was torn open all the way from his chest down to the left side of his stomach, ragged and fluttering in the mild current. For a second I was horrified, and then almost instantly realized something very strange was going on. If Jesse's suit was ripped that badly, he ought to have been dead. No ifs, ands, buts, or thighs. He should've flash-frozen just like the water vapor, hard as a rock without a prayer of survival. But obviously he hadn't.

"Uh, Jesse, how come you're not dead?" I asked, pointing at his suit. I don't think he'd noticed it yet, but when he looked down I heard him gasp, even through the radio. Then he looked up.

"This stuff is warm, Tyke. I mean *really* warm, like a bath tub," he said, pulling apart the rip and even lifting his shirt to show me that yeah, he was really exposing bare skin.

"But *how?* Liquid methane ought to freeze you solid in a heartbeat," I said.

"This is not methane. It's *water,*" Philip said, and as soon as he uttered the words I knew it was true.

"Tortola is a volcano. I didn't think of that," Jesse said, and I laughed.

"What's funny?" Philip asked.

"I just realized we're standing at the bottom of a pool of lava, that's all," I said.

"Yeah, well, we better be glad this pool of lava was here, or I'd be a frozen fish stick right about now," Jesse said.

"We can talk about all that later, boys. Right now I think we need to get out of here," Philip said.

That was a good idea, so Jesse swam over to the remains of the air lock and struggled to open it, with no success.

"Y'all come help me; the latch is stuck," he said, so Philip and I joined him in straining at the latch. I guess it got tweaked when we hit the ground because it did *not* want to let go, but finally it released all of a sudden, sending us tumbling head over heels into the bottles and cans again. We were able to shove the door open just barely enough to squeeze inside, and then we had to deal with the outer door. That one wasn't quite as bad.

At long last we found ourselves outside the pod. It was half-buried in a slushy region of ice-rock, and far up above us was the surface, glinting dimly orange. We swam up there and made it to shore with no mishaps, and then sat there on the ice-rock looking out at the bubbling water in the caldera. I wondered how many people had ever gone swimming in a volcano and lived to tell about it, much less had their lives saved by one. The water level was gradually rising, and I suspected there might be an eruption soon, although probably a gentle one. Kilauea is like that; you can get right up close to it and watch the lava pour out and take pictures and stuff without really being in any danger, as long as you can stand the heat. At the moment, the heat from Tortola was all that was keeping Jesse alive.

It was warm and humid and misty down there; not at all your typical Titanian weather, but I knew well enough that if we climbed a hundred feet or so and crested the rim of that crater, things would be mighty different.

Not that it mattered much, anyway. Without the pod we were doomed one way or another, since we'd never make it back up to the *Balboa* otherwise. We might last a few days, or maybe a few weeks at the most, and then that'd be all she wrote. We'd die from the cold, or suffocation, or hunger if nothing else, and there was absolutely nothing any of us could do about it.

I wondered how long Danielle would keep hoping and waiting for me, how long it might be before she stopped praying for my safe return and started praying instead that I'd died a quick and easy death. The thought made me sad. I wondered what our children might have looked like and what Danielle herself might have looked like with gray hair, and other things like unto that. Really depressing stuff to be pondering, under the circumstances.

"We can't stay here, boys. We've still got a job to do," Philip finally said, with a resolute tone to his voice.

"We'll never make it to Muwamanth without the pod. It's way too far. We'd run out of food and water and air before we could ever walk that many miles. I can't leave Tortola anyway, with my suit all tore up," Jesse said.

"You could wear one of the space suits instead," I pointed out.

"Well, yeah, but that still wouldn't help the situation with the air. We don't have enough to last us long enough, and that's a fact," he said.

We all three sat there gloomily for a few minutes, trying to think of some way out of this rat trap we found ourselves snared in. Things didn't look good at all.

"There's one other choice," Philip finally said.

"What's that?" I asked.

"You can go alone, Tyke. Take the rest of the supplies and hike over there to make sure the stones are put where they belong," Philip said.

I knew immediately what he was saying, and he didn't need to be explicit about what it meant, either. He was telling me to leave him and Jesse with no air, to die within hours, so one of us at least might have a chance to make it to Muwamanth.

It was a grim thought, and when I imagined exactly how Jesse and Philip would die, it made me shiver. Suffocation is an awful thing, and even though I knew the same fate lay in store for all of us regardless of what we did or which of us went first, it's still hard to talk about things like that.

But Philip was right, nevertheless. It was bad enough to come all the way to Titan and to die in the cold darkness all those millions of miles from home. It would be a hundred times worse to die knowing it was all for nothing.

"I don't know if I can make it," I said in a low voice.

"Yes, you can, if you're brave and don't give up. Here, I want you to have something," he said, and unsealed his suit to reach inside for a second. Then he took my hand, and lay a silver ring in my palm. It was somewhat like a class ring, and it was set with a star sapphire, midnight blue. I'd seen Philip wear a similar one occasionally, but never gave it much thought. Inside the band was inscribed the name *Barthélemy,* whatever that was supposed to mean.

"What's this for?" I asked, turning it over in my hands.

"It's the ring of an Avenger," he said softly.

"What's that?" I asked.

"An Avenger is a person who devotes his life to fighting evil, to making the world a better place, no matter how high the cost. You might say it's a secret society, or a club you have to be asked to join. There are only a few of us, and it's a serious thing even to be asked. You don't have to say yes, but I hope you will. It may give you the courage to finish this last task, whenever you're tempted to fear," he said.

"What do I have to do?" I asked.

"Swear the oath and keep it, that's all. Are you willing?" he asked.

I hesitated, unsure if I was willing or not. I take my promises seriously, and if I made one then I'd have to try to keep it. Not that I'd live long enough for it to matter *much,* of course, but a lot can happen even in a day or two. It was indeed a very serious thing to be asked.

But still, it's very hard to refuse the last wish of a person you love and know all too well that you'll never see again. It was the second time I'd had to say my goodbyes to Philip, and I think this time hurt worse than the first one did.

"I'm willing," I finally said.

"Then repeat after me. I swear before God Almighty, my Father and King, that I will fight evil to the utmost of my power and strength, in all places I may find it, no matter how high the cost," he said. That was a pretty strong oath, and again I hesitated for a second. Then I brushed it aside and repeated the words.

Philip unsealed my suit and uncovered my head, leaving only the respirator in place, and then with his thumb he smeared some oil from a crack in the ground onto my forehead.

"Then I anoint you an Avenger, Tycho Nicholas McGrath. Be faithful and true," he said, and slipped the ring onto my left middle finger.

I resealed my thermal suit, a little discomfited by the whole thing. I'm not accustomed to high-flown ceremonial stuff like that, especially not under such extreme circumstances. But Philip said no more about it.

I guess there was really nothing else to say.

Chapter Eleven

"Come on, we'll have to dive down and recover the rest of the air tanks, at least, and maybe some food and water," he finally said.

"No, not food and water. I won't be able to open my suit to eat or drink, anyway," I pointed out, and he nodded.

"True enough. Just air, then," he said.

So we swam back down to the pod and recovered as many tanks as possible, and then he and Jesse tied them to my pack so I could carry them easily and change them out quickly when I needed to. I had something like four days worth of air, and those two had a little less than twenty-four hours apiece. They'd run out just about the time I had to change my first bottle, and I wished there was nothing like that to remind me of the exact time. Sometimes you really don't want to know those kinds of things.

Then we said our last goodbyes, and I started climbing the crater wall.

It wasn't all that far to the top, and when I reached the southeastern rim I looked out across the black dunes of Shangri-la, extending forever in ridge after ridge all the way to the dusky horizon. Somewhere in that direction lay the hills of Xanadu, and near the center of them the Pillar of Heaven. With a little luck, I might just possibly have enough air and strength to make it that far.

The dunes were the hardest part. They were made of fine-grained black sand almost exactly like coal dust; in fact, I guess that's precisely what it was. I climbed up one side and slid down the other, trying hard not to lose my balance and go tumbling head over heels all the way down to the bottom. It happened a couple of times anyway, but I always managed to get back up and press on.

I hoped to eventually strike the main road across the desert which we'd seen briefly when we first touched down. It led directly up into the hills and it would also save me a lot of time and effort if I didn't have to keep climbing over dunes. The A'rum could fly, of course, so they rarely used the roads unless they needed to haul cargo long distances. I hoped that meant I wouldn't meet any of them on the highway.

I got thirsty after a while and there was nothing I could do about it, but I knew all too well that it would soon get worse. It was cold enough that I wasn't sweating too much, and that at least was a blessing. I needed to conserve water as much as possible for as long as possible, or I'd never make it.

In time I struggled over a dune very much like all the others I'd crossed, and found myself staring down at a road of ice-rock cobblestones. I got in a little bit too big of a rush trying to reach it and ended up rolling and tumbling all the way to the bottom, where I landed in a slimy tar-pit beside the ditch.

I struggled my way out of that last obnoxious obstacle, and once I was able to set foot on the road itself I made much better time.

Nevertheless, it still felt like I was moving slower than a snail. Even after several hours of trotting along at the fastest pace I could manage, everything still looked exactly the same as it did to start with. Nothing but powdery black dunes and tar pits, and the icy road threading like a white ribbon across all that blackness. Nothing ever seemed to change, and I began to get discouraged again. I wondered what Jesse and Philip were doing, and then wished I hadn't thought about it.

I don't believe I would have made it all the way to Muwamanth in time by myself. It's farther than a man can walk in only four days, unless he had some kind of vehicle.

But as it turned out, I didn't have to do it all by myself.

I was still trudging along the road, near hopeless, when I spotted a black speck in the sky. I didn't know what it was, but I'd seen enough of Titan by then to freeze till it disappeared. N'grumth had told me there were eagles in the desert big enough to eat a person, and even though I would be a deadly poisonous morsel for anything on Titan, I certainly didn't trust a bird to know that.

But it was too late.

Whatever it was had already seen me, and came swooping down out of the sky to land on the road right in front of me. Running wouldn't have helped at that point, so I stood my ground and prepared to defend myself if need be. To my relief, it turned out to be one of the A'rum, although that wasn't *much* of a relief. There was no telling how the King of Belet felt about the prophecy or what he might have told his own people to do if any of them saw us.

"Tick," it said, in its shrill voice.

"N'grumth?" I asked, uncertainly, and when he nodded I knew it was him. I was shocked to find him trespassing in a foreign kingdom like that; it was a breach of honor so horrendous that even the King's assassins hadn't dared to follow us across the border. It was an open question what the people of Belet might do to *me* if I got caught in their territory, but there was no doubt what would happen to N'grumth. Instant death, with not a prayer of mercy to be hoped for. No sane A'rum would ever dream of doing such a thing, and I wondered if he'd lost his mind.

"Yes, Tick. I've been looking for you for many hours. Where are your clanmates?" he asked.

"We crashed on Tortola; the volcano northwest of here. They couldn't come with me because we didn't have enough air for all of us, and Jesse's suit was damaged. We can't leave Titan without our pod, I'm afraid. But we wanted to finish the purpose we came here for, even if we never live to tell about it," I said, knowing he'd approve of that.

"Indeed. That was the only honorable choice," he agreed, as if he couldn't imagine that I'd even consider behaving otherwise.

"But how did *you* escape?" I asked, and I was almost certain I detected a note of pride in that twittery voice when he spoke.

"No one can catch me. I'm the fastest thing alive," he boasted.

"I'm glad to hear it," I nodded.

"When I ventured home I discovered the terrible destruction you made in the castle. Everyone was still in fear," he said.

"I'm sorry for that. It was the only way we could escape," I said.

"No, you must not be sorry, Tick. They were heretics who fought against what they knew had been foretold and what must be, therefore God used you to strike them down. They fully deserved it. I only wish you had killed more of them. But it was an excellent victory nevertheless," he said with approval. It sounded very much like something an A'rum would say, congratulating one of his friends and comrades-in-arms on a particularly bloody and glorious triumph in battle. Never mind the fact that these were his own family members we were talking about.

I will never, ever understand those people.

But it would have deeply insulted N'grumth to accept his congratulations with anything less than enthusiasm.

"Yes, we crushed them like gnats beneath our feet," I agreed, with what I hoped was sufficient zest and eagerness. It must have been, because he said nothing else about it.

"The King is very angry that you escaped. He believes the King of Belet is protecting you now, and the two of them are set to go to war immediately. The armies are marching even as we speak. You would never make it to Muwamanth on foot," he said.

"I don't have any other way to get there," I said.

"Yes, you do. I will have to carry you," he said.

"Can you do that?" I asked.

"Perhaps. I think so," he said. He didn't sound very certain, but I figured I had nothing to lose at that point. If he dropped me from way up in the sky and I got splashed against the ice-rock somewhere in Xanadu, then that was no worse a fate than suffocation.

"Let's go, then," I said.

"You will have to climb up on my back," he said, and I did, hearing him hiss when I touched his skin.

"What's wrong?" I asked.

"Your body is hotter than a lightning bolt. It burns. I don't know how long I can stand it," he said through clenched teeth.

"Should I get down?" I asked.

"No, hold on tight," he said, and then with a jump and a swoop we were airborne. Within minutes we were hundreds of feet above the ground, and N'grumth was steadily climbing higher.

I've never liked heights, even at the best of times. Clinging to the back of a giant bat almost a thousand feet above the desert took it to a whole new level. Most of the time I kept my eyes tightly shut and clutched N'grumth's leathery shoulders in a death grip. But every now and then I did crack my eyes to see what was ahead, making darned sure not to look down.

In front of us was Xanadu, the white hills gleaming palely in the half-light. We were already almost there, though it was still a long way to Muwamanth even after that. I wasn't sure exactly *how* far, but I was certain it had to be at least several hours flight. But I couldn't ask, and N'grumth was too busy flying to chat. Young and strong he might have been, but he wasn't built for carrying passengers.

It didn't take as long as I thought, actually. It was only about an hour before we landed in the courtyard at the monastery, and by then I could tell N'grumth was in severe pain. When I got off his back, I could see the reason. His entire back was scorched and seared like someone had taken a branding iron to his skin, and in places his flesh had actually started to melt and bubble. His breathing was ragged, and I don't believe he could have gone on much longer even if he had to.

"I'm sorry," I said, kneeling by his head.

Then he did something unexpected. With shaking hands, he removed the nugget of meteoric iron from around his neck and placed it carefully in my palm.

"Akiri," he said, staring at me intently; the A'rum word for one who has behaved with exceptional courage and honor. N'grumth had every right to grant me the title, I suppose, though I never suspected he thought so highly of me as all that.

My first impulse was to tell him he was far more deserving of the title than I would ever be, but that would have undercut everything he meant by the offer. Those who are most honorable and courageous themselves are almost always the ones most likely to praise others for the same things, and those who are most truly humble are usually those who are readiest to accept honor with simple thanks. If I ever learned anything from N'grumth, it would be that false humility is really a type of pride in disguise. So I humbled myself and thanked him.

"Thank you," I murmured, and he nodded slightly.

"Go," he said gently, jerking his head in the direction of the mountain. He wasn't being brusque; it was simply that he lacked the strength to say anything more. As badly burned as he was, I wondered if he'd even survive.

Well, he'd brought me here so I could go up to the mountain. I owed it to him and to many others to do just that.

Therefore I didn't stop to chat with the gaping monks. I ran through the black jungle to the foot of Muwamanth and started to climb. There was no path, since the A'rum could always fly and there had never been anyone else who needed to get up there. The rocks were every bit as slick and greasy as everything else on Titan, and terrifyingly steep. I wished for my metal spikes, but those were buried in the lake at Tortola, far beyond reach. Several times I lost my grip and slid dozens of feet back down before catching hold of another outcrop, my heart pounding in my chest. But gradually I made progress, and at long last there came a time when I threw my arm over the last ledge and pulled myself up onto the flat summit.

There stood the temple itself, whiter than snow, colder than death. They say it's forbidden to fly across the pinnacle, and anyone who visits that place (even the Kings) has to climb up the steps, whichever set are reserved for his land of origin. I was glad for that particular custom, because I don't know how I would ever have reached the top otherwise. I ran to the nearest set of steps (I think they were the ones for Belet), and quickly climbed up.

At last I was there, in that most sacred of all places on Titan, where no human being had ever set foot since the beginning of the world. And even though time was precious, I stood still for a little while to think.

My air gauge read just under three hours before I had to change my bottle, which meant Philip and Jesse were counting down the minutes till they took their last breath. And although I'm very awkward when it comes to prayers, I took a minute to offer one right then, with my arms and face lifted up to heaven like the A'rum do. I prayed for courage, and for comfort to Danielle and the others we'd left behind, for healing for N'grumth and peace for this warring world. And just as an afterthought, that Jesse and Philip and I might possibly be saved and make it home again somehow, though I couldn't imagine how that would ever happen.

The three corners of the temple are arranged in such a way that one of them points toward each kingdom of Titan, and I don't doubt that was intentional. Therefore I trotted over to the northern apex first, the one for Dilmun, and took one of the Guardian Stones from around my neck and placed it reverently in its spot. Then I did likewise for Belet on the west and Tsegihi on the south. Then it was done.

N'grumth had never said anything about what was supposed to happen next, if anything, so all I could do was hope and pray that I'd done everything I was supposed to do at that point.

Sometimes in the aftermath of a great deed, there comes a kind of quiet when you're not quite sure what to do with yourself. It was like that for me, anyway. My whole body was exhausted from crossing the desert and climbing the mountain, and even more so from clinging to N'grumth for so long. I couldn't face the thought of scaling Muwamanth again to reach the bottom; at least not till I rested for a while. So I sat down on the flagstones to gather my strength a bit.

It was a darned short rest.

A scant few seconds later, one of the A'rum appeared at the top of the Tsegihi steps, holding a space suit in his claws. Where he got it I couldn't imagine, and he spoke no English, but I vaguely understood his urgent twittering to mean that I should put it on.

There are times when you know better than to ask for explanations. You just do what you're told and hope there's a good reason. I swiftly put on the suit, leaving my thermal suit on underneath because of course I would have been frozen solid in a heartbeat if I'd taken it off to change. I had to hold my breath while switching the breathing gear, but that was all right. As soon as I was done, the A'rum turned his back as if he meant for me to climb on, the same way N'grumth had done.

Before long we were airborne again, and within an hour we were back out over Shangri-la. Here we met up with two other A'rum carrying space-suited passengers, who could only have been Jesse and Philip. But there was no time to ask what was going on, because almost before I knew it, I glimpsed the *Balboa* in leisurely flight just below the cloud deck.

"When we reach it, grab hold!" Philip called into his radio. The A'rum who carried us must have been some of the swiftest fliers among them, and the *Balboa* was moving at the slowest possible speed it could travel without crashing, but still, it was all they could do to keep up with it. As soon as we got close enough, I saw Philip grab one of the empty clasps where the landing pod had been, and lash himself to it with his belt lanyard. Jesse and I quickly did the same.

Then the A'rum dropped away, and the *Balboa* speeded up and began ascending again. Far below us, Xanadu was quickly disappearing into the murky shadows, and my last glimpse of the surface was of the Pillar of Heaven, gleaming white in a rare finger of sunshine. Then we entered the clouds, and it was gone.

The wind was awful at first, and threatened to blow us right off the clasps if we hadn't been tied down. But as the atmosphere thinned so also the wind decreased, till there was nothing but the emptiness of space. Once we were far enough out and there was no danger of being blown loose, we cut our lines and very gingerly crawled to the airlock using the magnets in our gloves and boots. I don't think I've ever been so glad to be back inside.

As soon as we got safely indoors and stripped down to comfortable clothes again, Jesse instructed the navigational computer to take us home. Then we all sat down in the seats and I was finally able to find out how this miracle had happened.

"Your friend N'grumth told the monks what was going on, and they sent some of the younger and stronger members to rescue us from Tortola, if there was anything left to rescue by then. I didn't know they could carry people on their backs like that," Jesse said.

"No, I didn't either. I don't think N'grumth even knew for sure if he could do it or not," I said.

"Well, anyway, it gave me an idea. We dived down to the pod to fish out the space suits and put them on while we still had some air left, and then I used my radio to get in touch with the navigational computer and have it bring the *Balboa* down low enough for the A'rum to fly us up there. We couldn't land it, true, but there was nothing stopping it from coming down into the atmosphere as long as it didn't have to actually land," Jesse said.

"That was a pretty good idea," I admitted. In hindsight I could see a thousand things that might have gone horribly wrong with it, of course, and I'm sure Jesse could, too. But desperate times call for desperate measures, as they say. Even if the *Balboa* had crashed or the wind had blown us off to fall to our deaths, we wouldn't have been any worse off at that point than we would have been if we hadn't tried it. But none of that mattered; it had worked, and it's hard to argue with success.

"It was a brilliant idea," Philip said proudly, and Jesse smiled.

"Well, you know, I was pretty hopeless at that point. I didn't know what else to do," he said.

"It worked. That's all that matters," Philip said.

"I don't guess they said anything about N'grumth, did they?" I asked.

"I don't think they knew any English except for a few words they memorized. They didn't mention him except to say he told them to come get us. Why do you ask?" Jesse said.

"Because he was in pretty bad shape when I left him with the monks, burned all over from carrying me. I hope he pulled through," I said.

"I hope so, too. None of us would be here right now without him," Philip said.

"He gave me his necklace before I left; I guess to remember him by," I said. I hadn't thought about it till then, but I pulled out the gleaming nugget of meteoric iron to show them. It had a hole pierced in one end for a string to be threaded through, although the one N'grumth used for that purpose had long since vaporized from the heat. But the nugget itself was unchanged, and I turned it over in my hands for a minute, remembering my friend and his strange and noble ways.

The A'rum are nothing if not lovers of grand gestures, of course, but it still surprised me a little bit that N'grumth would give away something so valuable. I suppose he would have known there was nothing else he possessed or could get which would survive for an instant beyond his frigid home world, but I wished I'd thought to do likewise.

In a way I guess I had, of course. I left behind the Guardian Stones, and whatever that might mean. And I suppose whenever Tortola cools off the A'rum might dig down and recover a king's fortune worth of metal from the remains of the pod. Most of it would go to the King of Belet, no doubt, but I hope N'grumth gets at least some reward for all the things he did. He deserves it.

I told Jesse and Philip what happened when I left the volcano and all the things I did at Muwamanth with the Guardian Stones. Then I took the sapphire ring from my finger and offered it back to Philip.

"Do you want this back, now? I mean, since it looks like we might all live, after all?" I asked.

"No, Tyke. You keep it," he said firmly.

"But. . . " I began, and he cut me off.

"Are you sorry you took the oath?" he asked, looking at me keenly. Philip has the bluest eyes I've ever seen, and they can be downright disconcerting when he stares at you that way.

"No, I'm not sorry," I finally said. It took me a minute or so to make up my mind about that, but it was the truth. I wasn't sorry for making the promise, and I didn't resent the necessity of trying to keep it. What else had I done all my life, after all, if not fight against evil in one way or another? I hadn't thought of it that way at the time, but it was so.

"I'm glad," Philip said.

"So how did *you* get involved in something like this?" I asked, gesturing vaguely at the ring on my left hand. There hadn't been time to ask him very much back there at the crater of Tortola, but now I was curious.

"Would you believe me if I told you?" he asked, and I laughed.

"After all this, I think I might believe almost anything. Try me," I said.

"Well, to begin with, did you know I'm over a hundred and sixty years old?" he asked.

I don't know what I was expecting to hear, but I can safely say that *that* certainly wasn't part of it. I was determined to be open minded, though, even if he told me there was a purple gorilla standing behind me reciting Shakespeare in sign language.

"Okay, then. What about it?" I asked, like it didn't matter a bit.

"That's nothing. Your Aunt Joan is even older than I am," he said.

"She looks really good for her age," I said dryly, and he finally laughed.

"All right, Tyke, you win. I'll tell you the story, and then you can decide what you think of it," he said.

"I'm all ears," I said.

"Well, as I said, it was a long time ago. I was only seventeen when they first asked me to become an Avenger, and honestly I wasn't sure I wanted to get involved at first. You run into some dangerous things at times, and I've always liked the quiet life. I did it mostly because my cousin asked me, and he was more like my brother in those days than anything else. Anyway, several months later we were up against a physicist who worked at the old White Sands Missile Range in New Mexico. He was a brilliant man, way ahead of his time in some ways, but he was also the cruelest and most evil person I've ever known. He nearly killed all of us in a motel in Tyler, Texas one night, and your Aunt Joan saved us by using his own equipment against him. You see, he did work on tachyons and gravity enhancement, and, among other things, a very limited kind of time travel. But before you get too excited, I've got to emphasize the *limited* part. One way travel to the future only, with no chance of ever going back. The machine was called a tachometer, I guess because of the tachyons. Anyway, Joan hit some buttons and dragged him to the year 2135 along with her before he could finish us off. I followed along a little later, as soon as I could find out where she went. I loved her, you see, and I knew that physicist I mentioned was just about to kill her. Coming forward myself was the only way I could save her. He'd already killed her first husband, Philip, so when I got here I took his place," he said.

My jaw dropped at that, and for a second I was struck speechless. There are times when it feels like the ground has opened up right under your feet and you're not sure what to think or believe about *anything* anymore.

"So you're not really Philip?" I finally asked, still thunderstruck.

"Well, I guess it depends on how you look at things. I'm the same person I've always been, and I've used that name for so long now that it feels like my own. But no, it's not the name I was born with," he said.

"What's your name really, then?" Jesse asked. I guess it must have been worse for him even than it was for me; he not only had to wonder who Philip really was, but he suddenly couldn't even be sure who *he* was anymore.

"Cameron. Cameron Parker. Cam to my friends. Surely you must have heard your mother call me that now and then, haven't you?" he asked.

I did remember Joan using that name once in a while, now that he mentioned it. Mostly at times when she was feeling especially glad or emotional and forgot herself in the moment. The last time I remembered her using the name *Cam* was when I overheard them talking after Callum's funeral, actually. I'd always assumed it was some private little nickname between the two of them and I'd never been curious enough to ask where it came from. Now I wished I had, even though I doubted they would have told us anything sooner.

"Yeah, I heard her use it before, but I never thought much of it," Jesse admitted, confirming my own thoughts on the subject.

"Well, now you know," Philip said.

I was quiet for a while, digesting all this new information. My Uncle Philip was a lot more interesting person than I'd ever been led to suspect before, and I wondered what else there was to know about him. Aunt Joan was turning out to have facets I'd never known about, too. They were almost like my parents, and yet for a moment I felt like I'd never known them at all. I wonder how many kids go for years thinking they know everything there is to know about their dull mom and dad, and then suddenly discover some depth they never dreamed of. And vice versa, of course. It made me wonder if you ever really know your friends, or the people you work with, or *anybody* for that matter.

That's a tough question, and I'm not sure I know the answer. No matter how well or how long you've known somebody, they can still surprise you.

"It must have been really hard for you to come here like that and give up everything you had, even your own name," I finally said.

"Well, yes and no. I did have to leave a lot of things behind, true, but I did what was right, and I've never been sorry for that," he said.

"Does anybody else know?" I asked.

"Only Joan. Well, Mike and Annabelle knew, but that's because they both came forward, too," he said. Those were *my* parents. I don't guess it should have surprised me; knowing where Joan came from made it logical to think my mother must have come from the same place. I just hadn't had time to make the connection, yet. But my father was a different story.

"How did *they* get here, then?" I asked.

"Annabelle tagged along when I came. Mike found his own way later, but I think that was an accident, actually. He managed to get hold of the tachometer somehow or other, and then ended up zapping himself by mistake. He knew about what happened to me and Joan, so after he got here he came to ask us for help since he didn't have anyone else to call on at the time," he said.

"That must have been strange, to have a complete stranger show up on your doorstep," Jesse said.

"Well. . . he wasn't quite a *complete* stranger, you know. His father was a distant cousin of mine, and one to whom I owed a deep debt of gratitude anyway. Mikey was family, sort of, and you never avert your eyes from a kinsman in need. I wouldn't have turned him away even if I hadn't owed Cody so much," he said.

This was all fresh news to me, though none of it was especially surprising. That was exactly the way Philip would have acted, and I couldn't remember my parents well enough to feel more than a detached kind of interest in who they were and what they did. I felt a little bit guilty for feeling that way, but what can I say?

"So that's how he met my mother?" I asked.

"Yes. We hadn't been in Tampa for very long at that time when he popped up out of the blue. Money was tight, and all we could do was give him a place to sleep on the couch. Annabelle was living with us too, and Chris was still a baby at the time. We had a pretty full house there for a while," he said.

No doubt they did; Aunt Joan had pointed out the house he was talking about several times when we happened to drive by there, and it was barely more than a cracker box. She used to tell us stories about how they had to let Chris sleep in an open dresser drawer because there was no room for a crib anywhere. I might have thought she was pulling my leg if I hadn't seen the place, but as it was I didn't doubt the story at all.

Chapter Twelve

We talked about that and other things on our way home, and I didn't mind the month in space so much this time. On the outbound journey I was half convinced we'd never come home, and that's a depressing thing to look forward to. But now I had every reason to think we'd make it home just fine, and when we did, then as far as I was concerned I never wanted to leave Kona ever again.

Maybe it was too much to hope for that the whole journey would go off without a hitch, though. We were passing through the asteroid belt when a piece of space debris smashed into the left engine, wrecking it instantly beyond all hope of repair.

The impact threw all of us to the floor, and then to the ceiling, and then anywhere else you could think of, as the *Balboa* spun out of control. It gave me flashbacks to when the pod crashed on Mount Tortola, except this went on, and on, and on. Boxes and cans and everything else fell all over us, too, just like then, and we were kept busy trying not to get hit too hard. I don't know how Jesse managed it, but somehow he struggled his way to the cockpit and fought the computer till he was able to shut off the other engine and stabilize us. Then he came back out.

We were all bruised and beaten from our wild ride, and it's a thousand wonders nobody had any broken bones.

"Is everybody all right?" Philip asked.

"I feel like I just took a shower in a washing machine, but other than that I'm fine," I said.

"Me too, but the left engine is out of commission. I don't know what hit us, but it was something big enough to do some major damage. There's no way we're getting that puppy up and running again," Jesse said.

"So how bad is it? Can we still make it home?" Philip asked.

"Well. . . yes," Jesse said. He sounded awfully hesitant when he said it, and that immediately caused alarm bells to start ringing in the back of my mind.

"I hear a *but* in there somewhere," Philip said wryly.

"Well, here's the thing. We can still make it home, but it'll take a lot longer, with only one engine," he said.

"How *much* longer?" I asked, and Jesse hesitated again before reluctantly meeting my eyes.

"About three months," he said.

All of us were silent at that. We had nowhere near enough food to last that long, and we all knew it. Fuel and cargo specifications for the trip had been unbelievably tight ever since the beginning, and we hadn't dared bring along anything extra beyond what was strictly necessary for survival. A three month delay was impossible. We had enough food to last us about one more week, or maybe a month if we immediately went on really tight rationing. But after that. . . well, you can live a month with no food, if you're very lucky. Two weeks if you're not. No matter which way you sliced it, we'd starve long before we ever got home. Water and air could be recycled and reused, but food is a limited supply.

I read a book once about a soccer team whose flight crashed in the Andes a long time ago, and before it was all over they started eating each other to stay alive. I wondered if that's what it would come to with us. One of us might actually survive long enough to make it home if we resorted to that kind of solution, but the thought of it was horrible. It kind of makes your skin crawl, when you think somebody might be looking at you with hungry eyes and wondering if you taste like chicken or not.

I decided it wasn't the time to suggest becoming cannibals.

"Are there any other options?" I asked.

"What do you mean?" Jesse asked.

"Anywhere else we could go, closer than home?" I asked.

"Not this time, Tyke. We're too far out. The only thing closer than Earth is Mars, and that wouldn't do us any good even if we did go there," he said.

I let my mind cast around for other solutions. Even weird and stupid ones, way outside the realm of possibility. When you're facing a dilemma, it's useful sometimes to brainstorm as many ideas as possible and then worry about analyzing them later. Katrina McClendon always told us that logic and creativity are like two horses pulling a cart. They make a fine pair when they work together, but if you try to merge them then the whole mess will blow up in your face.

I guess that's a joke only a bunch of science students would ever catch, but she was talking about the fact that two pieces of matter can't occupy the same space at the same time or you'll end up with a massive explosion. A particularly piquant illustration of the fact that creativity and logic are both vitally important things but must always be kept distinct. Come up with your ideas first, the wilder the better, and then evaluate them later to see if they're actually workable or not. But don't try to do both things at once.

So I let my mind roam anywhere it pleased, without worrying about practicality yet. I was hindered by the fact that I didn't really know a lot about space navigation; that's Jesse's specialty. But everybody hears things and reads books, and it so happened that I'd been reading that space book in the public library not long before we left Kona. A lot of it had talked about the various probes which had been sent out to this and that planet and what they learned there, but it had mentioned in passing that the probes couldn't carry a lot of fuel and therefore had to depend on a more creative way to reach their destination.

I decided it was worth mentioning.

"Could we use Mars for a slingshot, maybe? You know, a gravity-assist?" I asked hopefully.

"Nice idea, but I'm not sure we could handle the acceleration without either breaking up the ship or getting suffocated. The *Balboa* isn't built for things like that, and neither are *we* for that matter. But even if we did survive, I don't think it would help us. We still wouldn't be able to slow down enough with only one engine, when it came time. We'd shoot right past Earth like it wasn't even there," Jesse said.

"There's *nothing* we can do?" I asked.

"I don't know, Tyke. I'll have to think about it for a while," he said.

"Well, in the meantime, we better start rationing the food," Philip said grimly.

So that's what we did, and from then on out we were always hungry. Up to a point we were used to that kind of thing, from our time on the Moon. But somehow hunger is the kind of thing you never really get used to. I thought about food all day long, and then I fell asleep and dreamed about it all night.

We were close enough to Earth by then to make radio contact not entirely impractical, even though we had to wait twenty minutes or so between sending a message and getting an answer back. A very slow way to have a conversation, but doable sometimes. We told everybody what the situation was, even though there was nothing they could do except pray for us. None of them knew anything about physics or navigation, and they wouldn't have known how to fly another ship to come get us even if there had been one.

Jesse sat in the cockpit for hours, thinking about various ways to work things out and using the computer to analyze possible flight paths. He did find a way to use a double slingshot maneuver, using Mars to speed us up and then Venus to slow us down. That would have brought us back to Earth at a reasonable speed for re-entry, but unfortunately it wouldn't save us enough time to be worth the trouble. We'd still be dead by the time we got there.

"There's one other option, though," he finally said.

"So tell me. I'm all ears," I said.

"We can slingshot around Mars and then use *Earth* to slow down. Then, with just a little luck, we could land on the Moon," he said.

"You've got to be kidding," I said.

"When it's something that might actually keep us alive then no, I promise you I'm not kidding," he said, without a trace of a smile.

"So what then? Take off and head for Earth as soon as we land?" I asked.

"I wish it could be that simple. Unfortunately, the *Balboa* won't have enough thrust with only one engine to reach escape velocity after we land. We'll be stuck there till we can replace that other engine. But that's not a major problem. We can always rob one from the *Cabral;* I know those engines are still good. It might take a little while, but it's the only way I can think of that we might even possibly get out of this situation alive," he said.

"Another trip to Lakeside," I said wryly.

"I'm afraid so, but it's better than the alternative. If we even make it that far, that is," he added.

"You're still worried about the acceleration?" I asked.

"You should be, too. Like I said, the *Balboa* is not built for crazy stunts like that, and we're talking about putting her through *two* of them. She might not make it, Tyke, and that's no joke," he said.

"Yeah, I know," I said.

"No, you really don't. Even if we don't break up altogether, the hull might get breached, and if that happens we'd lose cabin pressure. Maybe slow, maybe fast. That's why we'll all have to wear space suits during the shot. They showed us videos of explosive decompression at the Academy. I promise you, I never want to see anything like that again, especially not in real life," he said.

I paused to think about that for a few seconds, and quickly decided I never wanted to see it, either. The pictures my imagination could supply were horrifying enough.

We made it through the slingshot around Mars all right, as it turned out. I felt like I was being slowly suffocated while a giant crushed me under his heel like a tin can, but other than that it wasn't as bad as we feared. I don't know exactly how high the g-forces actually got, but the *Balboa* didn't break up, at least. I know I felt ill and exhausted when it was over and my body hurt in every imaginable spot and a few unimaginable ones. That's not just a joke, either; I hurt in places I literally didn't even know existed before then. I bet you never realized you could strain the muscles underneath your tongue, did you? Well, neither did I. Not till then.

"One down, one to go," Jesse said, trying to sound cheerful about it. He looked just as rough as the rest of us, so his attempt at good humor didn't go over very well.

"I don't know if I can survive another experience like that one," I muttered.

"Oh, sure you can, Tyke. Besides, that was nothing. The other one will be *much* worse," he pointed out helpfully.

"Thanks, Jesse. I really needed to know that," I said.

"You're welcome. It'll be a while before we have to worry about that one, though. We'll have a chance to rest up and recuperate first," he said.

The only good aspect to Jesse's plan was that we didn't have to ration the food quite so tightly as we did before. Being slightly hungry all the time is much easier than wanting to gnaw your left arm off.

We were close enough to Earth to see the oceans and continents before we had to start our second slingshot, and we were in pretty close radio contact with the ground by then. That close to home there wasn't enough of a signal delay for it to matter much. Everybody was fairly optimistic, and it felt good to be that close to Danielle even though I knew we were speeding past her so fast we'd never be able to slow down in time without using gravity. But even though nobody was exactly pleased about the idea of having to repair the *Balboa* at Lakeside, we were all resigned to the fact and grateful that we had a way to survive at all.

We passed over Hawaii not long before Jesse took us into the dive, and if I'd had a telescope I probably could have picked out Kona down there on the southwest shore. The thought made me homesick in a way I hadn't been for a long time. But I told myself it didn't matter; I'd soon be seeing it in person, and then we could forget all about adventures in space for a while.

"Okay, folks, here we go. This one might be a little rougher than the last time, but not too much I hope. Cross your fingers," Jesse said, and I did. Both of them.

It was brutal.

It's a seemingly strange thing, but slowing down subjects you to just as many g-forces as acceleration does. At that point we were using Earth to shed the speed we'd picked up from Mars, plus the speed we'd already had on our way back from Titan, minus the little bit Jesse had been able to dump via our one remaining engine thruster. All very straightforward math, and simple on paper. But we still had nearly twice as much velocity coming into this shot as we did the other, and that energy can't simply disappear. It gets transferred to Earth, converted to heat, and other such things, but it always goes *somewhere*.

Including several places you don't want it to go at all, like metal fatigue. Have you ever bent a paperclip back and forth several times till it finally broke? That's called metal fatigue, and it's a major engineering problem whenever you build things. Put it under enough stress, of the right kind, and any metal will break instead of bending. Jesse was absolutely right about the *Balboa* never having been designed for slingshots and super-lengthy space journeys, and I guess all those things were taking their toll on the structural framework, little by little. That's why he was so afraid of the ship suddenly breaking up into pieces during the slingshot maneuver.

Well, it didn't quite do that. But near the end, a crack suddenly opened up on the left side of the ship and swiftly grew until it was as wide as my body and almost fifteen feet long.

We immediately lost all air pressure in the cabin, of course, along with most of our remaining supplies, which whooshed right out into space. We had on our space suits to guard against just such an emergency, of course, but if we hadn't been buckled in to our seats then Philip and I would have been sucked out right after the food in the blink of an eye. Or at least our exploded remains would have been. But as it was, I had to sit there with my eyes locked on that crack and watch it slowly and inexorably grow and widen for the next several hours, until Jesse finally was able to pull us out of the dive. He didn't dare do it any sooner than planned or we were dead; we wouldn't lose enough speed and we'd end up shooting right past the Moon with no hope of landing.

"Is there any way to fix that?" I asked when he came back out of the cockpit. His eyes got big when he saw the crack, and he swallowed hard. He'd known when it happened, of course, but I guess he never realized till that moment just how bad it really was.

"I don't know if we'll ever get it airtight again, but I'm sure we can seal it up at least. There's plenty of sheet metal at Lakeside, and we can do some welding," Philip said.

"That still won't be safe *at all,*" Jesse declared flatly, still staring at the crack.

"No, but it'll be a lot better than leaving it open to space like that, won't it?" Philip asked.

"Not by much," Jesse sighed.

"Well, every little bit helps. We'll have to do the best we can with what we've got, and trust that that will be enough," Philip said.

For the next three days we stayed as far away from the crack as humanly possible, and Philip told us to keep our lanyards tied to something sturdy at all times, just like if we'd been out in space. Which is exactly what we were at that point, for all practical purposes.

I think all of us probably aged ten years before we made it to the Moon, or at least it certainly felt that way. By the time Jesse brought us in across the Stormy Ocean, I was *thrilled* to see the place again.

But I guess that extra little bit of stress during re-entry was too much for the brave, longsuffering *Balboa.* She suddenly broke up into pieces over the Chocolate Mountains, dumping all three of us and the remainder of our supplies right out into the air at about ten thousand feet.

On Earth, such an event would have meant certain death, if not from suffocation then from getting crushed on impact. As it was, on the Moon we could look forward to a long, leisurely fall of almost an hour before we hit the ground. And then, depending on where we landed, we might still get squashed like bugs. You might be able to jump from any height into *water* on the Moon, but you definitely better not try it on solid ground or you'll be no better off than you would be from jumping off a five-story building on Earth and hitting the street. Seeing as how we were right over the Chocolate Mountains when the *Balboa* broke up, that didn't bode well. I had ample time to look forward to whether I'd hit rocks, or dirt, or even a patch of burnt-up wildflowers. I remember thinking I'd prefer to land on one of the meadows, and then at least my final resting place would be covered in poppies and lupines now and then.

Then Jesse keyed his radio. I think I've said before that you can't use radio on the Moon, and that's true for all practical purposes. But as with most things, there *are* exceptions. You can use radio as long as you've got a clear line of sight to the person you're talking to; it just won't work after they drop below the horizon. That makes it almost useless down on the surface. But ten thousand feet up in the air is another thing completely. We had no problem seeing each other at that height, and as long as that was true we could still talk.

"Swim for the lake," Jesse said, and surprisingly he didn't sound ruffled a bit.

"What are you talking about?" I asked. I knew *partly* what he was talking about; the blue-green water of the Okechobee lay just to our east.

"Swim through the air, like the A'rum did. We're high enough up and we've still got enough forward velocity that we might actually make it to the water," he explained.

That got my attention, and I suddenly went from contemplating the flowers on my grave to swimming as hard as I could.

Air is not a very buoyant fluid, just in case you wondered. You have to expose a lot of wing surface and expend a lot of energy to swim or fly through it, and we had precious little of either. But as Jesse pointed out, we did still have a good bit of forward velocity from the doomed *Balboa*, which meant we were falling at a slant already. It was uncertain whether that would carry us far enough to hit the lake, but every little bit helps.

That's why, if you ever find yourself in the position of falling from an airplane with no parachute (which I don't recommend, by the way), I suggest you do the same thing we did. Aim for the softest landing spot you can see and then buck hard to get there. You might survive or you might not, but anything that ups your odds is always a good idea.

Everybody has played that little game where you put your hand in the slipstream of the wind outside an open car window and let the force of the air push your arm up and down and back and forth. Well, you can do the same thing when you're falling, only using your whole body, and in that way you can somewhat decide what direction you go and where you'll hit the ground. That's what Jesse meant by swimming.

It's not an exact science, of course, or if it is then none of us were experts at it. Before long the three of us were separated widely. We fell lower and lower, and still hadn't made it out over the lake yet even by the time the ground was frighteningly close.

To make a long story short, I just barely made it or else I wouldn't be here telling you all this right now. But only by the very skin of my teeth. I hit the water maybe twenty feet from shore, and then, much to my surprise, skipped off it like a stone across a puddle. That hurt, quite a lot actually, and so did the next three times it happened. I thought crazily to myself that if I'd been one of the rocks me and Jesse used to skim across the river when we were little, I would have earned myself a good many points for that.

But finally I stopped skipping, and then sank to the bottom of the lake in my heavy space suit. The Okechobee is fairly shallow, just like its namesake in Florida, and that's especially true in the western part. I was lying flat on my back in a patch of weeds and mud when I opened my eyes, looking up at the sunlight glinting on the surface no more than twenty feet above me.

For a while it was hard to believe I'd actually survived, but once I got over the wonder of it all I immediately thought about Jesse and Philip. I knew it was highly unlikely we'd be able to make radio contact unless we were really close, but it was worth a try. I keyed my radio.

"Is anybody there? Jesse? Philip?" I asked, and then waited.

Silence.

Well, that was only to be expected, considering how far apart we probably were. I tried to get up and found that I couldn't do it because the movement of the water kept sweeping me off my feet, so I had to crawl on my hands and knees till I reached shore, maybe two hundred yards away.

I was back on the Moon for the third time.

Chapter Thirteen

I crawled up onto the rocky beach and took my helmet off, taking deep breaths of the warm gunpowdery air and letting it dry the sweat from my hair. It was late afternoon or thereabouts, as best I could judge. I had only the vaguest of notions where I might be; the western shore of the lake was all I really knew. I had almost zero chance of finding Jesse or Philip on my own, but I figured if they survived, they'd surely head for Lakeside Station, so that was my best bet for getting back together with one or both of them.

I knew which way was north from looking at the sun, so with no more ado I set off in that direction as fast as I could march along the lakeshore.

I soon found that the spacesuit was a real liability. It wasn't so much the weight, but it was cumbersome when I needed flexibility. So even though I was reluctant to leave it behind, I stripped it off and hung it up in a prominent place on a cedar tree down by the shore where it would be easy to find it again. I was barefoot underneath, but that's not such a big issue on the Moon. Yes, the rocks are sharp, but the low gravity keeps them from hurting your feet too much most of the time.

I had to swim across narrow fingers of the lake several times to cut off distance, but by and by I stumbled out onto a hill overlooking a vast plain of yucca plants and Joshua trees, separated from the lake by a strip of sand that rivaled the Thousand Mile Beach for the way it seemingly went on forever. I knew that place like the back of my own hand; it was Yucca Flats, and I'd been out there to ride the dune buggy with Chris and Jesse and Danielle many a time, in days gone by.

It was already after sunset by then, but all I could do was keep following the lakeshore till I dropped from exhaustion. I knew all too well that I'd never survive a night in the wilds. So I grimly trotted along the beach and now and then took a dip in the lake to cool off. There wasn't a breath of wind, and it was still early enough that running made me warm.

At last I came to the sandy banks of the Faithful River, which was low enough to wade across with no trouble at that time of the month. Back in the old days, Yucca Flats used to be called the Sinus Fidei, or the Bay of Faith. Sometimes they kept certain versions of those old monikers in more subtle ways than you might imagine, like giving them to the river that flowed across the plain, instead of to the plain itself.

I had nothing to eat this whole time, not even seaweed. Maidenhair doesn't grow in the lunar tropics, and I was unsure if the other kinds I saw were poisonous or not. I started to get weak after several days of not eating, and that slowed me down. It slowed me down even more when I had to climb up into the Lakeside Hills, even though I knew I was getting awfully close by then.

At long last I wearily stumbled my way through the gates, long after dark. It was already raining and cold by then, and in spite of my exhaustion the first thing I did was make a beeline for the cafeteria. I didn't even bother to turn the lights on first. I just grabbed the first can I could reach and yanked it open and ate it with my dirty fingers. Canned ham, it was, and by far the most delicious thing I've ever tasted in my life.

I somehow summoned the energy to make it from there back to the cabin I used to share with Jesse, and then collapsed into my old bed without a second thought. The rain on the aluminum rooftop lulled me into a dreamless sleep, and for a long time I knew no more.

It was the cold that woke me. It was snowing hard when I opened my eyes, and the house was dark and frigid. I hadn't had time or thought to switch on the power grid or anything else before I slept, and now I was regretting it.

I got up shivering and wrapped a blanket around me, the best I could do for warmth, and immediately headed for the control room. I used the underground connector tunnels this time, of course; no reason to go out in the snow at such an hour.

As soon as I got to the computer room and threw the main switch the power came on throughout the station, and it wasn't long before I had lights, gravity, and eventually heat. The system was doing its best when it came to that, but it takes a while to warm up an entire complex from dead nothing. Each cabin had its own separate heating system, of course, but I was still able to switch them on by remote control. I didn't bother with any of them except mine and Philip's, though. There was no point in heating the ones which nobody needed, but I still hoped Philip might show up soon. As soon as I was sure everything was running smoothly, I headed for the cafeteria again to find something else to eat and possibly carry some of it back to my cabin for later.

What I found instead was Jesse.

He must have come in during the night while I was asleep, and probably not too long ago, either, because his clothes were still wet from the rain and snow. He'd collapsed in the middle of the cafeteria floor, and I guess I wouldn't have seen him at all if I hadn't gone back in there. He was lying face down with one arm pointed up and the other one down, like you see in those chalk drawings at murder scenes, and for one heart-stopping second I thought he was dead.

I ran to check, and soon found that he was still alive, although barely. I tried to pick him up and couldn't do it; I was still too weak myself for that. So I ran back to the control room and switched off the gravity enhancer. After that I didn't have a problem carrying him to the cabin to put him in his own bed. Then I had to go to the main building *again* to turn the gravity back on and collect whatever I thought we both needed. I took some bouillon cubes and chicken soup for him, and a canned chicken and some energy drinks for me. Not much, I know, but the choices were limited.

I ate some chicken while I cooked the bouillon, and then got Jesse semi-awake long enough to feed him some. I'm not a doctor and I couldn't tell if his problem was starvation or hypothermia or just plain old exhaustion, but I figured feeding him something warm certainly couldn't hurt.

Nor did it seem to, because several hours later he woke up and got out of bed, seemingly no worse off than I had been.

He came into the living room and sat down in one of the overstuffed chairs beside me. I was watching a hundred year old sitcom when he came in, the kind of gossipy, formless thing you can watch in fits and snatches while you doze off on the couch and you still won't really miss much.

"How are you feeling, bro?" I asked.

"Cruddy, that's how. What about you?" he asked.

"Same here," I admitted.

"Never thought I'd see *this* place again," he said, glancing around the room.

"You should be glad to see it, unless you'd rather spend the night in a cave," I reminded him. Then I bit my tongue and wished I hadn't said it, considering that's exactly where Philip was probably holed up till morning. If he was even still alive, that was. But I didn't let myself think like that.

Jesse's face clouded up and I knew he was thinking the same thing, but he must have been no more anxious to talk about it than I was.

"So what happened to *you,* anyway? I must've landed ten miles out in the lake, and it tore an air hose loose when I hit the water, so I had to get out of my suit in a hurry and swim all the way to shore," he said.

"It's lucky you're the athletic one, then," I said.

"I'm not *that* athletic. I had to stop and rest while I floated for a while several times, and I bet it was more like twenty miles of actual swimming by the time I made it out of the water," he said.

"Well, I barely made it at all. I hit the lake right off shore and skipped about three or four times, but it didn't damage anything. I tried to call you on radio as soon as I got back to shore but I guess you must have been out of range. But I figured everybody would head for Lakeside anyway," I said.

"Yeah, I figured pretty much the same thing," Jesse agreed, and then there was an uncomfortable pause while we both thought about the one member of the expedition who was still missing.

"I wonder what happened to Philip," I finally said.

"If we both made it then there's a good chance he did, too. We'll have to wait till morning and see. There's nothing else we can do in the meantime," Jesse said.

He was right about that, so we tried not to think too much about Philip for the next two weeks of darkness. It gave us time to recover from all the things we'd been through lately, and that much at least was good. I wished we could have told the folks back home that we'd arrived safely on the Moon, but the radio at Lakeside had never worked and the one on the *Balboa* was strewn in chunks of wreckage across a fair-sized portion of Yucca Flats and the Chocolate Mountains.

I think besides Philip, that was what weighed on my mind the most.

"Do you think we'll ever make it home?" I asked Jesse one day, not long before sunrise. I was down in the pits just thinking about it, and I'm sure he was too.

"Well, I've been thinking about that. The only thing I know of is to try to fit together one ship that works from all the pieces we've got. We've got parts from the *Cabral* and the *Balboa*, and two more old ships up there at Desolation Island. Maybe we could cobble together one workable craft out of all that material," he said, sounding none too hopeful.

"I didn't think those old ships at Desolation were compatible with the new ones," I said.

"They're not, mostly. But we're not talking about doing things the right way. We're talking about rigging something up so it'll work long enough to get us home. I think the only thing we might need from those old ships is a stripped down hull, anyway, and that part shouldn't matter much. I think we can salvage everything else from what's left of the *Cabral* and the *Balboa*, if we can haul everything down here to Lakeside to work on it," he said.

"How would we do that? We'd have to scrounge half the Moon just to bring back what's left of the *Cabral* and the *Balboa,* and that's not even counting the trip to Desolation Island. We don't have a plane that works, and we don't have a boat at all anymore," I said.

"Well, we've still got that one plane with no navigation system. I could probably get it started, and then we could eyeball our way up the Lucky River and find the *Cabral* that way. We might have to bring her down in pieces, but I think it's doable," he said.

"I guess we could try it," I agreed. I was highly doubtful, to tell you the truth, but since I couldn't think of anything better, it was as good a plan as any.

As soon as the slush started to melt after the sun came up, we dressed warmly and made our way out to the hangar at the airstrip to get started working on the plane. If we had to visit the mountains, then we needed to do it as early as possible to avoid the afternoon storms.

As soon as we got there, we found Philip.

He was asleep on the couch in the mechanics' lounge, and he looked awful. Haggard and dirty and tired. Jesse quickly went to wake him.

"Dad, are you all right?" he asked, shaking him.

Philip took a deep breath and opened his eyes, looking tired.

"Yeah, I'm fine. That couch is definitely not the most comfortable place to sleep, though," he said.

"I don't doubt that. But how long have you been here? What have you been eating?" Jesse asked.

Philip glanced wordlessly at the old snack machine, which looked like he'd smashed it open. As best I could remember, there hadn't been anything in there except fifty-year-old chocolate bars and potato chips. They'd been so old and nasty when we lived at Lakeside the last time that nobody had ever touched them. Good for him we hadn't, I guess, but it must have been disgusting.

"You lived on *that* stuff?" Jesse asked, wrinkling his nose.

"Oh, well, I've had worse. It tasted a lot better than algae cakes," he pointed out, and I didn't doubt that at all.

"But how'd you get here, though?" Jesse asked.

"Well, I splashed down in the lake and followed the shoreline, just like I'm sure y'all must have done. But it was snowing really hard by the time I got here; too much to walk even another mile. And besides, I saw the lights on in the hangar, so I knew at least one of you was already at the station safe, and I knew there'd be heat in here," he said.

"How come you didn't call us, then?" Jesse asked.

"I tried to, but the phones didn't work," he said with a shrug.

"Uh. . . that's my fault. I didn't think to switch them on," I admitted, turning a little red. But honestly, who ever would've imagined needing them?

"Well. . . never mind. It's all over with, now. I sure would like a shower and some decent food, though," he said.

That called for a trip back to the cafeteria, where Philip broke out a can of sardines and quickly baked a pan of cornbread to go with it.

"If I had a penny for every fish and cornbread sandwich I've ever had to eat in this cafeteria, I'd be a rich man," I muttered.

"I've had to eat a lot more of them than you have, Tyke. I'm sure of that. Be thankful for what you've got, not for what you wish you had," Philip said. It was only a mild scolding, and I guess I deserved it. But it still didn't make me enjoy eating fish and cornbread any better than I did before.

"We've been thinking about a plan to get home," I said, to change the subject.

"Oh? What's that?" Philip asked, talking with his mouth full. Aunt Joan would have smacked his hand with a wooden spoon for doing that, but I guess under the circumstances he could be forgiven for having less-than-perfect table manners.

"We think we can strip down one of those old hulls from Desolation Island, and then refit it with parts from the *Cabral* and the *Balboa*. Maybe between the both of them, we can scrounge up enough pieces to make a working ship," Jesse said.

"Maybe," Philip said. He sounded skeptical, but then so was I.

"It's worth a try, at least. It's the only thing I can think of," Jesse said.

"Well, that's true, too. I'm not sure how much will be usable from either one of them, though," he said.

"If I remember right, it was mostly the front of the *Cabral* that got smashed up. The rear end is probably fine, and that's where the engines and most of the life support systems are located. And then the *Balboa* mostly broke up into pretty big chunks. We'll have to go out in the desert with the buggy and look for them, but they probably had a pretty soft landing what with the sand and the low gravity. We might could salvage more than you think," Jesse said.

I thought about that, and decided he might have a point. Besides which, it wasn't like we had a lot of other options to consider.

"It's worth trying, I think. But we better get up there and check out the *Cabral* first, while it's still early," Philip said.

"That's what we thought, too. We were on our way to work on the plane when we found you a little while ago," I said.

"Well, let me finish eating and take a shower real quick, and then we'll head on up there to see what's what," Philip said.

So that's what we did, and as soon as Philip was cleaned up we all three went back out to the airfield so Jesse could try to finagle a way to override the safety switch on the plane.

That part turned out not to be all that difficult, and before long he had the plane running strong and ready to go. Then we all boarded up and headed out.

Jesse took us up as high as he could, so we could eyeball a wider area and stand a better chance of not getting lost. Then we followed the Lucky River upstream; the same path we'd used (in the opposite direction) when we first got to the Moon. The first part of it was fairly familiar to me because it was the way we always used to go on our way to Trinity Bay to hunt crabs. But there was a certain point where we'd always left the valley behind to cross a low pass through the hills and finish following the Trinity river the rest of the way down to the Bay itself. Once we passed that point I wasn't familiar with much of anything anymore. I had only my memories of that one trip two years ago to rely on, and I'd had a lot on my mind at that time to say the least.

But Jesse was careful never to let the river slip out of sight, and we never got lost.

He landed us in the big crater lake which was the source of the river, blue as a sapphire and round as a marble, set like a jewel amongst the milk-white foothills of the Snowy Mountains.

"How come we're landing here? The *Cabral* is still thirty miles away or more," I pointed out.

"Yeah, but I'd really like to stay out of the canyon if we can help it. There are strong winds up there in the mountains and I don't want to end up smashing *us* into a cliff. Better to walk a little farther and stay safe, you know," he said.

It was hard to blame him for that, so I didn't offer any more objections. He taxied up as close to shore as possible, and then I splashed out and tied us up to a boulder.

"It's prettier up here than I remembered," I commented, looking back at the lake after we climbed up to the top of the rim-walls. I hadn't had the proper attitude to appreciate it the first time I'd been there, and even though I'd glimpsed it again from the top of Mount Bradley, I'd been too fascinated with the much-more-interesting view of the Grand Canyon of the Moon to pay much attention to a far-off lake.

But this time was different. Maybe because I'd seen so many ugly things lately, on the Moon and Titan both. I think that gives you a much deeper appreciation for beautiful things when you do see them.

"It's called the Lake of Eternal Peace," Philip said somberly.

I hadn't known it had any special name, but I guess Philip must have had plenty of time to learn those kinds of things while he was alone at the station for a year with not much to do except study in the Map Room. It sounded exactly like the kind of cheesy name the terraformers would have picked; grand, high-flown, and a little bit pretentious. I know I said I'd never laugh at their naming system again if I ever made it back from Tycho Crater, but I confess that one might have wrung a chuckle out of me in spite of myself. But then on the other hand, considering all those who died so close to that place and especially Callum, maybe it was an appropriate name after all. There are times when even the cheesiest of names ring truer than the namers ever intended.

So I didn't say a word while Philip gazed out across the water in silence, thinking of his lost child beyond a shadow of a doubt. I knew it without needing to ask or even wonder. They say there are certain things time never heals, and that's one of them. I wouldn't venture to say I understood how he felt, and I humbly pray to God that's one test I never have to face.

After a little while he took a deep breath and let it out.

"Come on, boys. Let's go," he said, and then we turned our backs on the Lake of Eternal Peace and started hiking northward.

There was no chance of getting lost now; not with the huge bulk of Mount Silverspur to guide us like a beacon toward our destination. We made good time, and reached the crash site in only about two hours.

Chapter Fourteen

It looked really bad when we got there. The cockpit was entirely crushed, and so was part of the fuselage on the left side. There was a long rip in the roof, which brought back vivid memories of pouring rain and blood and death.

"Are you sure we can do anything with this?" I asked, staring at it.

"Not the hull, no. It's mostly the rear end I want to save, if we can. The engines, the air and water purifiers, things like that. Like I said before, almost all the life support systems and other stuff were in the back, anyway. Everything but the command computers and the battery, but hopefully we can salvage those from the *Balboa*," Jesse said.

"So what do we do, then, start taking everything apart?" I asked.

"No, I'm afraid if we do that I might not know how to put it back together again. I've got a better idea. The reactor is the heaviest part, so if we take that out and leave it here, and then cut the rest of the rear end free, I think we could haul the rest of it back to Lakeside attached to the plane in one piece," he said.

"Are you sure about that?" I asked, still staring at the wreck.

"Well, ninety percent sure, anyway. If it doesn't work then we'll have to take it apart and take our chances, but I'd rather not have to," he said.

So we got to work removing the bolts that held the reactor in place, and Jesse was right about it being by far the heaviest part of the *Cabral*. But we finally got it out, and when it landed on the ground behind the ship with a thud, we got started cutting loose the rear of the plane from the front. Most of that was already done for us by the wreck, but it still took some tough laser work to finish cutting it loose. We didn't bother to keep the air lock, either, and that removed another big chunk of weight.

Finally what was left of the rear end came loose and rolled backward a little way, where it came to rest. The remainder of the *Cabral* looked in even worse shape than before, if such a thing were possible.

"I think that's all we need from here, if we can get this piece home. If there's anything else we can always come back for it later," Jesse said.

Without the reactor core or the airlock, the remainder of the rear end only weighed about as much as a small car, which is to say about two thousand pounds. That only amounted to about three hundred and fifty pounds in the one-sixth gee of the Moon, which meant that even though it was possible for the three of us together to pick it up and carry it, we had to really strain. It took us nearly fifteen hours to carry that heavy monstrosity all the way back to the lake, and by then we were so exhausted we could barely move.

Getting it attached to the plane was another issue. We finally managed it, though, by the simple strategy of putting it as near the edge of the rim-wall as possible and attaching it to the plane with a super-long piece of cable before we took off. Jesse did the best he could, but it was still one mean jerk when the slack in that line ran out. The rear end of the *Cabral* was yanked out over the lake and swung free, just like we intended, and then we were on our way.

"I hope we don't have too many more jobs like that one," I said, watching the big hunk of metal swaying in the wind below us. My arms and back still ached.

"We won't. Or at least I don't think so," Jesse said.

There was a *little* bit more work, though. When we got back to Lakeside, Philip cut the cable while we flew over the beach, to let the remains of the *Cabral* have a softer landing in the sand. Then as soon as we landed the plane we had to go down there and retrieve the thing, carrying it up to the hangar for storage.

As soon as that was done, we immediately had to get started scrounging the Flats for whatever pieces of the *Balboa* we could find. That meant ranging around in the dune buggy with a metal detector, after surveying the area from above with the plane for likely sites.

We found quite a few pieces, actually. The ones which were nothing but twisted metal and glass we didn't bother bringing back, but the ones that held potentially useful components we loaded up on a trailer and hauled to the hangar to sit beside the rear end from the *Cabral.* The real prize was the reactor core. Just like with the *Cabral,* most of the rear end had held together as one piece, scouring a deep pit in the ground at the foot of the Chocolate Mountains. After that we had almost everything we needed, but the two components we still desperately wanted to find were the battery and the command computer.

People sometimes think that heavy objects fall faster than lighter ones, but that's a mistake. In reality, a feather falls just as fast as a bowling ball, all else being equal. The reason heavier things tend to fall to the ground sooner than lighter ones goes back to that same buoyancy issue I mentioned before. Gravity has nothing to do with it. It's simply that heavier things don't float as well as lighter things.

So for that reason among others, we had every right to think that the heavier pieces of the *Balboa* would be found somewhere in the foothills of the Chocolate Mountains. That's where we found the reactor, and many of the biggest pieces of metal.

But expectations don't always pan out the way you think they will. We scoured those hills for days without finding a trace of the *Balboa's* nose. We ended up finding it almost by accident, way out in the middle of the flat desert smashed into a grove of Joshua trees. I can't imagine how it ever managed to make it that far, but it certainly did.

I think the Joshua trees helped to break its fall, because it was surprisingly undamaged. The nose cone is always the part of the ship which is expected to take the most abuse, so maybe that accounted for part of it too.

In any case, the computer seemed intact, and we were glad indeed to get it safely back home.

The battery was another story. We found *that* smashed into a dozen pieces against a rocky hill.

"Do you think the one on the *Cabral* is salvageable?" Philip asked, tossing aside a piece of the shattered one.

"Maybe, but I kind of doubt it. It's located right under the cockpit and that part of the *Cabral* got smashed up pretty bad," Jesse said.

"If I remember right, the lights and things did come on for a few minutes in one of those ships at Desolation Island. We might be able to use one of those batteries," I said.

"I don't think so. Radiation is bad for them, and I specifically remember Tabby saying the battery was no good on that ship," Jesse said.

"But did she mean it wouldn't hold a charge or did she only mean it was dead at the time?" Philip asked, and of course nobody had an answer for that.

"I guess we can find out. We've got to go up there and retrieve one of the hulls, anyway," Jesse said.

"How do you plan on doing that?" I asked.

"Well, those planes have wings, you know, and the hull by itself won't weigh much more than a glider after we strip all the heavy stuff out. I think we can pull it back with the plane we've got," he said.

So that's what we did, and at first things went fairly well. We had to fly by dead reckoning to find the place, and that's never either safe or wise, but this time it couldn't be helped. Jesse had every intention of coming back in the other plane we'd left there a year ago; the one that had a complete navigation computer.

The island was nowhere to be seen when we reached the general vicinity of where Jesse thought it should be, but that was only to be expected. We started circling in wider and wider patterns, hoping we'd catch a glimpse of it sooner or later. And finally we did. Philip spotted it first, far to the east, and Jesse immediately headed that way.

However much it made my skin crawl to think about another visit to Roachville, I knew it was necessary. So when Jesse touched down as quietly as possible near the other plane, I tried to remain calm.

"I sure hope the roaches are not out today," I said in a low voice, and Jesse only nodded. If he could handle it, then surely I could.

"If I remember right, I think the *Tyler James* is the one we need to focus on. The electrical system is screwy, but the *Mendeleev* had water damage and I'm not sure what that might have come from. It might have a leaky airlock, or even a hull breach," Jesse said.

"We definitely don't want that," Philip agreed.

Jesse started up the plane we'd left, and it turned over without a hitch. Then he moved it as close to the hangar where the *Tyler James* rested as he dared. The last thing we wanted to do was to rile up the vampire roaches.

They hadn't made an appearance so far, but then they hadn't shown up for a while that first time we visited the island, either. I didn't trust the place, and caught myself sniffing the air for that telltale odor they gave off. It was there everywhere, of course, faint and in the background. That was unsettling enough, but I knew if I ever got a strong whiff of that smell I'd probably break out in a cold sweat and start shaking. They'd come way too close to eating us alive the last time we were there.

And unfortunately, the *Tyler James* was in the very hangar which seemed to be most thoroughly infested with them.

"I think we'll pull her out on the tarmac, so we don't have to work on her in there," Jesse said, and I knew he had the same thing on his mind that I did.

We had to open the hangar doors to get the ship outside, and my heart came right up into my throat at the noisy screech the hinges made. Nobody had oiled them in half a century, so it wasn't surprising they'd squeak a little.

We attached a cable to the front end of the *Tyler James,* and then Jesse fired up the little plane to pull the bigger one out onto the tarmac, as far from the roach den as humanly possible. We still hadn't seen any, but I knew that could change at any moment.

Then we got to work, stripping off anything that seemed unnecessary. Engines, reactor core, command computer, all of it had to go. The only thing we saved was the battery, since we might possibly still need it. The whole job didn't take nearly as long as you might think, either; not with three people working feverishly to get it done and not caring in the slightest what happened to the pieces we chunked aside.

But at last it was finished, and the *Tyler James* sat there as a forlorn husk of its former glory, ready to be refitted with the pieces we'd scrounged from the other wrecks.

"All right, let's get out of here," Philip said.

And none too soon, either. I glimpsed a single roach crawling out from the shadows of the hangar onto the tarmac. He didn't seem urgently bloodthirsty or even specifically looking for anything at the time, but the mere sight of him was enough to get us moving in a hurry.

So we dragged that old wreck home, and from then on out it was mostly Jesse and Philip's project, since I know little to nothing about mechanics. They even ate and slept out there at the hangar, so they could keep working on it during the long snowy night when it wasn't possible to get back and forth between the airfield and the station itself.

There was nothing for me to do except help them lift something when they asked, but in reality I think I got in the way more than I helped. It was actually quicker for them to do things themselves than to show me how. I don't think I've ever felt so useless.

But time passed, and within six weeks they had the *Tyler James* reassembled, refurbished, and in as good a shape as we had any right to expect. All but the battery, that is, which, just as Philip had feared, wouldn't hold a charge.

"Should we try the one from the *Cabral?*" I asked doubtfully.

"I don't guess we've got any choice," Jesse said.

There was no problem about reaching the place now; not with the inertial navigation system on the plane we brought back from Desolation Island. It remembered the location of every spot on the Moon and could easily calculate how to get from one place to another with only the most minimal of input. All we had to do was tell it where we were and where we wanted to go, and it could take care of the rest.

So Jesse told it to take us to the Lake of Eternal Peace, and sure enough, the computer recognized the name and plotted a course to fly us there. Not that I ever thought Philip was making it up or anything, it just struck me as funny.

When we got back to the remains of the *Cabral* for the second time, we all hung back a little. Cutting loose the rear end was one thing, but the front was a whole 'nother issue. We all knew what was waiting for us up there in the crushed cockpit; the broken skeletons of Mr. Breyer and Mrs. Weiss, and probably the Andersons and the Rayburns, too, depending on how much cutting we had to do to reach the battery.

"You know what I think? I believe we should see this as an opportunity to give these people a decent burial after all this time. It's not right, that we should leave them here in a crashed plane when we've got the means to do something about it," Philip said, and of course that immediately cast a whole different light on things. What started out as a spooky mission to recover a battery while having to dig around with skeletons for company was transformed almost instantly into an errand of mercy and compassion for our fallen comrades. That was another matter altogether.

It's little things like that which make the world a kinder and more beautiful place, and that as much as anything else is what it means to fight evil, I think. With only a few short words Philip had utterly banished the darkness from that place, and I couldn't help but admire him for the way he did it. Always an Avenger at heart, I suppose.

I hope someday I can be even half so good.

Jesse and Philip took the hand lasers and started cutting their way forward toward the cockpit, while I came along behind them and collected the bones, making sure to keep them in their own little individual piles with a nametag attached. Aron Anderson was the first one; my classmate at the Academy and someone I'd known at least semi-well ever since I could remember, even though we'd never been especially close. Then his parents, Luther and Jenine. I hadn't socialized with them all that much in recent years, but I still remembered them well enough from all those road trips to North Carolina we used to make when I was younger. Sam and Jennifer Rayburn were next; Chris' wife Emily's parents. Those two I also knew, since they lived in Clearwater and Jesse and me used to tag along with Chris whenever he'd let us, and occasionally we'd stopped by at the Rayburns' house. I remembered Jennifer was blonde and liked to play tennis, and Sam was a landscaper at the country club.

But finally the wreckage was all sliced away, and we had Jason Breyer's and Peggy Weiss's bones sitting in neat little piles beside the others. Then we got started on the battery.

We had to cut the compartment open since the door wouldn't budge, but once we did, everything seemed to be in decent shape.

"Well, at least it's not cracked or broken," Jesse said, surveying it critically.

"Do you think it'll work?" Philip asked.

"No telling till we try it, but I don't see why it wouldn't. I'm shocked, though," he said.

We had to cut more metal out of the way to get it out of there, and once we did there was practically nothing left of the brave *Cabral* except some pieces of torn and twisted metal.

We buried the bones next to whatever other family they might have. Which is to say, Peggy Weiss we put next to Dr. Weiss and Bethany at the little cemetery in Lakeside, and Jason Breyer we put in the same place, next to his wife. We put all three of the Andersons down there, too. But the Rayburns we buried in the cave with Maddy and Callum. Philip cried a little bit when he went in there, but I don't guess anybody could blame him for that.

It didn't take long to do all the burials, though, and I felt good about having done it. I knew their still-living relatives back in Kona would appreciate it, too. I'm sure I would have, if the shoe had been on the other foot.

Then we fitted the new battery into our slapdash ship, and sure enough, it still worked. That was a huge relief.

"So are we good to go, now?" I asked anxiously.

"Not so fast, Tyke. I still need to check out all the systems and make sure they really work like they're supposed to. Not everything on this old puppy is put together the way it was intended to be, and that does funny things to computer circuits sometimes," Jesse said.

He was thorough about it, too, and if something didn't work right he was meticulous about running it down and doing his best to fix it. I don't think he was happy with the results.

"This heap runs like somebody built it out of spare parts in a garage," he complained one day.

"That's pretty much what we did do, Jesse," I pointed out.

"Yeah, I know, but I don't have to like it, do I?" he asked.

"As long as it gets us home, I don't care how it runs or what happens to it after that," I said.

"Well, maybe it will. I sure hope so," he muttered.

We waited for sunrise, when the air was most stable, and then Jesse took us out across the Sea of Tranquility for the rotational boost it would give us, heading east. Not that you get *much* of that from the Moon, but when it came to that ramshackle ship, he babied it in every possible way.

And I guess I can't complain too much; it mostly did what it was supposed to do, with a few notable exceptions. The heater went out almost immediately, which I guess would have frozen us to death if we hadn't had our thermal suits for protection. Jesse's was ripped, of course, but then the *Tyler James* never got anywhere near as cold as Titan.

I promise you it got plenty cold enough to make things uncomfortable, though, since all the food and water was frozen solid as a brick.

Not to mention the autopilot didn't work, which meant Jesse had to stay at the controls almost constantly and recalculate our course at least every few hours.

There were other bugs in the system, too, not nearly as life-threatening but maybe even more annoying in some ways. The lights only worked sporadically, and were liable to blink on or off at any moment, and for any length of time. That will drive you crazy after a while. And to add the final cherry on top, the lack of heat meant the entire plumbing system froze, which in turn meant the bathroom didn't work, either.

So, needless to say, we had a thoroughly miserable trip for three days. Jesse got almost no sleep at all, and there was nothing Philip or I could do to help him.

But again, I won't really complain too much. It kept us alive, and that was as much as we had any right to ask.

$$* \quad * \quad * \quad * \quad * \quad * \quad *$$

Three days after leaving Lakeside, Jesse brought us down into the Earth's atmosphere, and a few hours later we landed at the airstrip in Kona with no incident. As I've said many a time, those are exactly the kinds of trips I like.

As soon as the doors opened I was the first one down the stairs, forgetting all dignity as I threw my arms around Danielle. For her own part, she didn't pay the slightest bit of attention to how much I stank after three days with no running water.

"I knew you'd come back," she whispered in my ear.

"Of course. You couldn't get rid of me if you tried, beautiful," I said, and she laughed.

We sat on the beach that night watching the stars as we so often did, and I thought to myself that it felt like centuries since the last time we'd done that.

"I brought you something from Titan, just like you asked," I told her.

"Really? What is it? A bottle of lava?" she asked.

"No. Turns out I did have the chance to go swimming in a volcano while I was there, but I brought you something a little better than that," I said, laughing a little. Then I pulled N'grumth's necklace out of my pocket. I'd already strung it on a silver chain from the jewelry shop earlier that afternoon so Danielle could wear it. One of the few nice things about an empty world is that anything we want is ours for the taking. Nothing has any value at all except what it holds through beauty, love, or usefulness. And I think that much at least is a very good thing indeed.

"What is it?" she asked, turning the nugget over in her hands.

"It's a piece of iron from a meteorite. My friend N'grumth gave it to me, the one who saved our lives after the pod crashed. On Titan that's a precious jewel, the most valuable thing you could own," I said.

She slipped the chain around her neck, and I thought to myself that it really did look pretty on her. The nugget was only about the size of my thumb, which was perfect for an ornament. N'grumth might not truly comprehend what it meant to love someone the way a boy and girl love each other, but he knew very well what it meant to love a best friend. Danielle was that, too, so I hoped N'grumth would understand and be pleased that I'd given it to her.

"*Akiri,*" I murmured, and kissed her forehead. It was my right to grant that title to anyone I pleased, and I suppose giving it to Danielle was mostly an impulse born of love on the spur of the moment. But there was plenty of truth in it, too. She was in her own way more brave and honorable than I had ever been, and I wanted her to know I hadn't overlooked it.

"What's that mean?" she asked.

"It's a noble rank on Titan, for a person who behaves with courage and honor in the face of danger," I said, and she laughed a little.

"How do you figure I've ever done that?" she asked.

"You did it when you brought Derrick to the Moon," I reminded her.

"Well. . . okay, if you say so," she said.

"You did it when you asked to be the first one to take the vaccine back in Tampa, and you did it again when you went to the Crater with us the first time and then again when you agreed not to go to Titan. You do things like that all the time; you're just not loud and flashy about it like some people are. That's one of the reasons I love you so much," I said, and she smiled.

"That's very sweet. Thank you, baby," she said, and kissed me. It was as close to a perfect moment as I was ever likely to get, so I took a deep breath to steady my voice.

"Jesse and Leah are getting married next Saturday, and they'd still like for us to do it the same day. What do you think?" I asked. I was still a little nervous about the idea, but after several near-death experiences on the Moon and Titan, I think I was able to be a little more philosophical about things and not get so uptight about the small stuff.

"I think it's a great idea. I've never been to a double wedding before," she said.

"Me neither, actually. But it'll be fun," I said.

And you know, I think it was. We used the old Mo'Kuai'Kaua mission church in Kona, the oldest church in the islands and a relic from the days of the Kingdom of Hawaii. Johnny Weiss played the piano and Uncle Philip led the service, and Danielle has never been more beautiful before or since than she was that day in her long white gown. She asked Johnny to play the *Canon in D,* the same song we'd first danced to at that Candlemas party on the Moon, and I smiled when I heard it. She could be so sentimental at times.

I thought back to the first time I ever saw her, in Dr. Weiss's front yard on the day we left for the Moon. At the time, she was the last person on earth I would ever have imagined myself with. Now she was the *only* person I could imagine myself with. Life is strange that way, isn't it? Things never turn out quite the way you thought they would.

But in hindsight, I'm awfully glad for that.

Epilogue
Friday, December 25, 2156

Christmas is not so very different than any other time of year, in Hawaii. But then, it never was on the Moon either, or even in Tampa for that matter. It's a cultural relic, to think Christmas should be cold and snowy; a memory of Britain still lodged in our minds. They say the surest way to tell the origin of any group of people is to listen to the nursery rhymes they teach to their children and the carols they sing on holidays. I suppose the fact that we still sing to our children about London Bridge and snowy Christmases should say something about how long the memory of mankind really is.

That matters more than I used to think. The whole memory of every nation and tribe on Earth is preserved only in us now, and those of us who are thoughtful enough to care about those kinds of things can't help feeling it keenly. It tends to make you think a lot about your ancestors, even if you never cared much before. So in spite of the incongruity of place and time, we went to church this morning to sing some of those cold and snowy hymns anyway. In loving remembrance of all those who lived and died and praised God before us, if nothing else.

It hasn't been only me who's been pondering the past, either. Jesse has quietly started referring to himself as Jesse Parker, or what he calls his "real" name. Everyone kind of scratched their heads and didn't say much; I guess he could decide to start calling himself Eleanor Roosevelt if he really wanted to and there wouldn't be a soul in the world nowadays to tell him he couldn't. In a way it puzzled me just as much as it did the others, why he'd care so much about something like that. But then on the other hand, when I think about it in a different sort of way I can understand where he's coming from completely.

Chris hasn't shown any inclination so far to switch, and neither has Philip, actually. He and Joan *have* been a lot more relaxed about using his old first name, though. With her it's always Cam this and Cameron that these days, hardly ever Philip anymore. I'm not sure I'll ever get used to calling him that, myself. It's really hard to change first names, once you've gotten to know somebody very well. Which no doubt explains why Joan still uses that old name so frequently. He answers to both, so I don't guess it matters too much.

He's been telling me quite a bit here lately about the history and purpose of the Avengers. There are only supposed to be six of them at any given time, it seems, and he also let slip the interesting little tidbit that all six of them had been on board the *Cabral.* He and Joan. Katrina McClendon. Jennifer Rayburn. Jason Breyer. And most astonishingly of all, Aron Anderson.

At first I thought it was strange that all six of them should have ended up on the Moon expedition like that, but on second thought maybe it was exactly what I should have expected. They all knew and trusted each other long before the Orion Strain ever became an issue, so when it did, that was a bond which could be relied on. It's really amazing what all goes on behind the scenes that you never see or hear about, isn't it?

It didn't surprise me to hear that Katrina McClendon had been one of them. Her passion for having the truth at any cost and the way she constantly urged us to be heroes like Howard Ricketts and others made her a completely believable choice. Jason Breyer I could also understand, from all the comments I'd heard him make over the years about working for the good of mankind and how every action we took should be done in light of that. Jennifer Rayburn I simply didn't know well enough to draw any conclusions one way or the other. But *Aron?* The quiet, bespectacled, almost-friendless loner who loved to play chess and read pulpy science fiction novels? *That* Aron, who weighed a hundred pounds soaking wet and was my classmate for years, *he* was a member of a secret society devoted to fighting evil? The thought of it utterly blew me away, and I was reminded all over again how little we really know people sometimes.

Philip tells me I'm only the nineteenth holder of the Ring of Barthélemy since 1769. It's been worn by some really brave and remarkable people over the years, including Katrina McClendon and Philip's cousin Zachary Trewick, not to mention Barthélemy Chrétien himself in the very beginning. Hence the name, I suppose. Philip told me all kinds of stories about things those people did, some of them almost impossible to believe. It's a lot to live up to.

That still leaves three empty slots, of course, and Philip told me he's got those three rings, too. I guess he must have recovered them from the *Cabral* when we cut it apart to bury the skeletons and retrieve the battery. But anyway, if and when we choose, we can give them out to those who are willing to take the oath and keep it. At the moment I'm honestly not sure if there's anybody else to ask. I don't think Chris or Johnny would want to, and I know Emily and Leah wouldn't. Jesse might possibly, I guess. But the only person I know for sure who'd say yes and be glad to accept it would be Danielle.

I'll have to suggest her to Philip, when the time is right.

But other than her, we'll just have to wait till some of the younger kids grow up a little and we can see the mettle of their hearts and minds.

Anyway, other than that life has been quiet these past few months, and that suits me just fine. I've been busy re-creating species again, starting with the small ones first. You have to begin with herbivores and prey species, of course, or else there won't be anything for the carnivores to eat. But on the other hand, you have to choose carefully or they'll get out of hand and devastate whole areas. I've had a few notable successes, especially with some of the domestic animals. We have three cows now, at least, and a handful of chickens. It's awfully nice to have fresh milk and eggs again, even if it's only once in a while at this point.

Of the wild things, I've released some sea otters, several songbirds, and a few types of antelope. Sometimes it seems like the amount of work will turn out to be insurmountable, and I wonder if Earth will ever be like what it used to be.

The answer is no, of course; I don't even have to think about that one. But I hope that in time it will become something almost as good, and maybe in some ways better. For our children's sake, I hope that.

And to speak of that for a moment, mine and Danielle's first baby will be along some time in June, I think. A few weeks after Jesse and Leah's and almost the same time as Chris and Emily's second one. Even Philip and Joan have been talking about having a few more. Before long, this place is going to feel more like a nursery school than a town.

But I don't mind. I even look forward to it, ninety-nine percent of the time. There are times when I still worry, but not nearly as much as I once did.

And in the meantime, I'm content to walk barefoot in the waves with Danielle, and feel the wind in our hair, and be glad for all the things we have and the life we've been given. It could have turned out so much worse.

Life is sweet, and love is good, and for now that's enough for both of us.

The End

Continue reading Tyke's story in

Freedom

Book Four of the Tyke McGrath Series

Sample of

Freedom

The Tyke McGrath Series: Book Four
By William Woodall

Chapter One
Saturday, June 17, 2157

"Something just happened," Jesse said.

"What are you talking about?" I asked absently, not especially curious. We were right in the middle of our weekly Saturday night survivor search, but that had long since turned into a more or less perfunctory and dutiful kind of chore after so much time with no results.

"There was an energy surge just now, out over the Gulf of Mexico," Jesse said.

"Lightning, you think?" I asked.

"No, it's definitely not lightning. I'm not sure what it was, but it sent out a blast of neutrinos like you wouldn't believe," Jesse said.

"Really?" I asked, my interest piqued for the first time.

"Yeah, really. And it can't be a solar flare, either; the sun's been quiet for days, and besides it was much too localized for that," Jesse said.

"What do you think it could be, then?" I asked.

"I don't have the slightest idea," Jesse confessed.

"Where exactly did it happen?" I asked, rolling my chair over beside him to look at his computer screen.

"About thirty miles offshore from the mouth of Tampa Bay, actually," he said, pointing out the location on his screen.

"Really?" I asked again, even more interested.

"Yeah. The burst started at exactly 1:48:32 a.m. local time and ended less than a second later," Jesse said.

"Dang, is it already that late over there?" I asked. It wasn't even quite nine o'clock yet in Hawaii, and in Florida it was already well into the wee hours of Sunday morning. It made me sleepy even to think about it.

"Yup, 'fraid so," Jesse said.

"You're sure it wasn't just a glitch in the instruments?" I asked.

"No, I already thought of that. Everything checks out fine. Something weird definitely happened," Jesse said.

"Did you check it out with the visual satellite?" I asked.

"Yeah, clear skies and calm seas, nothing to see. Or at least nothing I could see in the dark," he amended.

"What about the infrared?" I asked.

"Well. . . that's pretty useless in the Gulf, you know, unless it's something really big and either really hot or really cold. Ocean temperatures are warm as bath water this time of year and that makes it hard for anything to stick out. That said, I *think* there might be two very small points of heat out there, but I can't tell for sure," he said.

"People, you think?" I asked

"Couldn't be. There was no ship, no plane, nothing like that within miles. There's no way people could have dropped into the ocean from nowhere, is there?" he asked.

"Well, no," I admitted.

"I'm not sure if those heat signatures are even real, much less what they could be. They're so small and so close to water temperature, they might only be a false return," he said.

"Yeah, but still. Maybe we should go check it out tomorrow, you think?" I asked.

"Yeah, I guess we better. Just in case," he agreed.

"So how do you think we should work this? Fly to Tampa and then take a boat out to those coordinates?" I asked.

"Yeah, we'll take some instruments with us, see if there's any residual radiation from that neutrino blast. Or anything else for that matter. Who knows, Tyke. Maybe it's an alien spaceship that crashed in the ocean and they'll give us a million dollars apiece for saving them," Jesse said.

"What would we do with it even if they did?" I pointed out.

"Oh, don't be a spoilsport. We could at least dump it all out on the middle of the floor, and then roll around in it like a pile of leaves and pretend we're the richest dudes in the world," he said, and I laughed.

"You're crazy, boy," I said.

"Well, hey, if we can't spend it then we might as well enjoy it some way or other," he said.

"You do know that money has more germs per square centimeter than a toilet seat, don't you?" I asked conversationally, and he wrinkled his nose. I didn't strictly know if that were true or not, but it sounded pretty convincing. When Jesse's in one of his silly moods all you can really do is mess with him in return.

"Oh, forget it, then. I'll just tell them to write me a check," he said.

"No other interesting little tidbits tonight?" I asked, getting back to business.

"Nope. Nary a blip," Jesse said.

We usually would have called it a night by nine o'clock, but we stayed till ten that time for fear we might miss something important. But nothing else happened, so we finally gave up the ghost and went home, leaving some of the equipment running just in case there were a radio signal or anything else to be detected. Then we left the university and walked through the silent streets of Kailua Kona till we made it back to the little strip of beach homes where we all lived.

The town looked reasonably lived-in nowadays; Philip and Chris and several of the others made it a point to keep all the yards mowed and the streets swept and those kinds of things, or at least as much as they could manage. It would have been a full-time job even if they hadn't had anything else whatsoever to do, but it made all of us feel a lot more at home than we ever could have felt if weeds and grass had been allowed to overrun everything. Which, believe me, doesn't take all that long to happen when you live in a place like Hawaii.

Philip and Chris had their hands full with lots of things besides mowing the grass, though. They had to maintain the electricity and the water system, fix the vehicles, and all those sorts of things, too. Even with help from Jesse and Hunter and sometimes the rest of us, I still didn't see how they kept up with it all. Not to mention the fact that Philip is also our preacher, dispute-settler, and general all-around leader.

We all had to wear several different hats, actually, with as few of us as there were, but the one job we all had in common at least part-time was teaching. We'd started using the old Kailua Kona High School a few months earlier since that was another thing which helped to maintain a sense of normalcy. Emily and Leah looked after the really little ones and the babies, and Aunt Joan taught the older ones except when she had to put on her doctor's hat and take care of somebody. Jesse taught advanced math and coached athletics when nobody needed him to pilot a plane or help with maintenance, and he also spent as much time as he could spare trying to teach Hunter how to fly so we'd have a backup airman if we needed one. Johnny taught music when he wasn't practicing or doing performances for us. Other than me, he was the only person in our whole group who got to spend almost all his time doing the thing he was actually trained for, and that's only because we all agreed music is an important skill which we didn't want to lose.

As for me, I was almost always busy with genetic engineering, so usually the only other thing I had to do was teach a science class twice a week and help Jesse with the survivor search on Saturday nights. Danielle was the chief cook and bottle washer, so to speak. She made sure we all got fed and that our clothes were clean, and she took care of the cows and chickens and weeded and watered the vegetable garden, and even helped me in the genetics lab now and then when she could spare the time. We were all busy as bees in the springtime, and occasionally that meant we had to pitch in and take over somebody else's job for a while, whether that involved changing a baby or changing the oil in a car. None of us could afford to be a slacker.

Everybody was sitting around a bonfire on the beach when we got home that night; another Saturday evening tradition. We were late, of course; that's what we got for poring over the instruments for an extra hour. But nevertheless everybody was still eating and socializing, so we didn't miss *too* much.

I grabbed a plate of chicken stir-fry and sat down next to Danielle on a palm log, hungry enough to eat the plate right along with the food. I attacked it with gusto, and she watched me with a half smile on her face.

"I take it you like the chicken?" she asked.

"It's delicious," I said with my mouth full, paying close attention to business. She laughed a little.

"Then slow down and enjoy it. I promise there's more if you want some; you don't have to inhale it," she said.

"But I'm *starving,*" I said, taking another bite.

"You must be. Did you not eat lunch today?" she asked.

"No, I was too busy," I admitted.

"Well, see, there you go. If you wouldn't skip meals then you wouldn't need to wolf it down like a python," she said. I made an effort to slow down just a bit, if only to please her.

"We found something interesting tonight," I said, as much to change the subject as anything else.

"Really? Survivors?" she asked.

"Well, possibly, I guess. It was a powerful energy surge that was over in less than a second, but we can't think of any good explanation for it. It happened about thirty miles from Tampa Bay, out in the Gulf," I said.

"That's strange," she said.

"Yeah, it is. If it had been on land I might have thought it was some kind of explosion, but what is there to explode in the middle of the ocean?" I said.

"A drifting ship, maybe?" she asked.

"No, we would've seen anything like that with the satellite, even in the dark. I don't have a clue what it was. But there were two possible point-sources of heat floating in the Gulf afterward, if they weren't just false returns. Jesse couldn't tell for sure," I said.

"That's interesting," she said.

"Maybe. It might all be a bunch of nothing, actually. But I think we might pay a visit tomorrow, just to make sure. Want to come? We'll only be gone for a day or so," I said. She and Jesse had both decided to accept the offer to become Avengers, leaving us with only a single empty slot remaining. But it also meant she was the top choice for going along on expeditions like that, even if she hadn't been already.

"I think I'll pass, this time at least. I'm still not quite back to normal yet," she admitted. That was undoubtedly true, even though she rarely mentioned it. Having a baby is hard work, no doubt about it.

"I'm sorry, babe," I said, and she shrugged a little.

"Eh, it is what it is. They always say the first one is the hardest," she said.

"I'm glad you can be so philosophical about it," I said.

"Maybe Joan is rubbing off on me. She talks like that all the time," she said, with a little laugh.

"Yeah, I guess she does. Where's Josie?" I asked.

"She's with Emily for a little bit, probably asleep," she said.

Just as I once thought, Kona was starting to feel like a nursery school. There had been three babies born that month, and that's a lot to handle at one time. Chris and Emily had a second daughter, Andrea, to join her sister Virginia. Danielle and I also had a girl, who we named Josefina because coincidentally we both had a great-grandmother by that name. Jesse and Leah had the only boy that time around. They named him David, though sometimes I think Goliath might have been more appropriate. He weighed nearly ten pounds when he was born and hadn't slowed down growing ever since. I think he practically killed his mother, being the small, petite little thing that she is.

But in any case, even though there was never a dull moment on the home front, I did sometimes find myself thinking it would be nice to get away from it all for a few days or so. We rarely did, mind you, but the trip to Tampa was a nice change of pace to look forward to.

The *Tyler James* had been officially retired from service as soon as we got back from the Moon, without the slightest regret. That meant our flight would take longer than it would have otherwise, since a regular plane can't match a trans-atmospheric vehicle when it comes to speedy arrival. One of our first projects when we got home from the Titan expedition was to hop over to Honolulu and fetch one of the corporate jets from the airport. The one we took had belonged to a pineapple company back in the day, and it had an incredibly realistic picture of several luscious, mouthwatering-looking slices of fruit painted all down the side. Every time I saw it I got hungry. But it had been the newest and the best jet we could find, and Jesse and I both agreed that the pineapple motif definitely had a certain kind of retro coolness. We christened it the *Pineapple Express,* since it didn't have any other name when we found it.

It was pretty luxurious inside, first-class all the way, and if we'd only had some pretty flight attendants to serve us chilled pineapple chunks in crystal fruit cups then it would have been perfect. But alas, we had to make do without.

We headed out early the next morning, but what with the long distance and losing five hours flying east, we didn't arrive in Tampa till almost nine o'clock that night, much too late to even think about mounting an expedition out on the Gulf.

"How's Hunter doing with his lessons?" I asked as we came in for a landing.

"Oh, pretty good. He's still a little green, but he works hard on the simulator and he's got in about sixty hours worth of flight time with me on the *Pineapple Express.* I might even be ready to let him take her out solo here before long," Jesse said, laughing a little.

"Good deal. Then *he* can fly us around sometimes," I said.

"Dang straight. I'm tired of being on call twenty-four seven. You ought to learn how yourself, Tyke," Jesse said.

"Not me, buddy boy. I hate heights," I reminded him.

"Got to overcome your fears sometime, you know," Jesse said philosophically.

"Easy for you to say," I said.

"Well. . . just think about it, okay? But anyway, what do you say we spend the night at the Academy tonight? We'll need some good computers tomorrow morning if we want to try to locate those heat signatures again," Jesse suggested.

"Sounds good to me," I said, even though if I were to be completely honest, I didn't much look forward to the idea. We hadn't been back to Tampa for over a year and I'd somehow managed to forget how oppressively quiet and empty it is. Spooky, even, in spite of the fact that I knew there was nothing that could hurt us other than maybe a snake or a spider.

The Academy was in better shape than most spots, of course, since we'd lived there as recently as eighteen months ago and also made sure the place was shut down properly when we left. So at least we had working lights and hot food for supper and all those kinds of things. Better than we could've had most anywhere else in the city.

We slept indecently late the next morning, with our bodies still set on Hawaiian time as they were. We didn't get up till almost noon, and then we had to spend at least another hour fiddling with the computer system to get it back online and reconnected to the satellite grid. However careful you think you've been about shutting things down properly, time still takes its toll.

But we did eventually get it working, and the first thing we did at that point was to take a quick look at the area by visible satellite, to see if there were anything obvious by daylight that we might have overlooked in the dark. There didn't seem to be, so then we switched over to infrared to see if we could spot those two little tell-tale heat signatures.

We still didn't find anything worth noting out in the ocean, and I chewed my lip thoughtfully.

"If those heat signatures after the explosion were really people then I'm sure they would've tried to swim for shore. Don't you think?" Jesse asked, and I nodded.

"Well, let's assume for a minute that's what they were. Could a person swim thirty miles across the ocean? And how long would it take if they did?" I asked.

"I'm sure they could. People have swum farther than that before. There's no way of knowing how long it would take without knowing what the currents were like and that kind of thing, but my best guess would be about eighteen to twenty hours," Jesse said.

"All right, let's make a sweep along the coast and see if we find anything that way," I said.

"Look there," Jesse said a few minutes later, at the exact same second that I saw it myself. There were two moving heat signatures on one of the islands at the mouth of the Bay, and I quickly switched back to visual to zoom in on that area.

Sure enough, there were two people walking on the beach. The resolution wasn't good enough to tell us much about them other than the fact that they were human beings, but that didn't matter. We'd find out who they were soon enough.

"Come on, let's go," I said decisively, and Jesse followed me without a word. We immediately drove to the closest marina and boarded a seaworthy boat to head out to Edgmont Key.

"Who could they be, do you think?" Jesse asked when we were well underway.

"Your guess is as good as mine, buddy boy. We'll find out soon enough," I said.

We landed at the old naval station on the southern tip of the island, and I tried not to pay attention to the skeletons. We didn't often see them in Tampa proper since most of the ones inside the city itself seemed to be hidden away inside homes or buildings, but here there were a lot of them scattered everywhere, still dressed in tattered slate-blue Defense Forces uniforms. But the station was set up in such a way that we had no choice but to pass through the building to reach the island, and that was rattling.

"I really hate places like this," Jesse commented as we crossed the main courtyard.

"Not real fond of them myself," I admitted, glancing at the skeletons again. It looked like they'd been on duty till the last possible moment and then died with their boots on, so to speak. Poor devils.

But finally we made our way to the northern wall and opened the gate, letting us out onto a breezy white-sand beach which was a welcome sight after the inside of the station. I kind of wondered why they bothered to build a wall around the place to start with, but I don't pretend to know the answer.

"So where do we go from here?" Jesse asked.

"Let's try the northern tip of the island. We might as well start where we saw them last," I said.

"Sounds good to me," Jesse said.

So with no more ado we set off along the beach at the best pace we could muster without wearing ourselves out. Walking in sand is hard work, believe it or not. It's all fine and well as long as you're going for a leisurely stroll, but it makes life difficult when you're trying for speed.

We found footprints of bare feet before we ever saw anyone, but finally we spotted the castaways far off down the shore. Jesse pulled out his ancient 45-caliber pistol and fired a round up into the sky to get their attention, not bothering to warn me first. Most people would have had a laser weapon, of course, but Jesse has always enjoyed the way that old gun kicks and smokes. It's also loud enough to wake the dead at such close range, and I clapped my hands over both ears.

"Dang, Jesse James, you could've said something first," I said.

"Sorry," he said, shrugging.

But it had the desired effect. Both people turned their heads to look, and before long we were both headed rapidly towards each other.

Then I stopped, suddenly uneasy for some reason.

"They look awfully familiar for some reason," I said doubtfully. They were still too far away to tell for sure, but I was almost certain I'd seen them somewhere before.

"Yeah, they do," Jesse said, scrutinizing them himself.

But even though we stopped, the other people didn't, and soon they were close enough to remove all doubt.

"It's impossible," I muttered under my breath. I always used to think it was just a tired old cliché when people talked about not being able to believe their own eyes, but I promise you it's not. Wait till it happens to you one of these days and then you'll see.

Because what I was seeing was literally impossible. I wanted to pinch myself but I *still* don't think I would have believed it. Standing right there on the beach in front of me, looking exactly the same as the last time I'd seen them fifteen years ago, were the very last people on earth I ever would have expected to meet.

We'd found my parents.

Chapter Two

I was too tongue-tied for words, and they seemed to be as well. But then Jesse broke the silence.

"Uncle Mikey?" he asked uncertainly, like he thought he might be dreaming.

"Jesse?" my father asked, and that was enough to break the logjam. Before I knew it I took a step forward, and then I was enveloped in arms and covered in tears, some of them mine I think. But when things had had time to subside after a little while, I still found that I didn't know how even to begin to ask all the questions that burned in my mind. Ever since I was four years old I'd thought my parents were dead, drowned in the Bay, and as far as I knew so had everyone else. Now here they were, looking barely older than I was myself.

I thought immediately of the story Uncle Philip had told us on the way back from Titan, about time travel and all the rest of it. Could that have been what happened? It would explain a lot of things, after all; maybe even that strange energy surge we'd seen on Saturday night. I couldn't keep my mind from chewing on the problem and analyzing every possible facet, but in the meantime Jesse had no compunctions about talking.

"But how can this be? We always thought y'all drowned in the Bay when me and Tyke were four years old. That's what the letter we got from the Defense Forces said; I've even seen it myself," Jesse said.

"We almost did drown. But we had the tachometer so we were able to escape by jumping fifteen years ahead. It's a long story, but we'll tell you everything as soon as we get a chance. But in the meantime where's everybody else? Who all is left?" my father asked.

"We're living in a little town named Kailua Kona, on the big island of Hawaii. There are twenty of us now, mostly family and friends. Mom and Dad, Chris, me, Veronica, Tycho; several others too, but I'm not sure which ones you'd know and which ones you wouldn't," Jesse said.

"We probably know several of them, actually. Is Katrina still with you? What about Amos, and Luther and Jenine, and the Bartows?" he asked.

"I'm afraid they've all passed away," Jesse said, in that uncomfortable way that people use when they have to regretfully inform someone that a friend has died.

"Oh, I see," my father said awkwardly.

"Well, I guess I should say Lucia is still with us. That's Amos and Katrina's daughter. And then Tommy and Amie Anderson are still alive, and Leah and Hunter Bartow. I'm married to Leah now, actually; we've got a little boy who was born just a couple weeks ago," Jesse said.

All this talk about death reminded me of something important, and I spoke up for the first time.

"I don't know if you know it or not, but there was a deadly plague that came through here just a couple years ago. It wiped out every warm-blooded life form on the planet, and there are still lots of spores in the ground. It kills within thirty-six hours after exposure, and I don't doubt you've both been exposed by now. So we better get you back into town and get you vaccinated, or this might turn out to be a pretty short reunion," I said.

"Yeah, Tyke's right about that. We better go while there's still time. We can talk on the way," Jesse agreed.

So that's what we did, and I found out quite a lot of things that day that I'd never known before; some of it stuff I wasn't quite sure I *wanted* to know. It turned out the boating accident had been no accident, for one thing; the Defense Forces had tried to murder all three of us that night. I never used to remember anything about the incident myself, but when my mother told that story it brought back vague memories of dark stormy waves and salty water stinging my eyes and nose, and fear and terror and other highly unpleasant things which I'd just as soon had stayed buried. I didn't want to think about that kind of stuff, not now and not ever, and when I heard that Hunter and Leah's father had been the commander of that mission it only compounded the issue.

But I kept my thoughts to myself till we got back to the Academy and at that point I gratefully refocused my attention on what needed to be done to prepare some anti-Orion serum. I knew exactly what needed to be done this time, but at least it occupied my mind and kept me from thinking about all that other stuff.

"So you're a great biologist now, is that it?" my mother asked, watching me work.

"Molecular geneticist," I admitted, kind of shyly.

"We always knew you'd do something wonderful like that," she said, and it was good to hear it even though it puzzled me.

"I always thought you wanted me to be a physicist or an astronomer. Isn't that why you named me after Tycho Brahe?" I asked.

"No, not exactly. Tycho Brahe was your daddy's hero back when he was in college, that's all. He wanted you to have somebody to look up to," my mother said, and I laughed a little bit.

"I think having you two around is going to end up destroying a lot of preconceived notions I've always had," I finally said dryly.

"No doubt, but it's never a good thing to let your mind get stale and fossilized, now is it?" she asked, and I laughed again.

"Well, no. No, it's not," I agreed.

The serum was finished, and as soon as I gave our two newest survivors their doses we were ready to leave. I cleaned up the lab while Jesse shut down the computers and the power supply, and then we all rode out to the airport to board the *Pineapple Express* and head home. It's a strange thing, but when you're headed west in a plane the sun barely seems to move in the sky at all. We gained five hours by the time we landed in Kona, and even though it had been almost sunset when we left Tampa, it was still early in the evening when we landed.

So then there were twenty-two of us in our little island paradise, and I have to say that my parents blended in pretty quickly. They were already thick as thieves with Uncle Philip and Aunt Joan, of course, but out of the younger folks only Chris and Jesse and I could remember them at all, even though they'd known almost everybody's parents at least socially back in the old days.

They found a house on the same strip of beach where we all lived, and we were always within walking distance if we liked. It was really hard at first, getting used to them being there, but before long things settled back into the old familiar pattern. They ended up taking over most of the teaching duties at the school since that was after all what they'd mostly always done before. It freed up Joan to help with the farming and Jesse to help with maintenance, so that at least was good.

My parents told me all kinds of interesting things over the next few months, actually, but one of the most thought-provoking tidbits they ever let slip was the simple fact that my father had warned the Defense Forces about the Orion Strain twelve years ahead of time, after he saw it coming with the tachometer. Not to mention Philip and Joan as well.

I could understand why Philip and Joan had never said anything; knowing the future is not nearly such a good thing as people sometimes think. It puts a burden on the knower, a straitjacket that he has to wear from then onwards. They carefully made arrangements so the XR planes would be ready at the right time, and I'm sure they did some behind-the-scenes negotiating with Dr. Weiss and various things like that, but they never let out a single peep that they knew anything. I didn't blame them for that, though; I knew they did it with everybody's welfare and happiness in mind.

No, what really interested me was what might have happened to the information Daddy had given to the Defense Forces. Philip and Joan didn't know the answer to *that,* and I couldn't help thinking it might turn out to be awfully important.

"I can't believe the Defense Forces wouldn't do something about a threat like that, if they knew it was coming," I said to Jesse one Saturday night.

"It's hard to believe they wouldn't, unless they thought he was lying," Jesse said.

"Well, true, but putting aside that possibility for a second, what would you have done if you were in their place?" I said, and Jesse thought about it for a few seconds.

"I think if I knew all that twelve years ahead of time then I'd start making some contingency plans, just like Mom and Dad did. There'd be no way of knowing what kind of germ they'd have to face or exactly what the circumstances might be, so first of all I'd try to assemble a team of the best microbiologists to be ready at a moment's notice to start analyzing the bug as soon as it appeared, hopefully to find a cure or a vaccination. And then just in case that didn't work, I'd either make sure I had an airtight facility to take refuge in for a while, or else I'd start building spaceships and considering where I might go to start over if the Earth turned out to be permanently unlivable or some such thing," Jesse said.

"Yeah, that's pretty much what I thought," I agreed.

"So then considering the fact that they would have already known the Moon is about to die before long and can't be salvaged, where do you think they'd decide to go instead?" Jesse said.

"I think I still would have gone to the Moon under those circumstances. Anywhere else they went they'd have to build airtight shelters to live in, and if you've got to do that anyway then why go far when you don't have to? Why even leave Earth for that matter?" I asked.

"I can think of a reason," Jesse said.

"Do tell," I said.

"If they wanted to start completely over, and I mean *completely* over, like permanently so, then they wouldn't build shelters on Earth and they wouldn't go to the Moon, either. They'd know it can't hold an atmosphere for very long. But there are other places that can. Mars and Venus come to mind, for example. Maybe they decided to work on terraforming one of those places. The technology exists, even if they might've had to do some hard digging to find it," Jesse said.

"I don't know about all that, Jesse," I said doubtfully. It sounded awfully far-fetched, even for a cold-eyed Defense Forces bureaucrat to sign off on. But then again, people have been known to do some pretty hare-brained things at times.

"It makes sense to me, at least. Think about it; if they devoted a lot of money and resources to the project, I bet they could have developed a workable space vehicle in five years or less," Jesse said.

"Maybe," I admitted.

"And then if they introduced a breeder gas into the atmosphere in one of those places, it'd grow exponentially and have the whole atmosphere converted in six months' time, tops. Ready for them to move in and comfortably start working on the rest of the process at that point. Once you could breathe and go without a space suit, things wouldn't be all that bad. No worse than living in a really harsh desert," Jesse said.

"Possibly," I said, still not sure whether I believed it or not.

"It's what I'd do," Jesse said, and I laughed then.

"This is *you* we're talking about, Jesse. But just for the sake of argument, even if you happened to be right, which one would you pick? Mars or Venus?" I asked.

"There are pros and cons to both of them, but on the whole I think I'd go with Venus," Jesse said.

"Why is that?" I asked.

"Because Mars is so much smaller, for one thing. It leaks atmosphere a lot slower than the Moon does, true, but it *will* leak it away. Venus never would; it's almost as big as Earth is," Jesse said.

"Hmm," I said, thinking it over.

"It'd be easy enough to find out," Jesse said brightly.

"How's that?" I asked.

"All we'd have to do is run a spectroscopic analysis of the atmosphere on both planets, to see what the composition might be. Then we'd know if anybody had altered them," Jesse said.

"I guess so," I admitted.

"We'd have to go up to the observatory for that," Jesse said.

"Let's go, then. You've got me curious now," I said.

It was almost nine o'clock, so we decided to call it a day when it came to the survivor search. Jesse shut down the computers, and then we drove up to the observatory on Mauna Kea after calling to let everybody know what we were doing. Philip recently got the telephone system working again, which is an awfully nice feature.

It took nearly an hour to reach the observatory, and Jesse parked on the gravel right outside the building. It was freezing cold up there, especially considering the fact that we were both in shorts and t-shirts.

"Hurry up, dude; it's freezing out here," Jesse said, clapping his hands against his sides while I fumbled with the door lock in the dark.

As soon as we got inside I switched on the lights and the heater, and grabbed a couple of blankets off the table which I'd brought up there for just such emergencies.

"Here, wrap up in this till the heater gets going," I said, handing one of them to Jesse and putting the other one around my own shoulders. It helped a lot, but I was still shivering while I set up the spectroscope. Being able to see your breath in the air while you work is not a good feeling, especially when you're not used to it.

"Is it working?" Jesse asked.

"Yeah, hold on just a minute," I said, adjusting the controls.

"Let's check Mars first, just in case. That'll be easier," Jesse said, and I shrugged.

"Whatever you say," I said, consulting the computer to find out where in the sky Mars ought to be at the time.

"Slight problem, buddy boy," I said after a while.

"What's that?" Jesse asked.

"Looks like Mars is behind the sun right now. There's no way to look at it for at least a month or two," I said.

"Well. . . try Venus, then," Jesse said, and I shrugged. It took several minutes to get the spectroscope set up and working properly, and then several more while it actually ran the analysis. Venus was low on the horizon by that time, just barely within range, but we were high enough on the mountain that I could manage. Eventually it was done.

"Now *that's* interesting," I murmured, staring at the readout.

"What's interesting?" Jesse asked.

"There's more oxygen in the atmosphere than there ought to be. About twelve percent, it looks like, and the rest of it mostly nitrogen. It's *supposed* to be ninety-six percent carbon dioxide," I said.

"Told you so," Jesse said, sounding satisfied.

"You really think they've got some kind of secret hide-out over there?" I asked.

The thought worried me, honestly. Much as I might have liked to think the world was safe at that point, it very well might *not* be if some of *those* folks ever decided to come back home. My parents' horror stories were still fresh and vivid in my mind, and the kinds of people who would do things like that are not at all the kinds of people you want to share a world with.

True, it was only by the sheerest of miracles that I'd ever been able to locate a cure for the Orion Strain, and without *that* the Earth was untouchable as poison. So we were probably safe at the moment, but that didn't mean somebody else might not come across the same cure sooner or later.

"I don't know what else it could mean. See if you can hack into the computer system at Southern Command and figure out what they were up to, right before the plague came," Jesse said.

It was a logical place to start since that was the military command zone in which Florida had been included, and if they'd taken note of my father's information at all then that would have been the commander who dealt with it. But hacking military computers is never easy, and the North American Defense Forces (aka the NADF) were by far the toughest nut on the tree when it came to security.

"That might not be so easy," I said doubtfully.

"I have complete faith in you," Jesse said, clapping his hand on my shoulder.

"Yeah, I bet you do," I muttered, but nevertheless I got started. Quite a few of the computers in the world were defunct by then, but the mainframe at Southern Command in Atlanta was still functioning, surprisingly. It was every bit as hard to crack as I thought it would be, but then of course I didn't have to worry about anybody noticing or caring, either.

Once I broke inside, I was able to access quite a lot of highly interesting and educational material. It turned out the Defense Forces had built six large colony ships at the personal direction of Colonel James Burns, who was the head of Southern Command. Each of them carried a thousand people, and his plan had been to send three of them to Venus and three of them to Mars, just in case one or the other expedition failed. There were tons of facts about the colonies and the planets themselves, all of it incidentally fascinating if you had a taste for things like that. For a science junkie such as myself it was like the heady aroma of meat and potatoes to a man who hasn't eaten in days, and I found myself getting lost in the data almost before I realized what I was doing.

"I guess there was no reason for us to hide out on the Moon, then," I finally said, with a wry shake of my head.

"Sure there was, if we wanted to survive. Do you really think they would've taken any of *us* along on those expeditions?" Jesse asked.

"Well. . . no," I admitted. Those colony ships had probably been reserved for high-ranking members of the government and the Defense Forces, along with whatever scientists and engineers they thought they needed in order to make a new life for themselves. A bunch of kids from a math and science school probably wouldn't have qualified, and neither would a motley crew of their parents, friends, and associates. We would have been left behind and forgotten beyond a shadow of a doubt, along with everybody else on Earth.

But that wasn't really important anymore at this point. We *had* survived, with no help from them, and for the moment at least we ruled the world. But twenty-two people couldn't stand against six thousand, if they ever found a way to come home. They'd barge in, shove us aside, and immediately take over and start running things however they saw fit. And judging from what my parents had said and some of the information I read in those files, none of us would like the way they wanted to run things very much.

But what could we do about it? We couldn't exactly wage war against our fellow survivors, and we wouldn't have wanted to do that even if we could have. Nor could we hope to hide from them forever. Refusing to give them the anti-Orion vaccine might keep them away for a while, perhaps, but they might still find it on their own someday. That was only putting off the problem, not solving it. Sooner or later we'd have to deal with those people, one way or another.

I only hoped it didn't turn out even worse than I feared.

Freedom
is available now from your favorite retailer!

Author's Note:

Avenger came about as the result of a request to hear more about Tyke's adventures from Mrs. Amy Magaw's fifth grade class in Orangeburg, South Carolina, after they read *Tycho* as part of a unit on space science. So here you are, kids. I know it took a few months, but I hope y'all like it. ☺

But since there's nothing worse in a sci-fi novel than rehashing the same old thing, I had to come up with some new purpose for Tyke and his friends to fulfill, and Titan provided an excellent opportunity. I'd been wanting to write a book about this strange and fascinating world for a long time, and this was a perfect lead-in for doing just that.

As usual, the science is pretty rock-solid, or at least as much so as possible when writing stories set in a place about which so little is actually known. The Xanadu hills are just as I described them, as is the Shangri-la desert and the Kraken Sea. Tortola is really an ice volcano located exactly where I placed it. The conditions of light, gravity, weather, temperature, and so forth are all matched as closely to reality as possible.

Anytime you're speaking of alien body chemistry (much less alien civilization) then the door is wide open to make things up, since there simply *are* no facts known. But I have tried to be consistent with the laws of chemistry and what would be theoretically possible, at least. An energy cycle based on acetylene rather than sugar is workable on paper, although whether it could actually work in the real world is anyone's guess. Budding is a type of reproduction which is known to exist even on Earth, but I did put my own twist on it in this case.

Alien societies have sometimes been used as a way of illustrating various points about our own society which the author doesn't like or thinks could be improved. I have not tried to do that here. My purpose is entertainment and education, not social commentary. There are a number of things about A'rum society which I don't personally approve of, just as there are a number of things Tyke and others in the book may think or do which I don't necessarily agree with or think wise. But as Katrina McClendon would have said, sometimes it's necessary to follow logic to whatever place it may take you, possibly including some places you don't like.

That's a concept which may seem strange to some people nowadays, since the honor of the intellect has sunk so very low in the world. But I do hope that by presenting it as a value to be admired that I might have done my own small part in reviving a thirst for the truth which sometimes seems almost dead in an age of sound bites and spin doctors.

That said, this book was mostly written for love of far horizons and wonderful things that no human eye has ever beheld, to satisfy that same yearning for exploration which has led human beings everywhere from the depths of the ocean to the threshold of the stars. I hope my readers will accept it in that way.

Sharp readers may have noticed that Tyke has a complex history which stretches far back into the past, and some of this was mentioned in *Avenger*. Many of his extended family members have been involved in the struggle against evil, and many of them have their own books which tell the story of *their* adventures. His parents (Mike & Annabelle) appear in *Nightfall*, his grandparents (Cody & Lisa) in *Many Waters* and *Bran the Blessed*, his Aunt Joan and Uncle Philip throughout the *Last Werewolf Hunter* series, and his great-uncle Brandon Stone throughout the *Stones of Song* series. In a way, everything I've written (so far) is the history of a single family. That wasn't originally planned, but I think it worked out well as a way of connecting the dots and creating a richer, more interesting world for my characters to inhabit and a deeper backdrop for the stories I write.

Tycho in particular has been a fun character to write about, so there will be at least two more books about his adventures, I think. After that point, it depends a lot on what my readers would like to hear. If you want to see more Tyke McGrath books (or something else), make sure to let me know!

William Woodall
September 7, 2013

Discussion Questions

1. People sometimes forget that beautiful things can be just as dangerous as ugly ones, as when Tyke and the others carelessly overlooked the dangers of Hawaii simply because it was pretty. Discuss this idea. Why do you think people might feel this way?

2. Tycho says that every event has its good points, no matter how awful it was, such as the fact that the Orion Strain made it possible for the stars to shine brighter because the earth is dark. Think about a time when something bad happened and see if you can pick one or two good things that came out of it.

3. At one point in the story, Tyke talks about how hope can sometimes make people sick at heart. What do you think about this idea? Has this ever happened to you or to someone you know?

4. The A'rum live in a world and a culture very different from our own. Suppose you were an A'rum who visited your town. What might you think of it? What things would seem strangest or most interesting to you? Would anything seem familiar?

5. On Tortola, Tyke hesitates at first before taking the oath of an Avenger. How would you feel, if you were asked to do this? Would you say yes or no? Explain why you think as you do.

6. Joan said that she expected her children to refuse any orders which were ungodly, but that had better be the only reason they ever had for disobedience. Do you agree with this idea? Explain.

7. Tyke says that going to school at the Academy has made him shy of talking about spiritual things, even in private. Have there ever been times when you felt this way? What could Tyke (or Philip, or Joan, or Jesse) have done to make things easier?

8. Tyke experiences several things which are hard to explain during the story. Discuss some of your own experiences of things which may have seemed inexplicable at the time.

9. At one point, Tyke says that Philip and Joan are turning out to have more interesting facets than he ever suspected before. Has there ever been a time when you thought you knew someone very well, and then suddenly discovered something new about them? Discuss that experience.

10.   The "theme" of a story is the underlying message or messages about life the author is trying to convey. It is the lesson or moral of the story, such as "Love conquers all". What do you think the theme of *Avenger* is? (There can be more than one.)

11.   Discuss the concept of the honor of the intellect; that is, the idea that we should follow logic wherever it leads us, regardless of whether we like it or not. Do you agree with this idea? How difficult do you think it might be to practice this virtue in real life?

12.   Philip revealed several facts about himself which Tyke and Jesse had never known before. Which of these facts were most surprising to you? Which of them do you think would have been most surprising if you were Tyke or Jesse? Give reasons.

13.   Near the end, Jesse began referring to himself as Jesse Parker, or what he called his *real* name. Why do you think he did this? If you were Jesse, what would you have done? Explain your thoughts.

14.   Tyke grants Danielle the name of *Akiri,* a title of A'rum nobility. Do you believe she earned this title? If so, give examples of things she did which were brave and honorable. If not, explain why you don't think her actions were enough to merit the title.

15.   Tycho and the other characters make several mistakes during the story, and they aren't always wise. What are some of the mistakes you think they made, and what should they have done differently?

16.   *Avenger* contains several unanswered questions about what will happen and how things came about in the past. List some of the things you were still curious about at the end of the book and speculate about how they might turn out or how they came to be.

17.   The A'rum referred to Titan as *the beautiful land,* which Tyke had a hard time understanding. Are there any aspects to Titan which you found to be beautiful, or would you agree with Tyke that for humans it will probably always seem like an ugly place? Explain.

18.   If you had been asked to join the expedition to Titan yourself, would you have wanted to go? Why or why not?

The Curse-Breaker Books
By William Woodall

Long ago, there was a Godly woman named Marybeth Trewick, who for various reasons found herself married to a rich but wicked man named Daniel who practiced all kinds of evil. She could only watch helplessly as her five sons grew up to become just as wicked as their father, and as her only daughter was forced to flee for her life lest she be killed.

But in the midst of her despair, God sent Marybeth a dream that after seven generations had passed, there would be five boys born to replace and redeem the ones that she had lost. These five would be breakers of curses and fighters against all things wicked and evil, and each of them would have the same vividly blue eyes, the same color as Marybeth's.

And even though the Curse-Breakers are each called to very different tasks in the world, the basic goal of fighting evil and loving God is always the same. These are their names and stories.

Brian Stone: The oldest curse-breaker, Brian's task is to save his brother's life and to remind men of Heaven by showing them the beauty of what could have been if the world had never fallen.

Cody McGrath: Two years younger than Brian, Cody is called to break the power of a dangerous sorceress. He's a dreamer of true dreams and a healer of the lost and broken-hearted.

Zachary Trewick: Four years younger than Cody, Zach is called to destroy one of the worst remaining aspects of his ancestor's wickedness; the werewolf curse which most of his family still embrace wholeheartedly.

Cameron Parker: Cameron and Zach are the same age, not to mention third cousins and best friends. Cameron has a big role to play in the struggle against the wolves, and later becomes the leader of all the survivors of Earth.

Brandon Stone: Brian's little brother, Brandon is three years younger than Cameron and Zach. He has a gift to know the meaning of dreams, and he is called to defend the weak and to uphold all that is righteous and true.

The Curse-Breaker Books form a collection of related stories about these five boys and sometimes their children. Each series tells the tale of a different Curse-Breaker (or sometimes more than one), but they also fit together in ways you wouldn't expect, in order to form a single unified storyline. It's helpful to read the books in order if possible, but it's not strictly necessary. You can read more about each series on the following pages.

The Stones of Song Series
By William Woodall

"There's a thing called magnanimity, or greatness of heart, and to me it's the most beautiful thing that ever there was. It means courage, but it's more than that. It means to cast aside all thought of yourself for the sake of another, like Moses in Gilead or the martyrs who died with a smile on their face. In its own small way it's a reflection of the Lord Jesus at Calvary, and therefore of God, the Light so beautiful that no one who sees it can ever turn away."

So says Cody McGrath, and in many ways that statement is the central theme of this series; the casting away of self for love of another, the scorning of selfishness in all its forms.

These are the stories of the Stone family: Brian, Jenny, Lisa, and Brandon, and some of the people they know and love, most notably Cody. All of them were called for great and glorious things, though sometimes only after great suffering and many mistakes.

Unclouded Day: Brian's life isn't easy. Abandoned by his father, abused by his alcoholic mother, and mocked by his classmates, his only treasures are his beloved little brother and his old guitar. This is the tale of his journey to find the Fountain of Youth, and perhaps to save the world.

Many Waters: Lisa is a small-town waitress with heavy burdens to bear. Cody is a young cowboy with big dreams and some very dangerous enemies. But when the two of them must face down an evil witch who tries to destroy their very lives, it seems that only a miracle can save them.

Bran the Blessed: Brandon hasn't always made the right choices in life, but he's never found himself in quite such deep trouble as this. But even though his life seems ruined forever, Bran still has a high calling to answer. . . if he can find the courage.

* * * * * * *

"I would absolutely, without reservation, encourage you to read this wonderful novel, even if you aren't the fantasy genre type. It was a blessing."
-Sue, *Reflections and Reviews*

"There are so many nuggets of truth in this book. It's about Heaven. It's about bad things happening for a reason. It's about deciding for yourself what truly matters most in life. It's a really good book!"
-Tattie, *Christian Fiction Ebooks*

The Last Werewolf Hunter Series
By William Woodall

Zach Trewick always thought he'd become a writer someday, or maybe play baseball for the Texas Rangers. What he never imagined in his craziest dreams was that he'd find himself dodging bullets and crashing cars off mountainsides, let alone that he'd ever be expected to break the ancient werewolf curse which hangs over his family.

But Zach is the last of the werewolf hunters, the long-foretold Curse-Breaker who can wipe out the wolves forever, and he's not the type to give up just because of a few minor setbacks. . .

Cry for the Moon: What would you do, if your family wanted you to become a monster? What if they wouldn't take no for an answer? When 12 year old Zach faces questions like these, he seems to have only one choice; *run*. Thus begins a long search for refuge, and perhaps redemption also.

Behind Blue Eyes: When a stranger kidnaps him from his own back yard, Zach soon finds that the past isn't quite as dead as he might wish. For the time has come at last for him to break the werewolf curse forever; and his family has no intention of letting that happen.

More Golden Than Day: When his girlfriend and then his cousin fall into the hands of the wolves, Zach has no choice but to take on his enemies for a second round. Only this time the stakes are horribly high, and if he fails he may end up losing everything he's ever loved.

Truesilver: When a family of wicked ex-wolves is accidentally awakened, Zach soon finds himself locked in a desperate fight for survival that he never anticipated. And even though he's sworn an oath to fight evil to the utmost of his power, there are times when courage is awfully hard to come by.

* * * * * * *

"If you are looking for a story about a boy who learns valuable lessons about family, love, friendship and God this is the book for you. I recommend this book to a pre-teen or adult. I truly enjoyed this book."
-Rae, *My Book Addiction Reviews*

"I found myself captivated with the story and could not stop reading until I reached the final page. Everything about this story is thought-provoking. Readers of all ages will appreciate this wonderfully told story,"
-Jancy, Kansas

The Tyke McGrath Series
By William Woodall

In the year 2154, the world has become a dangerous place. Extremist groups would like nothing better than to wipe out humanity completely, and even the people sworn to defend civilization against such threats have become deeply corrupt and untrustworthy.

When a virulent plague destroys all warm-blooded life on Earth, a small band of survivors clings to life on the partially-terraformed Moon. But fresh dangers lie in wait for the unwary; nor have they left behind all the wickedness in the hearts of men.

Nightfall: When Micah McGrath suddenly finds himself thrust into a dangerous and ugly future after a lab accident, his only choice is to make the best life for himself that he can. But when the secret police get wind of his research into time travel, he soon finds himself in deep trouble indeed.

Tycho: Tycho McGrath is a high school honor student in Florida when he discovers a terrifying secret: a man-made bacterium is about to wipe out all warm-blooded life on Earth within days. The only hope for survival is to flee at once, a plan which carries its own set of unexpected dangers.

Avenger: After spotting an SOS coming from the abandoned Moon, the survivors must organize a rescue mission. But the expedition quickly becomes far more complicated, leading them to the icy world of Titan in search of a holy mountain that no human eye has ever seen.

Freedom: When a cruel and power-hungry military commander on Venus decides to reconquer Earth, the only thing he needs is the formula for Tyke's Orion vaccine. The survivors soon find themselves locked into a bitter battle over the future of mankind, and who will inherit the Earth after all.

Elysium: What began as a simple mission to recover lost comrades in the Martian desert quickly turns deadly when Tyke and the others find *themselves* stranded on the Red Planet, with only the slimmest of chances to make it home again, or to fulfill the destiny which God has in store for them.

* * * * * * *

"Reminiscent of Freedom's Landing, by Anne McCaffrey, Tycho combines the best of traditional space-exploration sci-fi with modern apocalyptic fiction. For any fans of hard science fiction, it doesn't get much better than this." **- Liz, OH2 Reviews**

"This story was awesome! A must-read book if you like sci-fi." **-Scott, Georgia**

Trewick Family Tree

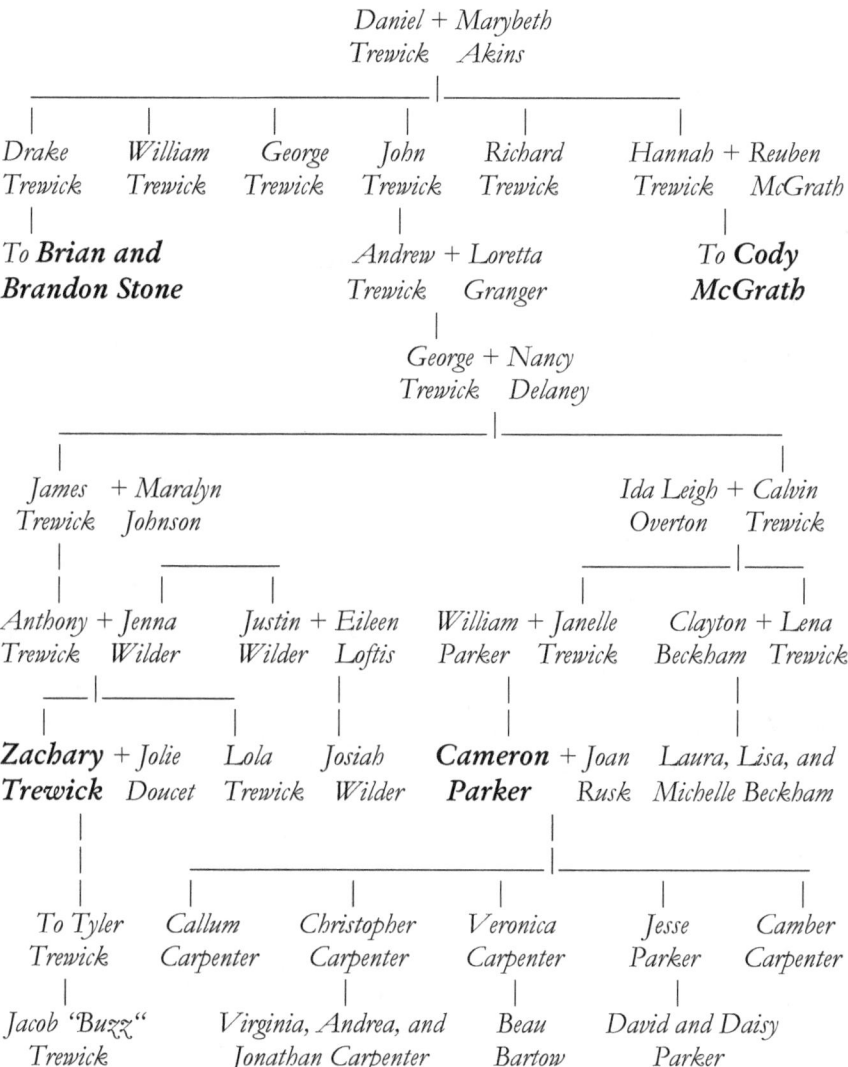

1. *Curse-Breakers are in bold.*
2. *Cameron Parker later changed his name to Philip Carpenter.*
3. *Tyler Trewick is Zach's great-grandson.*
4. *Lisa Beckham's husband is Logan Tygart.*
5. *Laura Beckham's husband is Heath Coates, son of Albert Coates.*

Trewick Family Tree

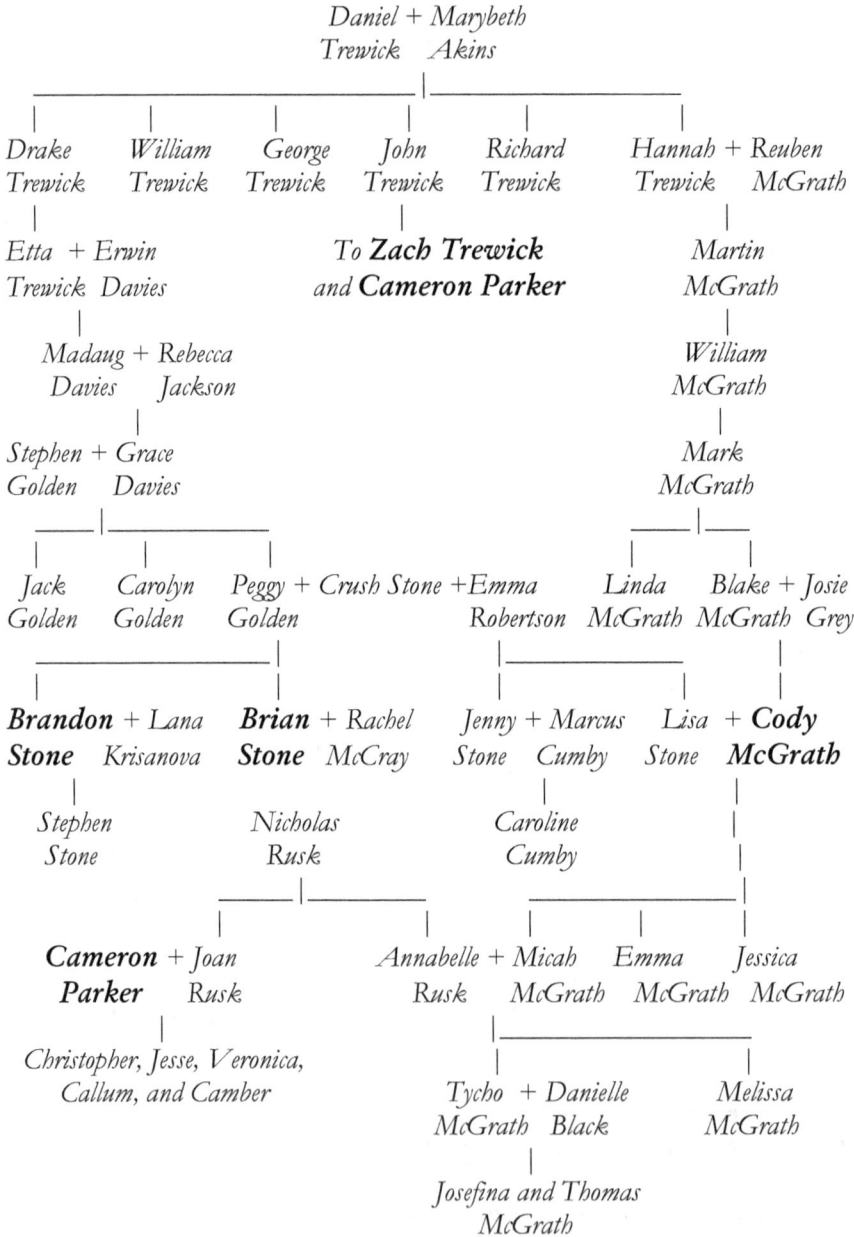

Doucet Family Tree

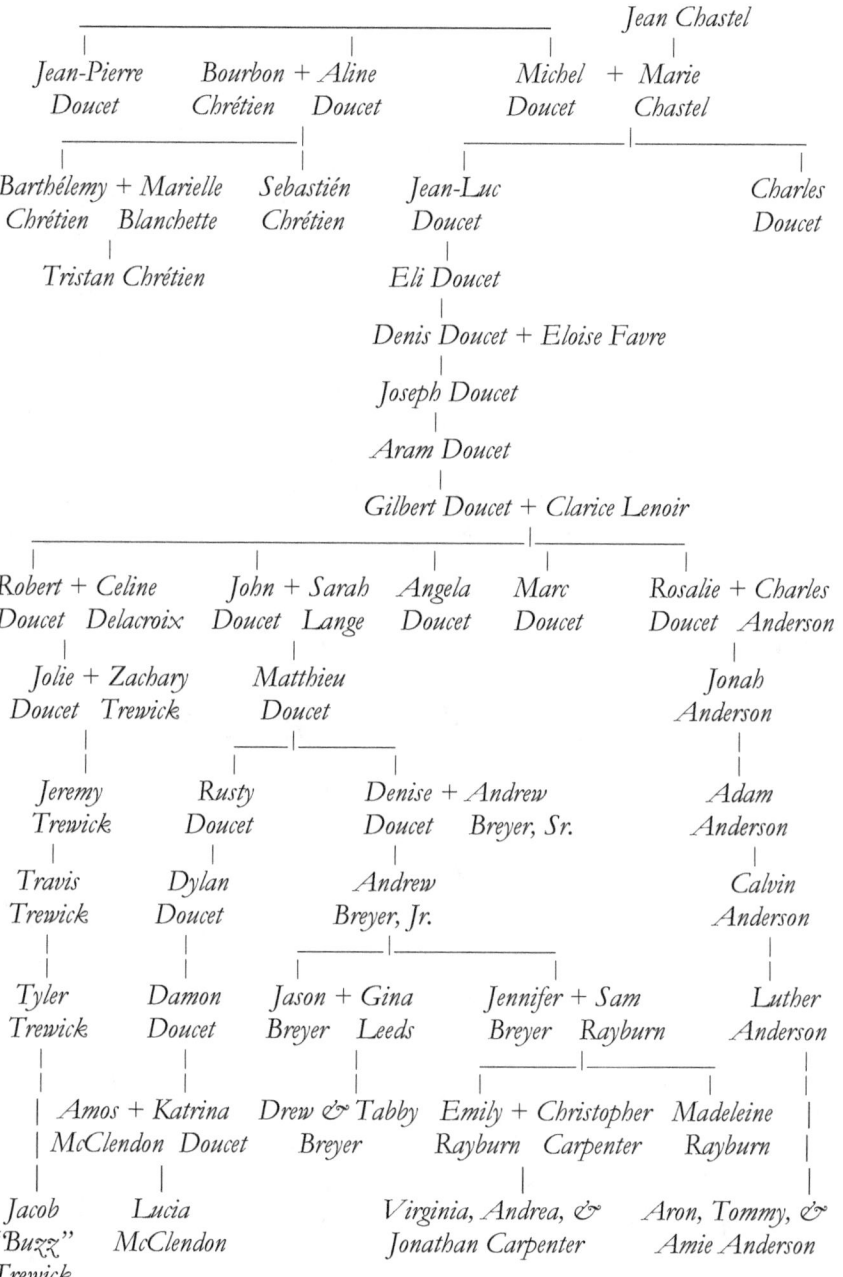

Bartow Family Tree

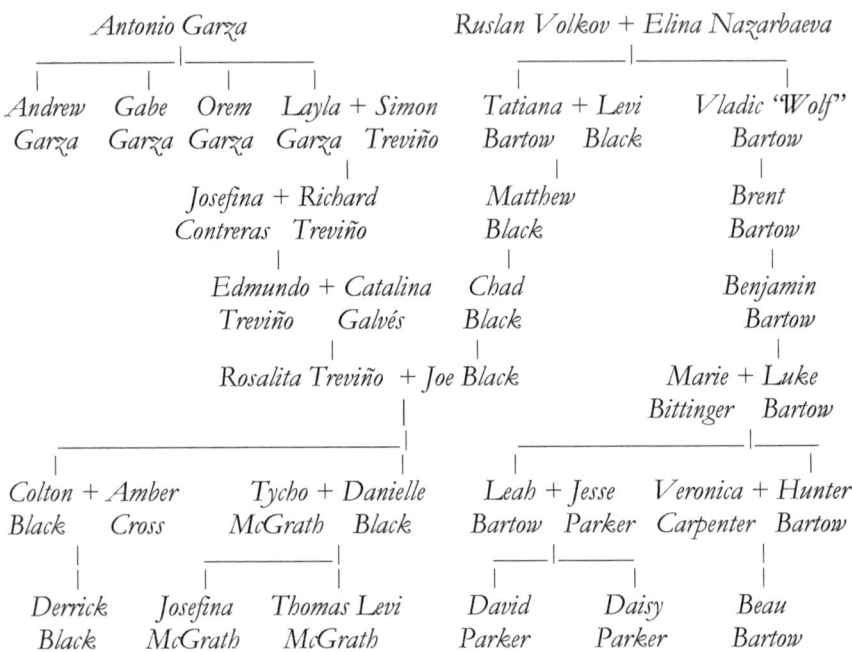

Jones and Golden Family Trees

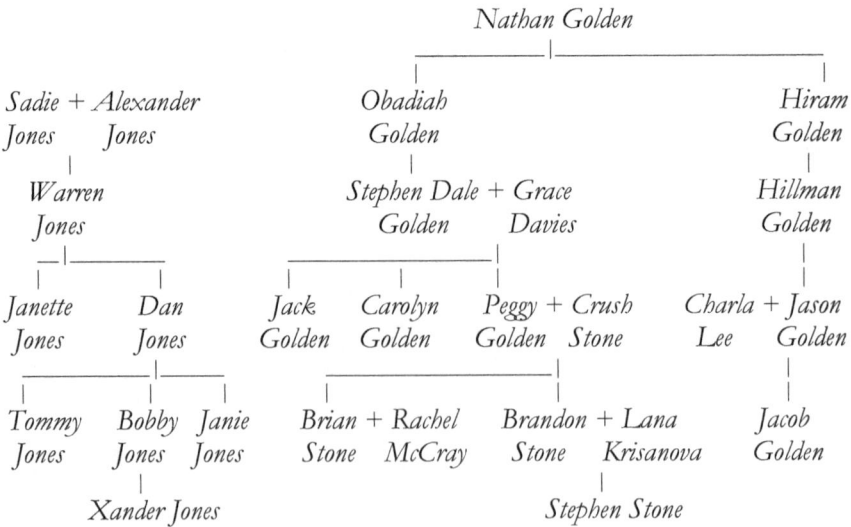

If you'd like to find out more about
The Tyke McGrath Series and other books,
please visit:

William Woodall's
Official Author Website

www.williamwoodall.org

Here you will find:

Free short stories
Discussion questions for teachers and book clubs
Free sample chapters of all my books
Photos of characters and locations for each story
Articles
Interviews
Quotable Quotes
Contact Information
And much, much more!

www.ingramcontent.com/pod-product-compliance
Lightning Source LLC
Chambersburg PA
CBHW050933120626
46552CB00001B/191